THE MAN IS A CACCIATORE

DANGEROUS DEVOTION
BOOK ONE

J R MOSS

Developmental editing by Eve Common— Read Ink Edits

❀ Created with Vellum

To anyone who has ever felt trapped in survival and searching for yourself.

IMPORTANT NOTE

This book is intended for adults only, and contains subject matters that may be difficult or disturbing for some readers.

Sensitive materials include:

Graphic: Blood, Violence, Cursing, Physical Abuse

Moderate: Death, Sexual content, Emotional disturbances, Mental Health Triggers, Alcohol and Smoking, PTSD, Panic Attacks, Dissociation

Minor: Torture, Kidnap, Emotional Abuse, Guns, Sexual Manipulation, War

EPISODE 1

Cassandra

A haze of cigar smoke filled the dimly lit first floor of Inferno, clinging to the air like a thick curtain. My pulse thrummed to the beat of the usual bass-heavy song I danced to, each note reverberating through my body like a promise. Whistles and catcalls rang out like sirens when I dipped back, my long onyx hair tumbling down like a black waterfall. I lived for this—the rush of adrenaline, the addictive high of cash floating down like snowflakes in late January.

My thighs gripped the cold metal of the pole as I spun, muscles straining, only to release and slide down slow, deliberate, and tantalizing. Every movement was calculated, every flick of my gaze, every roll of my hips. My routine was a bulletproof masterpiece, perfected over a year of study and sweat, and the high rollers on the edge of their seats knew it. This was as close as they would ever get.

Inferno was one of the hottest clubs on the east side; it sat just at the border of the Irish and Italian turfs, and I knew the Italians hadn't sunk their teeth into it yet from the tip I got from a few of the girls at the old club I danced at. I needed to know I was going to be protected especially after leaving Declan, and I wanted to be as far from the mafia families as possible.

Which was how I ended up here. I'd heard that Vinnie Ferrao, the owner, protected his girls—for a handsome fee. He paid extra for bodyguards, kept a running list of anyone his girls didn't want near them, and maintained a safe house. I didn't like the idea of handing over a large percentage of my pay, but I also knew I didn't have any other options. Not anymore.

My life attracted toxic men, or maybe it was just my fabulous personality; either way, I was constantly on the get-fucked end of the stick.

When I sat down for my interview after an extremely lengthy application process, it was more than I had expected but the rumors were true. Vinnie wanted to know why I was there and how he could keep me safe. I did write down one rule on my application: no private dances. My rule was non-negotiable, especially after working at my old joint, I swore I'd never let another man touch me again. I remembered the day I told Vinnie exactly how it was going to work.

"Look, Vinnie," I said, cool and composed, each word carrying the confidence of a seasoned negotiator. "I'm not like the blonde bunnies you've got prancing around out there." I gestured to the two-way mirror, where the black marble main floor stretched into view. An elegant maroon stage extended from the wall to the center of the club, anchored by a twenty-foot silver pole that caught every flashing color as lights streaked past it. "I'll bring in double the earnings in one night. You'll see for yourself that I'm worth the hire—on my terms." Still, bills were piling up, rent was breathing down my neck, and I had given my last $20 to a girlfriend from O'Malley's to get her daughter some fast food for dinner just the other day. So I played it the only way I knew how. I pushed back from the creaky thrift-store chair, counted to ten in my head, and walked toward the door. Pressure always worked on men like Vinnie—the kind who needed to impress their high-paying clientele and had a soft spot for women trapped in this dangerous world.

When I'd walked through the black doors to the club, I'd been hijacked by a woman with bleach-blonde hair. She said her name was Candy and had all but bragged about how Vinnie was the best, how I'd love it here. She'd practically confirmed what I heard about him being a good guy, told me about his tragic past—how he lost his wife and daughter to this cruel world.

It was odd how comfortable she'd been airing out this man's past. It made me feel for him, but I knew what I wanted, and once my mind was set, I didn't falter. I knew he was already desperate to help me; he wouldn't have called me in here other-wise, but I didn't want to assume I had it. Not until he offered me the job.

"Wait…" His voice hitched, laced with an exaggerated sigh of defeat.

I'd smirked to myself before turning back, already knowing I had him hooked. I let my expression fall neutral, but my emerald eyes narrowed, the predator in me watching the man sweat. He ran a hand through his thinning dirty-blonde hair. I loved seeing men in power look like desperate fools, it made me feel in control, something I felt like I had lost for a little while.

"Fine," he dabbed at his forehead with a handkerchief. "Prove yourself tonight, and we'll talk."

Now, three months later, I prowled along the edge of the stage, back arched and lips curved into a feline smile, I gave each of my high-rollers their due attention. Whiskey and vodka on their breaths, wedding bands on their hands, and desperation in their eyes—it didn't matter. As long as their money made its way into the thin straps of my G-string, I didn't care who they were.

It didn't take long for me to become a fan favorite here, which proved to Vinnie that I was a well-earned investment in his club. And I felt safe—safer than I ever had at work. I knew Vinnie's extra cost was well worth it, even if it meant it would take me a little longer to save up enough cash to get the hell out of Chicago.

Leo

The leather beneath me sighed as I sat back in the VIP booth on the second floor, ankle resting lazily over my knee. I flicked open my lighter, the flame flaring bright before I brought it to my cigarette dangling between my lips. For a brief second, the light sent shadows scattering, only for them to slink back into the corners. The snap of the lighter closing seemed louder than it should have.

I took a long drag, my gaze sweeping the club floor beyond the two way privacy glass. She was there—the black-haired dancer. Her presence burned like a beacon in the faceless crowd. My men had been coming here for weeks, leaning on Vinnie Ferrao. His place was the last club I hadn't claimed. I hadn't needed it before, but the Irish had been testing my patience, and Inferno sat too close to their border for my comfort.

The last few nights I'd dropped in, she was always onstage or making her rounds. Intriguing. Those calculating eyes, the way she flirted just enough to reel them in while keeping their hands at bay. No one got too close. No one got a private dance. I'd tested that theory myself—sent Gio down with a fat stack of hundreds. She turned him down flat. Watching her refuse was more entertaining than the show itself.

Vinnie fidgeted in the shadows near the booth entrance, practically begging to be addressed. I gestured with two fingers, wordlessly summoning him. Gio and Dimitri stepped aside, their forms as still and imposing as guard dogs waiting for the command by the only door.

They went everywhere with me—the only two men I trusted, aside from my underboss and my *caporegime*. Both had come to me at different times young, raw, and hungry, and they'd outshone the rest in all the ways that mattered.

"Mr. Romano—"

I held up a hand, cutting him off. I didn't need his fumbling words clouding the air. My focus was on *her.* The way the lights slid across her toned body, the strength in her movements. The leering crowd below only made my jaw tighten.

When I finally fixed my eyes on Vinnie, he visibly shuddered—and it made the corner of my mouth lift. I'd been wearing him down all week, showing up at the same time every night. He knew who I was and why I was here, but I wanted him to fucking submit, to beg for my protection. He was close. I'll give him credit—he's a tougher bastard than he looks. He'd survived two weeks of scattered pressure: alcohol suppliers suddenly cutting him off because I was leaning on them, a couple of sloppy drive-bys just to scare him. Then came the last week, with me piling on—unreasonable tasks, making a few of his dancers cry—and now, this stare-down.

"Now you may speak," I muttered, my voice low and commanding.

Vinnie shifted uncomfortably under my stare, his Adam's apple bobbing nervously. "Mr. Romano, I—I want you to know how much we've appreciated your presence here. Business has been booming. High rollers and—"

He wiped his neck with a stained white handkerchief, flustered, then changed tactics. "Look, Mr. Romano, I understand this deal is inevitable, but I need you to understand what this club does for these girls."

The way his tone shifted from nervous rat to protective father heightened my interest. I gestured with my hand for him to continue.

He dabbed at his forehead. "These girls here are under my care. I protect them. They pay me forty percent of their earnings each night, and I feel responsible for them." He paused, eyes dropping to the stage where the black-haired beauty continued to writhe below. Inhaling, he went on, "So I ask you to continue protecting them. They're all running from one danger or another." His eyes met mine—not desperate or nervous, but stern. I respected that.

"So these women are paying you to keep out the scum they're running from?" I took a slow drag of my cigarette.

His head bobbed. "That's right. Every night we have at least ten highly trained bouncers, the most state-of-the-art camera systems, and if they ever come to me needing a place to stay..." He dabbed at the back of his neck with the already damp handkerchief. "We have a safe house."

A plume of smoke billowed into the air around me as I considered his words. I liked this. I could work with this. And the extra cash I was sure he was pulling in from the girls—I could more than make up for the losses I'd taken.

"Have you met Angel?" Vinnie's voice cut through my thoughts.

I steeled my expression, though the question caught me off guard. My reputation as the Italian don of Chicago preceded me. I kept my tone cold, calculating. "And why the fuck would I care about some *provocatrice?*"

Vinnie blinked. "A what, sir?"

"A tease," Gio supplied from behind him.

Vinnie looked at him then whipped his head back to me. 'Oh..apologies. I only mention her because she's our best earner. Feisty, too."

Someone unfazed by me? I turned my gaze back to her, raising an eyebrow at the black haired *bella* collecting stacks of cash off the stage. The predatory curve of her lips as she met the eyes of those below was unmistakable. She was aware of the power she held. And when her sharp green eyes snapped up to meet mine—unapologetic, challenging—excitement flickered in my chest.

"Bring her to me," I said simply.

Vinnie practically sprinted to the stairs, eager to please. I leaned forward, stamping out my cigarette in the ashtray as I watched her move. The girl was trouble, I could already tell but she was going to be my trouble.

Cassandra

"Angel, baby..." Vinnie pleaded, practically sweating through his button-down shirt. Today he was ruining an off-brand burgundy shirt that smelled like he'd used too much starch while ironing it. His pudgy fingers trembled as he reached into his black pants pocket for the stained white handkerchief to dab his forehead.

"Don't call me 'baby', Vinnie," I snapped, crossing my arms. My glare flicked up to the VIP booth, where I'm sure those steel-grey eyes and wolfish smirk were watching this conversation. The all-too-handsome, enigmatic man who had been appearing more frequently was all the buzz this week.

The girls had been swooning over him for a month now, but he came scarcely, sending his goons instead–until this week. They tripped over themselves whenever he did show up, desperate to make an impression—especially if it meant this man I was now in a standoff with would notice them.

My gaze never left the two-way mirror where his presence haunted this club; my pride wanted to prove a point. "I told you," I said coolly, "I don't do private dances."

"Angel—please." He glanced at where my eyes were narrowed and then back at me, wiping his brow again. "Just this once, as a favor. Leonardo has been grinding me all week…" Vinnie's voice wavered, his desperation inching toward panic. "I just need him to be dazzled so he'll keep his word on protecting you girls before I finalize this deal."

Leonardo Romano. I'd heard the name before—not because of the club, but because in Chicago he was known as one of the most ruthless and dangerous men. You didn't want to cross him. Candy, one of the most annoying dancers who loved the sound of her own voice, mentioned her old man used to slip into his poker nights and said he had a nickname—*Lupe Nero*.

Breaking my stare, I glared back at Vinnie and pinched the bridge of my nose. "Fine," I sighed. "But I swear to fucking God, Vinnie, if he so much as touches me, I'll cut off your dick. Got it?" I knew Vinnie didn't have a choice, Inferno was on Italian turf and we all noticed the pressure tactics the past two weeks, and Vinnie promised us that his deal to protect us still stood even if Romano took over the "protection". I trusted him, there was no reason not to trust Vinnie. But Leonardo Romano? That I wasn't so sure of.

Vinnie nodded eagerly like I was his savior. I hated that look, because I was no man's saving grace. I'd rather walk across coals than have any man look at me like that. I was only doing this because I knew how it went with the underworld—I felt for Vinnie.

Vinnie treated me well, better than any boss I'd had over the years as a stripper, he even proved his protection when Declan did try to come in one night and his bouncers turned him away. Which is why when Vinnie asked for favors—a rare occurrence—I usually obliged.

My go at life had been one that seemed passed down from a previous one, one filled with absolute, shitty karma. Especially with motherfuckers like the one in the VIP booth, probably feeling like the king of the goddamn universe.

A sigh of relief blew from Vinnie's lips. "Your name suits you, you know that?"

"Yeah, whatever. Just lead the way already."

His cold, sweaty hand curled around my wrist. I gritted my teeth and yanked it back. "Just lead the way—you don't have to pull me like a leashed dog." I glanced up at where I knew the looming figure on the second floor was. I braced myself because I already knew this was going to be trouble.

Leo

This little vixen was definitely feisty—the way she glared at me with self-righteous contempt, her defiant features entertaining when she forced herself to do something she absolutely despised. My lip curved into a half-smile, my heart beginning to race. I pulled out another cigarette and lit it, watching her yank her wrist free from that weak man's grip. "Fuck," I whispered to myself.

I turned away, leaning against the glass, preparing for her arrival.

The moment my men let them pass and she stepped into view, my breath hitched. I took another drag of my cigarette to control my emotions as I studied her closer—her long black hair like silk, the sharpness of her emerald eyes as if she had fought darkness her entire life, and the unshakable confidence in the way she carried herself.

"You got a name?" I asked, my voice low, measured.

Her eyes narrowed dangerously, shifting from sharp to deadly.

"Angel." Her arms crossed over the fishnet dress that barely concealed the pasties beneath.

I stepped closer in a few short strides, my body towering over hers, but she didn't flinch. "What's your real name, Angel?" My tone left no room for bullshit. I certainly wasn't in the mood.

Her emerald-green eyes sharpened on me, a spark of defiance nestling into her irises like the twinkle in a jewel. It made my lip twitch. "And why do you need to know that?" she asked, popping her hip out and raising her chin.

My hands itched to wrap around her neck—to teach her who was in charge—but I kept them buried deep in my pockets. "Because I like knowing who's sizing me up...and I hate having my patience tested."

She didn't even get the chance to say anything.

"It's Cassandra Bennett."

Vinnie's pathetic voice slipped into our private moment, and the fierce resolve in Cassandra's eyes snapped to him, shifting into a fury that gave my heart an unfamiliar flutter.

"What the fuck, Vinn—" Cassandra started, but I interrupted.

"Cassandra..." Her name rolled off my tongue as smoothly as my accent, tasting like the most divine Italian chocolate. I smirked.

My gaze shifted to Vinnie. "I own you now, Vinnie. I'll hold up your pre-existing standards for the club. Now leave us."

I didn't care anymore about making Vinnie crawl—my sights were set on my new challenge.

Vinnie didn't need to be told twice. He scurried off, leaving me alone with her.

"Tell me, Cassandra," my words a dangerous purr, "will you dance for me?"

She didn't hesitate, brushing past me with her chin lifted high and shoulders squared. Her lithe form swayed through the veil of smoke like a phantom on her way to the small stage in the corner of the booth. A faint breeze carried the scent of vanilla and roses as she passed.

"Dio mi salvi," I murmured under my breath. If God didn't save me, this mysterious angel was going to make me do things I would never come back from.

Gio and Dimitri must have caught the comment because I noticed their shoulders shaking with silent laughter. I felt like a hound on a scent as I followed her fragrance through the haze.

At the steps of the small stage she paused, listing rules on her fingers like commands. "No touching. No talking. No whistling." Her eyes were as cold as the Chicago winters.

My fingers slid over the rim of my chilled glass on the side table as I studied her. No one has ever listed demands to me, not in a long time. "You didn't seem to mind it down there." I gestured with my chin, my gaze razor-focused on hers, as I entertained her stubborn resolve. Normally I wouldn't allow an outsider to embarrass me in front of my people but she felt different, I liked the fire in her and it ignited a predatory hunger in my heart.

She ignored my comment, grabbing the remote and flipping through tracks until she landed on one I didn't expect—*Death March* by Chopin, twisted with a metal flare. It was the kind of theme a valkyrie would choose going into battle, and by the hardness in her gaze, that's exactly what she was.

"I'll warn you—I don't care for the grinding the girls typically do." I rotated the leather chair I had been sitting in earlier to face the stage, then settled back slowly. A soft red glow lit up the room creating more of a seductive and sinful atmosphere that heightened my fascination with this woman.

"Good thing that isn't what you'll be getting." She gripped the pole so tightly her knuckles whitened. With a sudden swing of her leg, she lifted herself and spun, body blurring in the upstage lighting. Her movements were precise, sensual—more performance than dance.

A small smile played on my lips as I leaned back, falling under the spell of her grace. My mind raced with the need to know more. I signaled Gio over with two fingers, eyes locked on her.

"Find out everything you can on Cassandra Bennett—her address, her family, everything." My voice was deadly serious, leaving no room for debate.

"Yes, sir," Gio confirmed before pulling free his phone from his dark denim jeans, fingers flying as he connected with our tech guy uptown. I knew I'd have answers before this enthralling dance ended.

Cassandra

The song drifted to an end, and I sprawled across the stage floor, panting softly. I hadn't danced for his attention—I didn't give a damn about impressing him—but I had made my point: I was no one to fuck with.

Finally, I glanced up and found him standing near the edge of the stage. Unreadable. Silent. His steel-grey eyes held something dangerous—a simmering interest that prickled my skin. He looked unmistakably Italian: olive skin warmed by the low lights, dark hair neat but tousled just enough to seem careless, a jawline sharp enough to cut glass. But it was the scar grazing his right cheekbone that caught me. The pale, thin mark looked like a whisper of violence. I wondered, briefly, if it was still tender to the touch.

Focus.

Rising slowly to my feet, the silence was broken only by the click of my stilettos as I stepped down from the stage. He extended a hand, offering assistance I deliberately ignored. My fishnet dress lay where I'd tossed it mid-dance on the floor beside his seat. I scooped it up and pulled it over my head in one fluid motion before turning toward the exit.

"Favor complete," I said flippantly, tossing the words over my shoulder.

I made it two steps before a firm grip closed around my arm. He pulled me back—not roughly, but with enough force to spin me around so we stood face-to-face. My breath hitched, but I yanked at my arm just enough to prove I wouldn't be handled.

"What?" I snapped, my gaze challenging his as he raked a hand through his hair. I knew I was pushing buttons—that this man could easily unholster the gun he most likely had on him and blow my brains out without blinking—but something about him told me I could push, at least a little. And I needed to make it clear he doesn't own me before my goal of leaving Chicago is ruined.

Only then did I register how tall he really was. Broad shoulders blocked out the dim light, his presence commanding the space between us. For half a second, intimidation crawled up my spine.

His eyes hardened, though his voice carried something else I didn't even want to place. He leaned down, eye level now. "I'd like to see you again. Not here, not as a favor to Vinnie. Just you and me."

Sizing him up, I tilted my head. "I don't think that's a good idea. I'm not getting a good vibe from you."

The slow, dangerous smile that spread across his face made my blood heat—and not in a way I liked. "Most women either kill to be alone with me or stutter in fear." He leaned closer, tucking a loose strand of hair behind my ear, his thumb brushing over my cheekbone with infuriating delicacy. "But you—you look at me like I'm nothing."

His voice dropped to a velvet murmur. "It's…refreshing."

How fucking infuriating.

I slapped his hand away, glaring up at him with my jaw set. "Maybe it's because I have a brain and standards, Mr.…?" I knew exactly who he was, but I wanted to hear him say it, and I knew it would get under his skin.

His eyes flickered, dangerous amusement shading darker. "Romano." The name left his lips like a warning. Then, after a beat, softer: "Leonardo Romano. But those I deem worthy call me Leo."

Leo. The audacity.

Before I could scoff, he lifted my hand and pressed a kiss to my knuckles like some outdated knight out of a storybook. The warmth of his lips burned against my skin, and I yanked my hand back so fast it might as well have been fire. This man was no Prince Charming, and I didn't need another man trying to play that part again.

"Have a good rest of your evening, Mr. Romano," I said icily, spinning on my stilettos and storming out of the booth without looking back.

As I stalked down the dim hallway and down the stairs, I muttered under my breath, mimicking his ridiculous introduction. "Romano. Leonardo Romano." I added a cheesy James Bond accent for good measure, sarcasm dripping from every syllable.

I spat on the floor to seal the curse in my mind. What a pompous dick.

Guys like Leo were all the same. I knew their type—I'd dated their type. Possessive, controlling assholes who thought the world owed them everything. I rubbed my temples, forcing him out of my head. I had sworn after my last ex that no man like that would get within ten feet of me again. And I sure as hell wasn't about to let Leo Romano change that.

BY THE TIME my shift ended and I stepped outside, the sticky dawn was already lighting up Chicago. My skin felt too tight, my clothes suffocating. Tugging at the strap of my bra, I groaned in frustration. Everything about tonight crawled under my skin like a rash—and Leo Romano was the culprit.

The stagnant air felt like swallowing oil. I coughed, resentful of Chicago summers, though winter was worse. "You win some, you lose some," I muttered, shaking my head.

The concrete crunched beneath my white sneakers as I scanned the parking lot for my black Honda Accord. Finding it, I unlocked the door and flopped into the driver's seat, tossing my oversized knockoff Louis Vuitton purse onto the passenger side. The sharp scent of a new air freshener clung to the humid air. This car was my baby. She had been through too many moves and runaways with me.

At one point, she had been the only home I had. And yet I'd filled her with garbage, barely protecting her from the elements. If she were sentient, she would have quit on me years ago.

Before I could shut the door, a sleek black SUV rolled up fast, cutting across the lot to park directly in front of me, blocking me in. My stomach dropped. The window lowered, and there he was—Leo, smug as ever, face slightly obscured by tinted glass.

A slow exhale left me, and the knot in my stomach unwound into something sharper.

"That outfit isn't nearly as impressive as your fishnets," he drawled, his Italian accent thick.

"Mr. Romano." My voice was flat as I reached for the pepper spray in my center console. "It's extremely inappropriate to contact me outside the club. You have two more warnings before I call the police."

He chuckled darkly, the sound raising goosebumps along my arms. My gut twisted, though my face stayed blank. He pushed the door open and stepped out, moving with deliberate precision—slow, predatory, controlled.

He rounded my door in a few strides, gripping the frame and leaning in so close I caught his cologne—bourbon, smoke, and something warm I hated to admit smelled good. His jaw ticked, and the faint stubble suggested he hadn't been home in at least a day.

"The police?" he scoffed, lips curling. "*Principessa*, I own half the cops in this city. But sure, let's play your little game."

Amusement laced his tone, but the threat beneath it curled tight in my gut.

"I'm exhausted, Mr. Romano," I said evenly, slipping a yawn into my voice. My right hand clutched the pepper spray, hidden in my purse. "And I'd like to go home."

His eyes dropped to where I hid my hand, something flickering there—frustration, maybe something else. My heart hammered in warning.

"You know," he said softly, voice low and intimate, "most people don't tell me no twice and live to talk about it."

I arched a brow, defiance flaring. "Then I guess I'm special."

My left hand gripped the door to close it, but he held it firmly open, leaning in further so our faces were inches apart. My pulse spiked, and I caught the way his eyes lingered on my neck, right where the skin fluttered with my heartbeat.

"You know I could make your life very…complicated." His jaw flexed. "Especially if you keep being difficult."

"I'm not being difficult, Mr. Romano." My voice was clear, unwavering. "I just want to go home."

The silence stretched, his gaze burning into mine, daring me to flinch. I didn't.

Finally, he released the door and straightened, his hands curling into fists at his sides. "Fine. For now."

His self-satisfied grin vanished, replaced with an unreadable hardness, and he walked back to his car. Sliding into the back seat with infuriating grace, he disappeared as the SUV pulled away.

I let out a long breath.

"Asshole," I muttered, cranking the engine and speeding out before he decided to circle back.

Leo

My fingers drummed against my knee, impatience gnawing at me as I watched dawn break over the skyscrapers. I was fucking tired, up for almost twenty-four hours handling loose ends. "Did you get the information I asked for?"

Gio, seated in the passenger seat, handed me a thin manila file. "Everything you need is in there," he said, his tone measured but carrying a weight of caution. "But, boss…"

I narrowed my eyes on the back of his head, my jaw already tight. "What?"

"You're not gonna like what you see."

The air in the car thickened as I yanked the file from his hands and flipped it open. My gaze skimmed the neatly typed contents, each line sharper than the last. Apartment address. No living family; Italian mother, veteran father with enough battery charges to tell me she had grown up in a dark world.

Her bank statements were a mess, but her savings account showed she had a goal and couldn't seem to keep the money in it, sending it through her Venmo or Cash App to other women in Chicago. That intrigued me. Was she helping the girls at the clubs she worked at like Vinnie was? The interest turned into a hunger for more. Medical history—nothing notable other than a few broken bones from when she was a kid and one broken rib in her early twenties. Then my thumb paused as I reached the next section.

Her dating history.

The names were a who's who of low-life criminals in multiple states—two in for grand theft, another serving life for murder. But it was the last name on the list that made my blood pressure spike.

Declan fucking McCalister.

The file crumpled under my grip as my hand tightened. "McCalister," I growled, the name sour on my tongue.

"I told you, Boss," Gio said quietly, shaking his head. "She's either very brave… or very fucking stupid."

I shot him a look sharp enough to cut steel. "Shut the fuck up, Gio."

He raised his hands in mock surrender, though I didn't miss the smirk he tried to hide—or the low chuckle Dimitri stifled from the driver's seat. I wasn't in the mood for commentary.

Of all the men she could've tangled with, it had to be him. Declan McCalister—the Irish mob prince himself. I clenched my jaw until the ache throbbed at my temples. The Irish—especially Declan—had been stirring up trouble on my turf. First poaching girls from my clubs, then robberies at some of my nicer restaurants, then the final straw was torching one of my warehouses.

And with Cassandra working in my newly acquired club? Who the fuck knew what that little Mc-Asshole was plotting. He never did have a good track record with his girls.

I flipped back through the file, eyes landing on her address. Neutral turf. That explained her quiet confidence—the way she'd stared me down tonight like I wasn't worth a second thought.

That little vixen had known exactly who I was. She knew my name, my reputation, and still had the audacity to look at me like I was nothing more than dirt beneath her heels.

A slow wicked grin tugged at my mouth, steadying my pulse. Oh, Cassandra.

She might think this was over—that walking out tonight had put distance between us. But she'd underestimated me.

What a fun little game we were playing.

Cassandra

I parked my car a block away from my apartment in New City. Same issue as always—no damn spots closer to the building. I sighed, gripping the steering wheel for a second longer before forcing myself to move. The quiet street hummed with the distant sound of sirens and the occasional buzz of a car speeding past, but I'd long since learned to tune out Chicago's chaos.

I'd been living here almost five years, and this city wasn't anything special—just another place until I needed to run again. I snagged my purse, locked the car, and started walking. The air was muggy, dawn rolling in.

My neighborhood wasn't the best, but it wasn't the worst either. It was neutral ground touching all three families' turfs. The Irish had the smallest slice in the West End row houses, the Italians owned the North Riverfront and Little Sicily in the East, while the Russians held the South side docks. The central part was neutral territory—a pact created by the families where they could do their business.

My apartment was a classic brick walk-up, run down, with a fire escape too rusted to be considered safe. The smell of water damage always hit like a slap in the face when I stepped inside. I pulled out my keys and flipped to my mailbox key. The metal ground together as it opened, snagging the pile I quickly flipped through them. Nothing but bills. I slammed it shut with a sigh.

The dark-painted stairs creaked and groaned as I climbed three flights. The hall was never well lit, and Frank, the building manager, didn't give two shits. I'd given up asking him to fix the rotting wood on the second-floor landing after Mrs. Heath almost broke her ankle last year.

My phone buzzed with another message, this one not from Declan but from Jewel, a young seventeen, almost eighteen-year-old cashier I had become close to at the local convenience store. She was always the only one running the small shop when I stopped in at odd hours of the night. When she confided in me that she was planning on running from her daddy, who was a disgusting pig with a special place in hell, I had given her my number and promised to pay for her bus ticket when she was ready. This was the text, and fuck, I had just made the funds tonight for it, but that meant I'd have to dodge Frank for another week about rent—and he was already losing his patience.

But I wasn't going to not help her. My heart raced as I replied, "Meet you tomorrow morning at our spot we discussed." I kept it vague. We'd already made the plan in person. I knew all too well how important it was to have a go-bag and a strategic escape from years of experience with garbage humans.

Tucking my phone back into my purse, my hand wrapped around the worn bronze knob as I jiggled the key into the stubborn lock. Finally exhaling, once I was inside, I could scrub this entire night from my brain and crash.

But as I twisted the doorknob, something felt off.

The soft murmur of a voice—his voice—met my ears the moment I stepped in. I froze in the threshold, my breath catching as I scanned the dimly lit living room.

Declan.

There he was, lounging on my worn-out couch like he owned the place, one leg propped on the coffee table, a cigarette hanging from his lips, with those unfair messy, dark curls that made me want to fix them. Then he shifted in his seat, the lamp throwing his sharp features into shadow, highlighting the jagged scar at the corner of his mouth and the cold glint in his ice-blue eyes.

"Gotta go." His tone was clipped as he finished his call, shoving the phone into his pocket. His eyes zeroed in on me.

"You're ignoring my calls, Cass." His Irish drawl thickened the words. He crushed the cigarette out in the ashtray I kept because of him—a habit I hadn't been able to break, not even when I'd broken off everything else.

"I thought I'd stop by to see why you're icing me out," he added, that cocky, knowing smirk curling across his lips.

I sighed heavily, tossing my bag onto the table and sliding off my shoes. I kept my tone calm, even, bored. "For starters, I was working, Dec. And second, I don't owe you anything—not anymore."

Declan's smile faltered. The way he stared at me sent a familiar tension crawling under my skin. He didn't move right away, just studied me the way he always did—like I was his, even when I wasn't.

Finally, he rose, slow and deliberate, the predatory movement so ingrained it looked natural.

"Is that so?" His voice dropped lower, the predatory smile returning darker this time, twisting at the edges. "Or maybe you're avoiding me because of someone else?"

He stepped closer, his black boots scuffing my wood floors. I crossed my arms, my heart pounding faster, palms slick with sweat I didn't want him to see. "What the hell are you talking about?"

He stopped just shy of me, his tall frame dominating the space and I couldn't stop my gaze from drifting to his small splattering of brown freckles across his nose. "Romano." He practically spat the name, disdain rolling off him like poison. "Heard you were dancing for the Italian bastard tonight."

Shit. My eyes snapped up to his. He knows already?

I kept my expression blank, my voice steady. "It wasn't like that. Vinnie needed a favor, so I helped him out."

Declan's eyes narrowed, his gaze boring into me like he could see right through the lie. "You expect me to believe that? You told me you didn't do private dances."

"I don't, Dec."

He moved closer, his voice a low snarl, cutting me off before I could explain. "Romano's got a reputation, Cass. You working there—on his turf—makes you his property. Whether you like it or not."

His words hit like a punch to the gut, but I didn't show it. My arms tightened across my chest as I tilted my chin. "Then where the hell should I work, huh?"

A vein pulsed on his forehead. Panic crawled into my chest. "You're working for the enemy, Cass! Fuck, couldn't you have just stayed at O'Malley's? You were better off there than crawling for Italian money."

I groaned, running a hand through my hair as frustration bubbled. "O'Malley was a goddamn pervert, and you know it. And let's not pretend you didn't make things worse. You were in there every other night starting fights because someone looked at me too long."

Declan started pacing—always a sign his temper was about to

snap. Slowly, I slid my hand toward my purse on the table where I kept pepper spray and a taser.

"You don't understand, Cass." His voice rose, spit flying. "You working there now makes you a liability, a target." His eyes flashing, cold and calculating.

His fists clenched, but instead of striking out, he turned sharply, pacing like a caged animal. "This isn't just about the damn club. You're working on his side now. That puts you in the middle whether you want it or not."

I shook my head, exasperated. "Jesus, Dec, it's not my fault you and Romano are at each other's throats. I don't care about your turf wars, and I'm not his anything."

Declan stopped, his gaze colder than I'd seen in months. Then something shifted—desperation flickered in his eyes. "Come work for me," he said suddenly. "I've got that restaurant. It's safe."

Safe. The word hung between us. For the briefest moment, I saw the old Declan—the man I'd once loved. He stepped closer, brushing a lock of hair behind my ear, his touch gentle, almost out of place.

Declan's Irish pub Flanagan's was a decently attended place, lots of drinkers and I'd heard the bartenders make money, but nothing like stripping. Besides, I knew he and his dad used that place to launder cash. It was a dirty business just like the rest of them.

This was when Declan was most dangerous—one minute an uncontrollable lunatic, the next pleading. The whiplash shredded me.

"Declan…" I sighed, shaking my head. "No. I like where I work. Vinnie treats me fine, and the money's too good to pass up."

"Cass…"

I grabbed his hand where it rested against my cheek, holding it for a moment. "Your wars are between you and the Italians. Not me."

His hand tensed under mine, eyes darkening. For a second, I thought he might say something real. Instead, the dangerous glint returned. "Maybe not. But you know what happens to girls caught in the middle."

I'd only heard stories—girls poached, missing, dead. Casualties of mob wars. And strippers like me? We were at the bottom of the totem pole. Used as informants, currency, leverage. Either way, we got hurt. But most of us were so desperate for cash we took the extra opportunities despite the risks. I wasn't any different—too broke to escape this underground world. But I wasn't going to sell myself out. I just needed to dance long enough to stack enough cash and get the hell out of this city.

His thumb brushed my cheekbone again, fire simmering in his gaze. And damn it, his touch still got to me.

"I know," I murmured, letting his hand fall. "And I'll be careful."

Declan lingered a beat before pulling away. His expression softened, just slightly. "Alright. But if Romano gives you trouble, you call me. Understand?"

My chin dipped. I bit back the ache in my chest. "I'll be fine." Even I didn't even believe it.

He leaned down, pressing a soft kiss to my forehead. When he pulled back, sadness tucked itself into his smile. "You always did have a soft spot for me, Cass."

With that, he turned and left, the door clicking shut behind him.

The second he was gone, my knees buckled. I sank onto the chair by the table, burying my face in my hands. A shaky breath ripped out of me.

"It's been three months," I muttered. "It'll get easier."

EPISODE 2

Cassandra

Sweat glistened on my arms and chest, sliding down my back in thin, cool rivulets. My feet pounded the pavement, which vibrated occasionally with the passing CTA train, while my favorite playlist blasted through my earbuds. The runner's high had hit five miles ago, and for the first time all week, I felt invincible.

Every year I told myself I'd run the Chicago Marathon—and every year, something got in the way. If I was honest, though, it wasn't the *something*. It was me. I had a library of excuses for why I couldn't accomplish things—and never enough courage to actually follow through.

For now, I'll keep blaming it on my bad karma and commitment issues.

The endorphin release was exactly what I needed. Seeing Declan this week had not been helpful. He and I had a complicated relationship, to say the least. It was a fast-burn romance straight out of a smut novel—*a broken girl running from her past, a troubled boy surrounded by his demons, and both looking for sanctuary in each other.* Sounds romantic as fuck when I fantasize about it that way.

Fuck. I missed him—especially the softer side he rarely let anyone see. I shook my head, cutting off the thought before it could run its course. *Remember why you left, Cass.*

I couldn't miss him. There was a reason I left. I needed out before things escalated—because that was when the romance stopped, when the passion and heat between us turned volatile.

Dammit. Frustration swelled in my chest, and I lengthened my stride, using the emotion to push myself harder—to reach my goal of ten miles in under two hours. But the video loop of memories kept playing—like a sick psychological experiment designed to induce the exact responses I was trying to outrun.

The breeze off Lake Michigan carried the stench of sour whiskey from the run-down pub up ahead. My stomach twisted as the scent hit, shoving me back into the memories until I was drowning in them again—the sound of glass shattering, Declan's voice echoing through the marble hall, and my own heartbeat pounding like it was trying to escape my ribs.

"Declan, I can't do this anymore!" I shouted, slinging my duffel bag over my shoulder.

"To hell you're leaving!" Declan spat, his face flushed red, that familiar vein in his forehead pulsing dangerously.

"Move, please." I settled my voice as calm as I could, clinging to some semblance of control. My eyes dropped to the white marble floor of his family's mansion—unable to meet the gaze of the man who had become both the one I yearned for and the one I feared.

He leaned in close, hand pressed against the door, effectively trapping me. His breath was hot against my face—reeking of aged whiskey—and he whispered, "Make me."

It was a threat. A challenge. He was losing control, teetering on the edge that made him a loose cannon. Fuck.

"Declan McCalister, you let that girl leave this instant!"

Abigail's stern Irish accent echoed through the room. Seconds later she appeared, rounding the corner with her usual commanding presence. I peered around Declan slightly, keeping one eye on the man looming over me and the other on my red-haired savior.

"How dare you speak to this woman with such disrespect," she scolded, her greenish-blue glare cutting into him like a blade. Abigail wasn't a woman you said no to. A first-generation immigrant, she'd lived a hard, fast life—especially with Finnegan, her husband and the current Irish leader, at her side. When she spoke, it commanded respect and obedience, just like her husband.

Declan straightened, his anger still simmering but less overt now. "Mother, I—"

She cut him off, tone unwavering. "Your father and I taught you better. Now move."

Unfortunately, I wish I could say she was telling the truth about that. But when you raise your oldest son to be the next-in-line mob boss, you can't exactly win Mother of the Year. Still, I wasn't going to say that out loud—not when she was saving me from her son's wrath.

Declan glanced down at me, then back at his mother, before huffing in annoyance. Reluctantly, he stepped aside—just enough for me to squeeze through the door. My shoulder brushed his as I did, and he grabbed my wrist. His grip was tight but not painful—a silent plea for me to look at him one last time.

"Where are you going?" he whispered, his voice raw, his eyes swirling with a hint of fresh tears.

The pain in his ice-blue eyes—the betrayal—took everything in me not to falter. "I'm renting an apartment in New City. I'm sure you'll find me," I said flatly, holding back the emotion twisting my heart. It felt like someone had thrown it in a blender to make a fucking margarita, throwing my dignity atop it for garnish—and then added salt on the rim for good measure.

Cheers to that, Cass.

His grip loosened, his hand falling to his side. I turned and walked quickly, forcing each footstep forward and blinking hard to keep the dam of tears from breaking.

Séamus had an unreadable expression as he opened the door to the black SUV waiting outside, and I slid in, tossing my duffel on the seat beside me. Only when the door shut and I was shielded from view did I let the tears fall.

HE LOVED ME. And I still—

No, Cassie. Stop.

My nails dug into my palms as I sprinted now, pushing harder, as though I could leave it all behind. The scent of burning hotdogs from a corner cart hit me—greasy and sharp—making my stomach churn the way memories of Declan always did.

Why couldn't I let him go? Even after everything he'd done?

My favorite coffee shop across from Oz Park came into view, and I channeled everything I had left into those last few feet—every ache, every frustration, every ugly, cry-filled night—into the run.

The smell of freshly brewed coffee mingled with the fumes of the city as I thudded to a stop. Lifting my wrist, I pressed two fingers to my pulse point and glanced at my watch.

Nice.

Leo

Oh *Dio mio,* this woman could run.

Gio parked the black Bentley close enough for me to see her. I watched her chest rise and fall, sweat sliding down her neck and disappearing between her breasts. The crowd parted around her like she was a goddess—too beautiful to touch.

In my spare time this week, I had taken to memorizing Cassandra's routine. This run was one of her regular routes. I scoffed at the irony—my little *topo* running while I stalked her like a feline predator.

Gio's voice broke through my thoughts, followed by a car horn blaring somewhere nearby. "Boss, do you want to keep watching her, or should we head back to the estate?"

Clenching my fists, I growled, "We'll leave when I'm ready." I had business to attend to. Stalking women was beneath me as the *don*—but this guilty pleasure I couldn't resist.

Fuck—I lost her. My eyes scanned the crowd until I spotted her, coffee cup in hand, crossing toward Oz Park. Her usual routine. I loved how predictable her patterns were—but her mind, *that* was what kept me interested.

"Alright, Gio, let's head back now. But I want someone tailing her for the rest of the day," I ordered.

"Anything specific you're looking for?"

"Just… observe. See if anything out of the ordinary happens." My voice trailed off as I watched her sit on her usual bench, people-watching like some normal woman in Chicago. It made me grin wickedly—too fucking adorable. She needed someone to watch over her, whether she realized it or not. The city chewed up women like her and that was kind in our world. Especially women like Cassandra Bennett who didn't ask for saving but saved everyone else around her.

"You got it, boss."

The briefing earlier this week had brought me news about her visit from Declan McCalister—the Irish prince himself. The information made me see red. After composing myself, I decided I'd keep eyes on her and everyone who thought they had a claim on her. Now that she was at my club and in my sights, she only belonged to *me*.

Owning Inferno brought in a decent amount of extra income—it picked up some of the losses the Irish caused us. And knowing Declan's old girl was raking in some of that cash for me brought a sweet sort of revenge.

From what Dimitri had gathered from his intel collection the other night, Inferno was well-staffed with the best girls in town. I don't know how Vinnie—that weak-spined bastard—managed to pull that off. After looking over all their employment information, most of the girls had one thing in common—they were all running from some criminal, or trying to make enough cash to leave.

Inferno was a safe haven, in its own fucked-up way—and I liked that. It felt like a good deed, instead of the usual bloodstained acts we had to dish out in this business. Deep down, I was a good man—maybe even a reasonable one—but sometimes good men had to do unreasonable things.

Cassandra

I'd noticed the black SUV tailing me today—and for the past week. The only problem was that I didn't know if it was Irish or Italian. Either way, it was bad news, but I wasn't going to let it stop me from living my life. My daily ritual was the one thing that helped me feel normal, even when I knew my life was anything but.

After sitting in the park for thirty minutes, people-watching and enjoying my victory coffee—a hot cappuccino—I ordered an Uber back to my apartment.

The sun was finally starting to set, allowing Chicago to breathe a bit from its scorching heat. The Uber driver—who I was almost positive was still in high school—weaved recklessly through rush-hour traffic. I couldn't help but let my hatred for this city sit on the back burner as I admired it. The east side of Chicago—or more importantly, the touristy section—was all trimmed lawns and modern sculptures, and I secretly loved it.

Especially the Magdalene sculpture in Grant Park. When I saw her for the first time, it was spring, and she was surrounded by tulips. She was stunning even with her Frankenstein rusted automobile parts. By summer, vines and flowers would crawl up her skirt, allowing her to blend with the environment and enhance her surroundings.

Personally, I related to her—well, except for the *enhance* part. That I did poorly at. But blending in, shape-shifting? That was what I did best. How I stayed strong. How I survived. I loved her for how effortlessly she belonged here. Maybe I hated her for it too.

As the overly Axe-body-sprayed Toyota Camry pulled up to my building, two familiar figures stood at the entrance. I couldn't stop the smile that spread across my face, though concern followed fast behind. Séamus—one of Finnegan's longest-standing bodyguards, mid-fifties—was always in an off-white shirt and green windbreaker.

His blue-grey eyes were hard most of the time unless he was speaking to someone he cared about. And Bran, the quiet, reserved one with buzzed black hair, a Bulls hat he wore everywhere, and an all-black wardrobe, only showed up when instructed to watch—or take someone out.

Stepping out of the vehicle, the smell of exhaust fumes canceled out the overpowering, fake scent of cedarwood and sage body spray I'd been subjected to for forty-five minutes. "Séamus. Bran." I acknowledged as I approached them, dipping my chin.

The two men, usually stoic and cold, softened when they saw me. That was hopeful. Maybe they weren't here to kill me after all.

"Cassie, it's good to see you again," Séamus said, his eyes crinkling at the corners, that deep Irish voice oddly comforting. Bran offered me a small smile, though it never reached his dark green eyes.

"Likewise." My gaze flicked between them and I caught the glimpse of Bran's gun tucked in his pants. "I'm assuming you're both here on orders?" I didn't need confirmation—I knew Declan had sent them. I just needed to know *why.*

Séamus gave me a guilty smile, tucking his hands into his windbreaker pockets. "Yeah, sorry, darlin'. He had us come watch ya."

I ran a hand over my hair, brushing back the loose strands from my ponytail that tickled my forehead, and sighed. "You guys want any coffee or something to eat before your long night?" I gestured toward the door.

Séamus and Bran interacted with me the most while Declan and I were together. They knew everything that happened between us— everything—all the way up to the last night I stayed at the McCalister household. Séamus had let me sob the entire car ride to my new complex, which took me months to find in secret and even longer to save up the money for first, last, and the security deposit on the shit- hole. I thought it was going to be impossible to save the extra cash I was making at O'Malley's by doing degrading private dances and keeping it a secret from Declan.

Séamus gave me a look that said *I'm sorry about all this.* "Thanks, Cassie," he said softly.

Bran offered me an apologetic, grateful smile.

"Anytime," I replied, patting both men on the shoulders before guiding them up to my apartment. The two men followed close behind me up the three flights of stairs in silence.

Opening the paint chipped door, I gestured for them to come in and sit at my worn kitchen table, its laminate cracking and peeling. Thirty minutes later, the apartment smelled of steak, potatoes, and sautéed greens—something I remembered was their favorite back at the McCalister estate.

I placed my secondhand porcelain plates before them and refilled the half-empty coffee cups, their rims chipped from years of use.

"Cassie, you've done too much," Séamus said warmly, his protest softened by gratitude.

Bran dug in immediately, flashing me a smile of appreciation as he chewed. He had a new scar running through his thick dark brow, but it didn't take away from his kind face. Bran had to be in his early thirties, but he never spoke enough for me to ask questions.

"Just eat. You've got a long night ahead of you," I said playfully.

Joining them with my own plate, we ate quietly. Every now and then, Bran groaned with satisfaction, while Séamus's phone lit up with notifications he would have to respond to.

Having dinner with them filled me with a strange sense of comfort and familiarity. It reminded me of a time when I'd felt at home at the McCalister estate. I cut another piece of steak, mixed feelings of guilt and sadness swirling in my chest. I didn't think I'd ever feel that way again.

Leo

"FUCK!" I slammed my fists onto my desk. The Mick bastards were getting in my way.

Gio had informed me as soon as I walked into my damn house after being out all damn night dealing with some rats, that Cassandra let those two Irish pieces of shit into her home last night. I needed to know more—details, connections—how deep she's entrenched.

"Gio!" I barked.

He entered immediately. I glared at him, my fury barely contained.

Through gritted teeth, I said, "I want you to look into Cassandra's relationship with the Irish prince." My jaw ached from the tension I had been holding all week over this woman.

"Yes, Boss," Gio said quickly before turning and exiting. My men knew not to ask questions when I was like this; my fury knew no bounds, and especially when my little *topo* was involved. I'd had a permanent migraine from this woman, and I was pretty sure the only cure was her. One day she and I would laugh at all the stress she had caused me in order for me to protect her.

The door clicked shut, leaving me alone in my growing frustration. I turned and strode to the window overlooking the garden of my estate. Dragging a hand through my disheveled dark brown hair, I gripped the ends tightly. My hydrangeas and salvia, some of my favorite flowers, were in full bloom recently and yet not even their beauty could ease this agitation.

My mother would be telling me to sit and eat some of her homemade Stracciatella soup. She always made it for me as a kid when I had exams or an important deadline.

"My love eases the weight on the heart, Leonardo, and I made this soup for one of my greatest loves."

Her cooking did have healing powers, and I never told her no—the consequences of that were a smack behind my head with a wooden spoon.

My hand gripped my phone tighter as I looked down at the dark screen. I had never felt such a need to own someone before. And this nagging feeling—that I needed to kill every man who had ever spoken to her—was relentless. My hands shoved aggressively into my pockets as I paced.

Moments later, Gio returned—his steps smooth and deliberate. He carried a folder, clutching it tightly like the soldier he was. Gio had been with me for a while, pretty much rose through the ranks beside me in this business. He also saved my ass on occasion, especially when we were negotiating with the Russians for a piece of their armory trade. When I was promoted, I didn't hesitate to make Gio my personal bodyguard. I always knew I'd be given the don spot, considering my father held it before me. Dimitri came soon after, highly recommended by Gio; it helped that they were cousins. Gio was ten years older than Dimitri, who was around twenty-three—young but hungry. With his military background and Gio's approval, I didn't waste any time making him my second bodyguard.

"This is everything I could gather, Boss." He handed me the folder and waited patiently, his hands in the pockets of his dark-wash jeans.

Still standing in front of the window, I opened it and flipped through the papers.

"Dated Declan for a year; lived at the McCalister estate for the same length…still friendly with the Irish mob…left three months ago," I read aloud. I flipped to a series of photos pulled from various sources—her smiling, walking with people I recognized from the Irish mafia. I methodically wadded the file into a tight ball.

My steps were sure and purposeful as I strode toward the classic brick fireplace and tossed the crumpled folder into the unlit grate. Then, with a flick of the switch, flames erupted, consuming the pages. The photos shriveled and turned to ash—black and flaky, it crumbled into dust like the Irish mob would soon do.

Gio stood silently nearby, a loyal shadow. We both watched the fire for a long moment, the air growing hotter, matching my internal struggle. What did she see in Declan? He was impulsive—probably Finnegan's weakest link in his business, in my opinion. My father would have offed me already if I acted the way Declan did. We already knew he was the one commanding the fires to our warehouses and poaching our girls from the dozen or so clubs we owned, selling them off. Cassandra probably didn't know the extent of this asshole's crimes.

If I wanted her to accept my protection I needed to make a bigger gesture, push more of myself into her world. I wanted to be deeply rooted in her life as if I had been there all along, and absolutely impossible to get rid of—like an Italian cypress.

"I want you to send Cassandra a bottle of Italy's best wine and two dozen roses tonight after her shift. Make sure she knows it's from me," I ordered, forcing my voice to sound calm as I gripped the mantle with one hand.

"You got it." Gio pulled out his phone and began typing, making the arrangements.

I glanced back at the flames, watching the last of the photos disappear into embers. A metaphor for what I would make sure happened to any man from her past. She would only remember me—one way or another.

Cassandra

Another flawless shift. The bucket of money from my last stage performance was overflowing—I knew for a fact I'd made close to eight hundred dollars in tips for the night, I didn't want to think about the 40% Vinnie would be taking later. My heels clicked confidently as I headed back to the dressing room to change and head home for the evening.

The other girls were already at their personal stations, counting money and peeling off glittery costumes. The room smelled of dollar bills, sweet perfume, and…roses?

"You got a delivery just a minute ago, Angel," Candy's high-pitched voice called out.

A delivery? That was unusual. I never received deliveries at work unless it was takeout, and even that was a rare treat.

I hurried to my station and stopped short. Two dozen red roses sat in a crystal vase beside a bottle of Giacomo Conterno Monfortino. I knew that wine—it was expensive, and far too fancy for this setting. My eyes narrowed as I reached for the card nestled in the bouquet.

The paper felt heavy in my hands as I opened it.

Thinking of you, principessa – L.

Leo. Of course.

I sighed, rolling my eyes. I tossed the card in the trash beside my vanity. The roses were beautiful, and the wine was tempting, but I couldn't accept them. Not from him. I knew it meant something—it always did. It's how I got consumed by Declan, and all the other men. Accepting gifts, help, or anything else meant they owned me, and that always meant trouble.

"Here, Candy." I grabbed the flowers and bottle, passing them to her. "These were meant for you."

Candy's face lit up, her grin so wide I could see all her too-white teeth. "See, ladies!" she said loud and proud, strutting around the room with the roses like a trophy. "When you look like me and work as hard as I do, the men start eating out of the palm of your hand."

The other girls groaned—annoyed but not surprised by her arrogance. It was Candy, after all. Candy and a few of the other girls here were big personalities, but this was the first strip club I worked at where we had each other's backs. We all knew the dangers of being a stripper in Chicago, especially when the mobs and gangs were involved. Poachers were constantly coming in as "high rollers," trying to tip large or whisper sweet nothings about a life of luxury and being cared for. But all the girls here were runaways from abuse, crime families, or survivors of trafficking. We saw the signs, and we had Vinnie kick them out. He was good for that—good to us. Which is why I stayed.

I let myself chuckle softly at Candy's continued theatrics. She was entertaining when she wasn't a pain in my ass. Candy and I competed for the top-earner spot often, but she was a sore winner and a sore loser. We were like day and night: she had the blonde, fake-playboy-bunny look, while I was the dark-haired siren.

Although neither of us would ever admit it—because I sure as shit wouldn't—the opposites thing worked in our favor if we played it right. She and the other girls had a special place in my heart since I arrived at Inferno, and I had kept things close to my chest, but I would give these girls everything I owned. My hand drifted over my heart as it twinged with a deep ache. I hated that I would be leaving them eventually, but I couldn't stay in Chicago.

After shoving my things in my locker like some high-schooler after P.E. class, I locked it and grabbed my knockoff Gucci bag I'd bought back when I was living in NYC, right before I moved here. It was a celebratory purchase on my way out. My boyfriend at the time had just been charged and imprisoned for murdering a man he was only supposed to rough up, and honestly, it was for the best. He was emotionally manipulative and a narcissist. The sex was fucking awesome, though.

Stepping into the parking lot, the smell of fresh asphalt assaulted my nose, and the sound of nearby construction and hollering filled the humid air. It was probably getting close to five in the morning, and the drive home was filled with early-riser traffic and the people who loved to brag about being part of the five-a.m. club doing their workouts and whatever the fuck else they did each morning.

My hatred for that life stemmed from my own lack of normality in this world and my inability to find security in this underworld I'd been dragged into and now couldn't escape, no matter how many times I ran. I just had too many daddy issues.

Shouldering my apartment door open, I kicked off my tennis shoes and flopped onto the outdated sofa, propping my feet on the coffee table. My gaze fell on the ashtray still filled with Declan's cigarette ash from when he visited last week. He'd kept Séamus and Bran gatekeeping the place, and I didn't hate it. I knew it would keep the creeper Leo Romano from knocking on my door.

I groaned, covering my eyes with the crook of my arm. *Fuck all these overbearing men.*

Two minutes later, the intercom buzzed, jolting me upright. I stared at it, scowling. "A visitor? This early?" I muttered. Dragging myself over, I pressed the button. "Hello?"

A familiar voice came through, warm and rough with age. "Is that any way to greet your favorite auld fella?" he chuckled.

My heart stopped. "Oh my God—Finnegan?" I pressed the buzzer immediately. "Come up!"

When the knock sounded, I flung the door open. "Finnegan!"

My face broke into a genuine smile as I took in his thin but sturdy frame. Finnegan McCalister might have been the leader of the Irish mob, but to me, he was the kindest man I knew—like a father. When Declan brought me home like a stray dog, Finnegan hadn't hesitated to welcome me, immediately pulling connections to get me any work I wanted on his side of town. That raised the flag that this wasn't just any household but someone important, and over time I was clued in that I'd stumbled into the home of one of the three most dangerous families in Chicago—just my luck. *Cue the whomp-whomp-whomp sound effect.*

If it hadn't been for falling for Declan hard and fast, I probably would have run for the hills. But again—daddy issues galore. Declan was also really fucking cute with those few freckles across his fair skinned nose, and those ice-blue eyes—especially when they were filled with adoration instead of death—could make me melt instantly.

"Cassie, my sweet lass." He pulled me into a strong hug. Séamus and Bran stood behind him, watchful as always. I smiled at them over Finnegan's shoulder.

When we pulled back, I held his shoulders, peering into his ice-blue eyes that mirrored Declan's. The weathered lines on his face radiated quiet strength and warmth. "I've missed you so much," I said, my voice catching.

Finnegan cupped my cheek, his hand warm and gentle. "None of that, lass."

Dipping my chin, I stepped aside to let the three of them in. "Make yourselves comfortable."

I busied myself in the kitchen, making coffee. When I returned with three steaming cups, Finnegan had already settled at the dining table. I sat carefully beside him, my smile unwavering.

"To what do I owe this surprise visit?"

Finnegan set his cup down with a soft thud, his warm eyes darkening to something more serious. "Well, Cassie, my dear, Declan informed me about your little situation with Leonardo Romano." His gaze lingered on my face, searching for any hint of deception.

I sighed, rubbing my temples. "Yeah, it's complicated…"

"Ye need to be careful, my lass. Romano's not a man to be trifled with. He's got a reputation…." Finnegan leaned in closer, his voice dropping to a whisper. "He doesn't take kindly to refusals—especially when he thinks he owns something."

My eyes hardened, but I kept my voice calm and cool. "Nobody owns me. Not Declan. Not Leo. Not anyone."

His eyes warmed in a way that made my instincts prickle with warning—as if I were both a daughter and indebted to him. "Ye always were a resilient one." He reached for my hand, squeezing it a bit harder than reassuring. "I know you and Declan had a falling out, but just know we miss you." Something was off, and my instincts were telling me to be on guard.

My back stiffened slightly, though I didn't pull away. Séamus and Bran exchanged a look I couldn't decipher before simultaneously sipping from their mugs.

"I know…" I forced a smile. If I was going to survive whatever this was, I needed to play along.

Finnegan nodded, his expression unreadable but still unthreatening. "As broken up as he is, you were always too good for him."

My brain was screaming at me, my pulse racing. "Thanks, Finnegan. Your words are too kind."

He let out a loud, rumbling laugh—the forced sound echoing off the apartment walls—and it startled me. "No one has ever called me too kind before." He patted my hand, his eyes piercing into me with a warning. "Be safe out there, lass. This world isn't for the faint of heart —or the reckless."

He stood, and the rest of us followed suit. I walked him to the door, Séamus and Bran flanking us protectively. Finnegan turned to me one last time, his voice low, soft, and affectionate. "Cassie… ye will always have my protection. You're like a third daughter to me, and if you ever need anything, I'm only a phone call away."

I swallowed hard, my eyes stinging as tears threatened to fall. Now he sounded like the man I'd lived with—but his warning still worried me. I hugged him tightly, holding on as if he could keep me safe from every-thing swirling in my life. "Thank you for checking on me. I love you."

Finnegan hugged me back, his strong hands steady. He whispered softly, "Tá mo chroí istigh ionat, my heart is inside you, my lass." The words sounded endearing but as they settled over me I felt it more like a collar tightening around my neck.

When he pulled away, he brushed a stray tear from my cheek. "I'll be seeing ye."

With that, he left, Séamus and Bran following him silently—like an omen. I closed the door and stood there for a long moment, the weight of his words settling over me and making a cold shiver slither down my spine.

Leo

"Boss, Finnegan stopped by Cassandra's apartment last night," Gio informed me as we drove toward our next meeting, I had some business with the Russians about when their next shipment of guns would be arriving.

An afternoon shower pelted the front windshield as I stoically sat in the back seat, staring out at the window droplets running across the glass. Chicago pulsed with life outside—the rhythm of the city an ever-present thrum. My thumb tapped restlessly against my knee as I considered Gio's words.

"Keep watching her," I said finally, my voice low and measured. "If the King of the Irish is visiting her personally, that means he's worried she'll run her mouth." My little *topo* was strategic, living on neutral turf, knowing if either of us hurt her it would break the agreement between the three families. But Cassandra was also defiant and constantly left that territory for the sake of her daily activities, which —even in this short time I had known her— I could see were precious to her.

Gio nodded, glancing at me in the rearview mirror. "Anything else you want done, Boss?"

I pulled out my phone and typed out a message to my men: Let me know the next time she ends up on Italian turf...alone. I slid the device back into my pocket, a slow curve pulled at my lips. If she's going to expose herself, I'll show her what that sort of defiance invites.

Between Declan, Finnegan, and those two goons standing outside her building, they were making it far too difficult for me to get near my little *topo*. She refuses to dance for me again at the club, even when I threaten to get rid of Vinnie. The little vixen just smirks at me with challenge. She's too fucking smart—and I like it—but the blue balls

I've had for the last two weeks are starting to make my fuse shorter and shorter.

Just the other day, I shot one of my men in the foot for bringing me the wrong coffee order. Now they're all on edge, probably counting the rosary for me to get laid. Unfortunately for them, I wouldn't touch another woman unless it's Cassandra Bennett. She was all I could think about, dream about, jerk off to. It was infuriating.

I leaned back into the seat, fingers steepled as I let the thoughts turn over in my mind. "I'll just have to start playing dirty," I muttered to myself, the words hanging like a promise in the air.

The mere thought of getting Cassandra alone—*truly* alone—lit something dangerous inside me. Fireworks ignited low in my groin as I pictured her face, her fiery emerald eyes, and her body close enough to touch.

Exhaling a deliberate breath, I ran a hand through my hair. She had a deeper hold on me than I'd anticipated. It irritated me—and made me question my self-control. She was a puzzle I had to understand, knowing she kept secrets about her softer side while simultaneously pushing my boundaries at every turn—it was addictive.

The sound of a car horn blared nearby and I shifted uncomfortably, adjusting myself in my seat. This last week had been fun—like hunting prey—but I was growing tired of waiting. My restlessness to pounce was becoming impossible to ignore.

EPISODE 3

Cassandra

The Chicago sun beat down on my bare shoulders as I hurried along the short walk to my favorite pizza joint, Vita al Pomodoro, off West Taylor Street in Little Sicily. Vita al Pomodoro came into my life a little less than two and a half months ago when I got off at the wrong subway stop after a long run up the east side in the late afternoon. I was starving and was drawn in by the smell of toasted bread and the warm feeling I got when I looked into the window. I brushed the back of my hand over my forehead, wiping away beads of sweat that formed like dew on a misty morning. My eyes darted around for what felt like the hundredth time, scanning my surroundings.

Well, this place was a safe haven until Leo Romano came into my life. I had been sticking to Italian territory to avoid Declan. It wasn't that I didn't feel safe here. It was more like I was trying to avoid more drama, and with Leo constantly up my ass, Declan had been texting me constantly about my whereabouts.

I was far from stupid. I knew the risks of continuing my weekly habits, but it wasn't fair that I had to change everything I enjoyed—everything I cherished—just because I had one unhinged ex-boyfriend and one Italian stalker. This only made me want to try harder to keep my normalcy, to leave this fucking city.

During the two bus rides to get here, I couldn't help but notice every dark SUV that idled behind the bus or beside it, the window tint a shade too dark for anyone to see inside. Then the smell of freshly cooked dough and tangy tomato sauce reached me, cutting through my nerves. Relief washed over me like the comfort of a hot shower. Soon, I'd be inside, stuffing my face in peace.

When I reached the door, I gripped the overheated metal handle and tugged it open. Bells clanged above my head, breaking the quiet tension buzzing in my ears. I stepped inside and inhaled deeply. The familiar aroma of garlic, oregano, and basil wrapped around me like an old friend. A soft smile tugged at my lips as saliva pooled in my mouth.

Maria passed by, her presence as comforting as the smell of the pizza itself. She was an older, robust woman with brown hair pulled back in a simple bun, exuding warmth and charm like it was second nature. She made everyone who walked through the door feel at home —but with me, it felt personal. Like family.

She paused, then turned back to me with a broad smile. "*Cara*, welcome back."

"Hey, Maria," I said, mirroring her smile. "It's good to be back. You have a table open?" I glanced around at the busy little restaurant. They were fully staffed today, and the sound of laughter, Italian conversation, and the faint hum of a female singing *Ave Maria* coming from the speakers brought a sense of ease to my tight chest.

She grabbed a menu from the front counter and started guiding me, her hips swaying with her tightly wrapped apron. "I have your usual spot in the back open." Her voice calling over her shoulder as she began guiding me to the back.

My lip tipped up on one side, loving how well she knew me. In all fairness, I came here at least once a week. They expected me every Thursday night. "Perfect." We weaved through the crowded space, avoiding servers with hot trays of delicious home cooked meals and passed by booths with framed images of Maria and Marco during their years in Italy over each one. The restaurant resembled what I would imagine an Italian family kitchen would look like, with tables covered in adorable table clothes, handpicked flowers in small vases in the center, and pale walls with grape themed wall paper on the top edges outlining the space and giving it a tied-together look.

Sliding into the booth, I watched as Maria disappeared for a moment, returning with a glass of water. She set it down in front of me and tilted her head, studying me with a knowing glint in her eye. "You want your usual, or are you feeling spontaneous today?"

I chuckled, not even looking down at the plaid-colored menu. "No, I need my usual. I'm looking for comfort right now. My life has been…too spontaneous lately."

Maria nodded as if she understood everything without needing the details, taking the menu I held out. "Coming right up."

As she left, I leaned back against the booth and let out a long, tired breath. Between Declan's men staking out my apartment complex, the constant feeling of being followed, and fucking Leo Romano being a relentless, thorn in my side at the club, my nerves were shot. I needed this pizza—the warm, familiar weight of comfort food to take the edge off and maybe drown some of the cortisol in my system.

Leo

My hands had been steepled in front of me, resting on the cool, hard surface of my mahogany desk, as I listened to my second and cousin, Ciro, and my *caporegime*, Nico—who was in charge of our soldiers and operations—drone on over the conference call. Their voices grated in my ears like a rusted cheese grater scraping across metal. My jaw ticked, the tension building with every passing second. Fucking Cassandra. The slick, infuriating ways she kept slipping out of my grasp at the club. One minute she was in the spotlight, the next she was disappearing into the shadows like a ninja. She had a way of always being too busy, conveniently so, when I was at Inferno. I only knew this because Dimitri had told me he was able to talk to her countless times when he went alone.

My gaze had narrowed on her name, scrawled in sharp, angry letters on the notepad in front of me. I needed to get the upper hand.

She thought she could outsmart me, outmaneuver me. I wouldn't allow it. Not anymore.

"Boss?" Nico's voice cut through my thoughts.

I blinked, shaking my head and forcing myself to focus. They were talking about the Russians and our upcoming shipment we expected from them. Recently, a new Pakhan had been chosen, Aleksander Sokolov. His father, Ivan, had passed from cancer just last spring. Aleksander and I had similar styles of running our families, which made our relationship with the Russians easy. We also had a common dislike for the Irish, especially Declan.

When I spoke to Aleksander earlier in our meeting, he had been on board with keeping our ties strong since the Irish were creating tension along their boundaries as well. It was a stupid move on their part. The Irish were not known for common sense—only brute force. When we eventually retaliated, I knew the Russians would stand behind us—as long as the turf was divided evenly.

"Fine," I barked, my voice sharper than I intended. "Just keep our men in line. If they step out of bounds and fuck up this deal, you warn them that I'll personally find them and blow their fucking brains out."

Ciro chuckled. Of course he did. He was never fazed by my temper. He'd grown up with it, after all. His mother and father had been murdered in their sleep by some low-level gang looking for money when he was just five years old. The bastard had been lucky enough to be spending the night at my family's house when it happened, but that night changed everything. From that day forward, he was my brother, not just my cousin.

"Ciro, be there to make sure the shipment goes smoothly tomorrow night," I ordered, though the tension in my tone remained. He knew how important this new shipment of weapons was for us, and we couldn't afford to lose our good standing with the new Pakhan.

His response came with a knowing smile I could practically hear through the line. "That black-haired *bella* from the nightclub still leaving you with blue balls, Leo?"

Nico's loud laughter followed, grating in its own right.

My fists clenched, the veins on the backs of my hands bulging. "Both of you, shut the fuck up and mind your business."

Ciro didn't stop. He laughed this time, louder, cockier. "Yep, definitely blue balls."

"Boss, how have you not fucked this stripper yet?" Nico chimed in, his voice full of amusement.

My patience finally snapped. My fist slammed down onto the desk, sending pens and papers rattling. "I'm ending this call before I put a hit out on both of you," I growled and hung up before either of them could get another word in.

Leaning back in my leather chair, I rubbed the bridge of my nose, inhaling deeply in an attempt to calm the storm in my head. "Fucking Cassandra Bennet," I muttered under my breath. That woman was a thorn in my side, digging deeper every goddamn day.

Then my phone buzzed in my pocket. I pulled it out, my irritation temporarily forgotten. A text from Gio lit up the screen: *She's on our turf, and she's alone.*

A dangerous smile spread across my face. "Perfect."

I moved fast, making my way to Vita al Pomodoro without a second thought. By the time I arrived, Gio and Dimitri were already waiting for me out front, their stances stiff with anticipation. I paused at the entrance to adjust my suit jacket, tugging the sleeves down and smoothing out the wrinkles before combing my fingers through my dark brown hair. I could feel the tension in my jaw, the sharp ache that came from clenching it too hard for too long.

Dimitri opened the door, and the bells overhead jingled as I stepped inside. For a brief second, the sound eased the tightness in my jaw, but the relief was fleeting. My eyes scanned the bustling restaurant, noting how people averted their gazes the moment I met them. It was instinctive, almost primal, the way they looked away, as though the weight of my stare alone was too much to bear.

A familiar robust woman named Maria–who I knew was Marco's wife–greeted me, her voice warm, her presence radiating that unshakable familial energy I always associated with this place. "Mr.

Romano," she said, her tone laced with respect. "It's a pleasure to see you again. Can I get you a table?"

I softened my stare for a brief moment, just enough to keep things polite. "I'm looking for a woman who's here," I said, my tone low and sharp. "Long black hair, emerald green eyes, hard to fucking get." The last part slipped out more agitated than I intended.

The woman chuckled softly, shaking her head. "Ah," she said, gesturing to the back of the restaurant. "You're looking for our sweet *Cara*, Cassandra."

My eyes immediately found her, seated at a table near the back. Her long black hair cascaded down her back, and even from here, I could see the tension in her shoulders, like she was bracing for something. Perfect. I nodded my thanks to Maria and began striding toward her, each step deliberate, purposeful.

When I reached her table, I slid into the booth across from her without invitation. The vinyl seat hissed beneath my weight as I settled in.

At first, her eyes were soft, almost hopeful, as though she were expecting someone she cared about to sit across from her. For a split second, the sight of her like that made something stir in my chest, something foreign and unwelcome. But then she realized it was me, and her gaze sharpened into a glare so deadly it could start a war.

"*Principessa*," I purred, smirking as I leaned back in the booth. I hid the flicker of envy that rose in me when I saw that softness in her eyes moments before. That angelic gaze wasn't meant for me. And for some reason, I hated that.

Cassandra

A heavy breath left my lips as I set my half-eaten slice of pizza down on the grease-soaked paper plate. The thing was practically see-through, like my patience at the moment. My appetite was officially gone, replaced by a burning anger and the faint, unwelcome feeling of butterflies that made my eyes feel like they could shoot laser beams. That's how fucking infuriated I was to see Leo Romano sitting across from me.

At first, I thought it was Marco, the restaurant owner, coming over to say hi like he always did. But no. Of course not. This wasn't a friendly visit from someone I liked. My little sanctuary—this place where I could escape the insanity outside—was tainted. Ruined. Just like that, my temporary reprieve had been shattered.

This shouldn't have been a surprise. A flicker of annoyance at myself tightened my chest. I should have expected the man who'd been desperately seeking me out to seize any opportunity outside the club to make himself known.

"I didn't realize they just let anyone into this establishment," I quipped, wiping my hands on a paper towel as I fixed him with a cold, steady glare. I'd been cleverly avoiding him at the club, keeping busy with clients, or picking up shifts behind the bar, even cleaning the damn bathrooms. That's how desperate I was to keep out from under this wolf's paws. "I thought Maria and Marco had better standards than that."

Leo's grin was wicked, that smug, infuriating glimmer of intrigue and challenge lighting up his grey eyes. "Oh, *bella*," he said smoothly, leaning forward to rest his forearms on the table. The motion caused his sleeves to slide up, revealing an obnoxiously expensive Rolex and tanned, veiny hands. Hands that I knew were as capable of violence as they were of charm. "Speak to me again with such disrespect," he continued, lowering his voice in that cold, deliberate way of his, "and I'll make sure you're never allowed to return here again."

It wasn't the words themselves that got me. It was the way he said them—controlled, quiet, and edged with menace. The kind of threat that made you sit up straighter without even realizing it. And I did. I straightened my spine, my body reacting instinctively to the silent authority in his voice.

His smirk deepened as his eyes flicked over me, catching the subtle shift in my posture. "There we go," he said, his tone dripping with cocky satisfaction. "You're a difficult woman to get alone."

He leaned back then, clasping his hands in front of him on the table as if we were about to negotiate some high-stakes deal. The calmness of his movements. The way the pink scar on his cheek stood out more with his cocksure, predatory grin. Or the way his steel grey eyes, crinkled in a way that made him look too fucking attractive. It made me want to risk everything and punch him in his too straight nose.

"Apparently, I haven't made it difficult enough." My eyes bounced around the room at the patrons, who became quieter, stealing glances at us. "Mr. Romano, do you remember how I told you it was extremely inappropriate to contact me outside the nightclub?"

His eyes narrowed slightly, his hands tightening around each other in response. "I do."

Good. I leaned forward this time, mirroring the cold edge in his voice. It was nice to see reprimanding had an effect on him. "This is your second warning."

"And what will you do?" he asked, his lips curling into an amused smile. One that made me forget I was mad. "Call your little Irish boyfriend on me?" The laugh that followed wasn't warm, wasn't amused. It was harsh and sharp, the kind of laugh you'd hear right before someone got a bullet in their skull.

For a moment, I felt the blood run cold in my veins. But I refused to flinch. I would not let this man intimidate me, no matter how dangerous his reputation—or how dangerous he was. "I gave you an ultimatum, Mr. Romano," I said firmly. "Either—"

"Cassandra Bennet." His voice dropped lower, smoother, like a blade sliding from its sheath. "What makes you think the authorities—most of whom I own, by the way—would ever side with you?"

I sighed and leaned back, crossing my arms over my chest. I wasn't going to win this power game, not at that moment. Time for a new strategy. "Leo," I said carefully, my tone calmer, "if you know who my ex-boyfriend is"—I emphasized the word *ex* for good measure—"why the hell would you pursue me?"

He studied me for a long moment, his grey eyes unreadable, calculating. Then he smiled, with teeth that looked too sharp to be sweet at the moment. "You're indeed a dangerous prize to be won," he said softly, a glint of challenge sparking in his gaze. "The Irish are nothing but a minor inconvenience for me. Like a gnat buzzing around my face." His voice turned colder, his eyes sharper. "And with any pest, the best way to eliminate them is to crush them beneath my hand."

Holy shit. My stomach churned at the weight of his words. How the fuck—actually, what the fuck—was I going to do about this?

Before I could even think of a response, his hand shot out like a viper, grabbing mine and uncrossing my arms. His grip wasn't tight, but it was firm enough to keep me from pulling away immediately. His thumb began stroking over my knuckles in a way that felt too intimate, too delicate for the words he had just spoken. Our hands rested on the table, and the gesture—while soft on the surface— carried a possessive weight beneath it that sent a chill down my spine.

"*Principessa.*" His eyes flicked to my lips before meeting my gaze again. "I am a very persistent and patient man." He rotated my hand so his thumb could brush over the tender skin of my wrist most likely feeling my rapid pulse beneath. "But my patience is wearing thin in this little game of ours." He pulled my hand closer to his mouth, his lips ghosting over my knuckles in a way that made my pulse hammer in my ears. The motion was maddeningly romantic, but also terrifying.

I pulled my hand away quickly, cradling it in my lap like I'd just been burned. "Leo." I averted my eyes to the photo of Maria and Marco standing in front of the Leaning Tower of Pisa. "I wasn't playing a game with you. This is one-sided." I brought my focus back to his steel-grey eyes, the look of a wolf starving for a kill resting just below the surface. "I don't know what you think you're trying to win, but I am not a prize to be won."

His eyes flashed with something—frustration, maybe, or perhaps amusement—but I didn't care. I stood abruptly, pushing the bench back with a screech that made a few heads turn. "Stop following me. Stop harassing me at work. And stop ruining my dinners."

Not waiting for his response, I stormed out of the restaurant, catching Maria's surprised gaze on my way out. I forced a tight, apologetic smile and pushed the door open, stepping into the muggy evening air. I wasn't surprised to see the same two guys from the night I danced for Leo, especially the one covered in tattoos who would talk to me on occasion and who happened to look like a snack on two feet. I think his name was Dimitri. I gave them a tight smile that didn't meet my eyes before continuing my stomping that felt like a childish march toward the bus stop.

As I stalked down the street, my stomach growled, reminding me that I'd left an entire pizza uneaten—and unpaid for—back at the restaurant. "Fuck!" I shouted into the busy street, to the universe, and to karma, the vindictive bitch that clearly loved screwing with me.

Leo

The seat felt colder after she left, my eyes locked on the door long after she stormed out. My chest burned with an unfamiliar fire, one that clawed at my insides, tight and unrelenting. "Damn it," I muttered under my breath, pounding a fist on the table. The sound echoed across the quiet restaurant, drawing a few more stares I didn't bother acknowledging. "Either she's incredibly brave or incredibly stupid."

My declaration came out more like a threat than a need. Control slipped through my fingers more when I was with her than it ever had in my life. I didn't want my little *topo* to see me as a monster. I wanted her to see me as… fuck. What did I want her to see?

I forced myself to stand, throwing a wad of cash on the table to cover the untouched food and a little extra for Maria. My movements were sharp, my temper frayed. I didn't care about the hushed whispers or the lingering eyes that followed me as I crossed the room. I gave Maria a curt nod as I passed, her warm demeanor meeting the ice in my own.

She and Marco were good people, and their little restaurant took in a good profit, which I had my claws in, but on occasion I would have Nico cut them some slack, especially because they made food as good as my mother's—not that I would ever admit that out loud. If my mother ever found out, she would cut off my nuts and serve them to me in an Italian wedding soup.

Shoving the door open I was greeted with car fumes, and blaring horns of rush hour outside, Gio and Dimitri were at my sides immediately, falling into step like the obedient foot soldiers they were. I didn't pause, my strides long and purposeful. "Call Vinnie and tell him

I want to speak with him about Cassandra," I ordered, my voice tight, coiled like a spring.

"Yes, boss," Gio replied without hesitation, already pulling out his phone as we approached the waiting black SUV.

Before I reached for the car door, Gio glanced up from his phone. "He said he'll be at the club in five minutes, boss."

I gave him a single nod, more of a dismissal than an acknowledgment, before ducking into the back seat. The door slammed behind me with enough force to rattle the entire vehicle, but it didn't make me feel any better. "Drive."

The driver didn't hesitate, pulling the car smoothly into the flow of Chicago traffic. A bus hissed at a stop, and I saw a familiar head of black hair, which only made me clench my fists in my lap, my knuckles turning white. Why was Cassandra under my skin deeper than I was under hers?

"Take me to Inferno," I said flatly, continuing to watch the city chaos unfold around us, with car bumper to bumper, the curse words of drivers as they flipped each other off, and people heading to the subway lines after a long day of work. Christ, if only my work ended like their nine-to-five jobs. So simple, so easy, and I knew they were all ungrateful.

"Yes, sir," the driver replied quickly, his eyes focused on the road.

Silence filled the car, but it wasn't a calm silence. It was thick, oppressive, like the electric air before a storm. My knee bounced restlessly, my hands steepled in my lap as my mind continued to spiral around the never-ending drain.

Cassandra. Her name lingered in my mind, each syllable like a match striking against the kindling of my frustration. She had rejected me for a third fucking time. And she had the audacity to threaten me with law enforcement again, as if I didn't own half the badges in this city.

My teeth ground together, the sharp pain radiating through my jaw, a small, grounding comfort. If it weren't for this...need to win, this infuriating stripper would have been dead at that point. She had disrespected me more than once, pushed me in ways no one else dared to, and yet…

I closed my eyes and inhaled deeply, forcing myself to steady my breathing. The slow exhale didn't calm me as much as I'd hoped, but it reset something in me. Cassandra Bennet was like a splinter in my mind, an irritation I couldn't ignore, no matter how much I wanted to. She was dangerous, but not in the way I was used to.

This woman had challenged me, defied me, and it pushed me to a place I hated going—a place of confusion, of vulnerability. I should hate her. I should want her gone, out of my life, erased from my problems entirely. But instead, I wanted to be near her. I wanted to hear her sharp, cutting remarks, to see the fire in her eyes when she glared at me. I wanted to touch her again.

My gaze drifted down to my hands, the same hand that had touched hers only moments ago. Her skin had felt impossibly soft, delicate, almost fragile beneath my own. And yet she was anything but fragile. The memory of her warmth stirred that strange, clawing feeling in my chest again, something I didn't recognize and couldn't name.

I hadn't been able to resist brushing my lips over her knuckles, testing what it would feel like to bring that softness closer to me, to take it for myself. But even that brief contact hadn't been enough.

I straightened in my seat, adjusting my suit jacket with deliberate precision. My mind was made up. Cassandra would submit to me. She would beg for me. Because if she didn't…

My fingers curled into a fist, nails biting into my palm. If I couldn't have her—if I couldn't taste her defiance and break her down, piece by piece—then no one else ever would. I'd see to that personally.

And God help anyone who thought they could take what I had already decided was mine.

Cassandra

The car beeped, locking with a soft click. The humid evening air clung to my skin as I shifted my work bag on my shoulder. Then I heard the sharp whirr of a car window rolling down and a familiar voice, low and edged with frustration. "Get in. Now."

I whipped around, startled, my heart already skipping a beat. Declan's face stared back at me from the back seat of a sleek black car, his expression rigid and agitated. *Fuck.* First it was Leo, and then Declan. Why couldn't the men in my life leave me the hell alone?

My throat worked as I tried to swallow the lump there, knowing full well I didn't have a choice. I walked toward the car, my stomach twisting into knots. I hated when he looked like this; he was so unpredictable, and unpredictability with Declan was scarier than any nightmare came to life.

As soon as I slid into the back seat, the smell of cigarettes and whiskey filled my nostrils. Declan reached across me and slammed the door shut with more force than necessary. "Drive," he barked at the driver. The car lurched forward, speeding into the flow of traffic and away from Inferno. Vinnie wasn't going to be happy that I was late.

He turned to face me, his usually sharp features caught somewhere between anger and relief. His jaw was tight, but his eyes...they betrayed something softer, something more desperate. "I've been out of my mind with worry." His hand shot out, grabbing mine with a grip that was almost too tight, opposite of the firm but gentle grip that I'd felt from Leo.

My eyes scanned his face, searching for something—answers, maybe, or some reassurance that this wasn't about to spiral into chaos. But his expression was a storm, one I couldn't quite read. "Why were you worried?" A part of me needed to hear his answer, to feel like he still cared about me. But another part of me screamed to run, to get out of this car while I still could. I was sure the traffic would stop as I tucked and rolled.

His eyes flashed dangerously, the kind of cold fire that always made me feel both safe and suffocated at the same time. "Because, Cass," he said, his accent thickening with his frustration, "I heard a certain wop made an appearance at that pizza place you like so much."

I stiffened as his grip tightened on my hand, the force of it pressing my knuckles together, making the bones grind. The contrast hit me like a jolt. Leo's touch had been possessive but controlled.

Declan's was raw, unfiltered, and driven by something far more volatile.

"Dec, I didn't want him to show up," I said quickly, my voice pleading for him to calm down. "But he's been following me." My eyes locked on his, trying to reach the part of him that wasn't consumed by rage. "I'm sorry you were worried."

My free hand brushed over his, attempting to soothe the storm I could see brewing in his eyes. For a moment, it worked. His grip loosened, and regret flickered across his face, like he'd just realized what he was doing.

"I'm sorry, Cass," he said quietly, running a hand through his hair. His jaw clenched as he looked away. "I didn't mean..." His voice trailed off, as if saying the words would make them too real. Then his gaze snapped back to mine, sharper. "Tell me everything. What did that bastard want?" His voice dripped with venom at the mere thought of Leo Romano. "Did he hurt you?"

I held onto his hand, still running my fingers over his knuckles as if trying to anchor him—and maybe myself. My heart ached for this man I used to love so freely, the man I missed despite everything. "No, he didn't hurt me," I said, my voice steady, though the weight of the situation made my chest feel tight. "But he's playing some weird possession game." I let out a frustrated sigh, the absurdity of the whole situation bubbling to the surface. "I keep turning him down, I promise."

The desperation in my voice was undeniable, as though I needed him to believe me, to see that my loyalty to him hadn't wavered, even after everything. I didn't understand why I needed him to feel my loyalty, to know that I still cared so much about him, but in the depths of my heart I felt that I still yearned for him, and that little call kept me soft.

Declan's eyes narrowed, the predatory gleam in them sharp enough to make me hold my breath. His body tensed, every muscle coiled. "He's trying to get with you? That fucking Italian piece of shit." His hand tore away from mine, and before I could react, he punched the roof of the car with a force that made me flinch.

The sound reverberated through the car as I shrank back slightly, trying to keep my breathing steady. His rage was palpable, almost suffocating. "He thinks he can just waltz in and—" Declan cut himself off, sucking in a sharp breath as he visibly worked to regain control. "And what did you tell him?" he asked, his voice lower, more dangerous. "What exactly did you say to make him think he has a chance?"

"I haven't said anything to make him think that," I said quickly, my voice firm but tinged with exasperation. "He probably considers my refusals some twisted sign that I'm playing hard to get." I looked away then I felt the sting of unshed tears pricking my eyes. Pressing my forehead against the cool glass of the window, I watched the city lights blur past. My voice softened to a whisper, as though I were confessing to the window. "Dec, I still love you."

The hitch of his breath at my words made the flutter in my chest start again, replacing the hammering. He reached for my chin, gently turning me back to face him. His ice-blue eyes had softened, the anger melting into something that made my heart squeeze painfully. "You do?" he asked, his voice barely above a whisper. His hand tilted my chin up, his thumb brushing over my bottom lip in a gesture so tender, so familiar, it broke something inside me. "Cass, after everything…you still love me?"

I nodded, letting my eyes speak of the longing I felt for him. He pulled me into his lap, his arms wrapping around my waist as he buried his face into the curve of my neck. His breath was hot against my skin, his voice muffled but raw. "You know, I've missed you every fucking day. Every day you've been gone has felt like an eternity in Hell."

My arms wrapped around his neck, holding him tightly as tears slid silently down my cheeks. I had dreamt of this moment for three long months—missed the feel of his arms, the sound of his soft voice, the way his words could be so gentle despite the chaos that surrounded him. "You and your family mean the world to me," I murmured, pulling back just enough to cup his face in my hands. I needed to see his eyes, those glacier-blue eyes that had always captivated me.

"Fuck, Cass," he whispered, his grip on me tightening as our foreheads rested together. Our lips hovered inches apart, and then he kissed me—softly, hesitantly, his lips trembling as though he was holding himself back.

When we broke the kiss, my breath hitched. "We can't…" I whispered, my voice shaking. "I can't risk it again. Not after…not after last time."

The memory hit me like a punch to the gut—the way his temper had boiled over, the snap of his fist against my cheek, the searing pain of his grip in my hair. I shuddered at the thought, even as I stayed in his arms. He was everything I wanted and everything I knew I couldn't have.

Pain flashed in his eyes, his voice breaking as he whispered, "You think I don't know that? That I don't hate myself every day for what I've done?" His jaw tightened. "I'm trying, Cass. I'm trying so fucking hard to control my temper." His gaze darkened, a dangerous edge returning. "But the thought of you with another man…any man…" He trailed off, his voice like ice. "And then there's Leonardo Romano…"

"Dec," I said softly, brushing my thumbs over his cheekbones. "I'll keep rejecting him. If I feel the slightest danger, I swear I'll call you." My voice was gentle, though the weight of everything we had been through hung heavily between us.

He covered my hands with his, his anger giving way to vulnerability—the kind that always shattered my defenses. "You promise?" he asked, his Irish accent softening. "Promise me you'll come to me if anything happens." He kissed my palm tenderly, his voice tight with determination.

But then his walls slammed back up. "Forget it," he muttered, pulling away. He turned to look out the window, his expression closed off once more. "Let's get you back to the club, God forbid Leo finds out his little whore is late." He tossed me off his lap to the seat beside him like I was trash. I gaped at him, feeling that comment cut so deep into my heart that what little mending had happened reopened and was bleeding out again.

I exhaled slowly, the connection between us severed. Moving as far over as I could, I kept my gaze out the window as the car rolled on.

"Take us back to Inferno," Declan's harsh tone felt like salt in the wound.

Silence filled the space, but our fingers remained intertwined. It was the only evidence that what we'd just shared had been real—raw, fragile, and something neither of us was ready to fully let go of yet. Maybe I was destined to always be fucked up, to live life only receiving the scraps of anything good.

Leo

Smoke, musk, and the clawing stench of cheap perfume filled the air as I carved my way through the crowd toward Vinnie's office. The music from the club pulsed through the walls, reverberating beneath my feet and amplifying the tension already coiling in my chest. Gio had informed me that Vinnie would be at Inferno, and he better have been, because waiting had never been one of my virtues.

Not when I had seen my little *topo* earlier and been reminded— once again—of how stubborn she could be.

I reached the dull silver door handle, its cheap, scratched surface cold beneath my fingers, and thrust it open without hesitation.

Vinnie jumped to his feet immediately, his thin, dirty blonde hair already plastered to his head with sweat. The pathetic sight made my lip curl in disgust. "Mr. Romano, sir, you needed to see me?" His voice wavered as he hastily wiped his sweaty palms on the thighs of his wrinkled, knockoff suit.

A moment later, Gio and Dimitri entered the room, flanking me like shadows. Their presence only added weight to mine, a subtle reminder to Vinnie of exactly who he was dealing with. I crossed my arms over my chest, the motion tightening the fabric of my Versace suit sleeves and making them ride up just slightly. My voice came out cold and sharp, giving him no room to question my intent. "Yes. I need to discuss matters regarding Cassandra."

His shoulders stiffened at my tone, his nervous energy rippling off him like heat from the summer Chicago pavement. "Of course," he said quickly, gesturing to a chair across from his desk. "Please, have a seat."

The sight was insulting—a peeling, beat-up dining chair that looked like it had been dragged from a garage sale. My lack of movement must have made my displeasure clear because Vinnie scrambled around the desk, awkwardly gesturing toward his own oversized pleather chair instead. "Here, sir," he stuttered, offering it like a peace treaty.

I sat in the worn-out chair, the legs creaking under my weight. The dust-covered desk in front of me only added to the insult, but I decided to indulge the moment. Let him sweat. Vinnie lowered himself into the pathetic dining chair across from me, shifting uncomfortably as it groaned beneath him.

"I would like Cassandra to be my personal waitress and entertainer every time I come in," I said, my tone leaving no room for argument. I steepled my hands on his filthy desk, my eyes locking on his like a predator watching its prey.

Vinnie swallowed hard, "Angel won't like this." His knee bounced beneath the desk like he was already preparing for the fallout. I didn't miss the fact that he called her Angel and not Cassandra. I wondered if she made that rule. Who was I joking—I knew she did. "She and I made a deal when she first arrived three months ago—she doesn't do private dances for anyone." He was bold enough to hold my gaze, something I noticed he did when he spoke from a protective point of view.

Leaning forward, I narrowed my eyes, my jaw ticking with irritation. "I don't give a fuck." The words came out like a low growl, cutting through the thick, stale air. I was done being denied—by Cassandra, by anyone. "She will be my private waitress and entertainer."

I turned to Gio, giving him a small nod. The sound of a pistol cocking filled the room, sharp and deliberate, as Gio leveled the gun at the back of Vinnie's head, intentionally pressing the cold barrel roughly to the back of his skull and nudging it.

Vinnie froze, his face draining of all color. He looked like a ghost, a fat, sweaty ghost, his hands trembling as he gripped the edge of the chair like a child riding their first rollercoaster.

"You will tell her what I want," I said, my voice colder, more calculated. "And if she denies you…" I leaned back, my movements slow and deliberate, letting my words sink in. "You will inform her that if she doesn't comply, I'll have Gio blow whatever fucking brains you have left out of your skull." I knew my sweet little *topo* was a kind woman, soft on the inside despite the bitter, harsh exterior she let everyone see.

Vinnie nodded frantically, his sweat trickling down the sides of his face and soaking the neckline of his cheap blue dress shirt. "Abso… absolutely, Mr….Ro…Romano."

"Good," I said firmly, rising to my feet in one smooth motion. My broad shoulders filled the room, making the space feel even smaller. I crossed the room in a few long strides, reaching for the door. "I'll be in tomorrow night. Make sure 'Angel' understands our arrangement."

I pushed the door open and stepped out, Gio and Dimitri falling into step behind me as we exited the club. The sound of bass felt like a war drum going into battle, and it made an uncontrollable smile spread across my face. I glanced to my right and in the far corner, I saw Cassandra talking to some sad sap thinking he was getting some sort of special treatment from her. *Tomorrow, bella*, I shall have you.

The sticky night air hit me, but it did nothing to temper the fire simmering in my chest. Pulling a cigarette from my jacket, I lit it with a steady hand and took a long drag. The bitter smoke filled my lungs as I exhaled slowly, watching the plume swirl into the dimly lit street. "Arrange for Vinnie to pay Cassandra double on the nights I come in." My words were confident as my gaze fixed on the faint, flickering glow of a streetlamp across the street. "I'll make sure the funds are deposited to accommodate the stipend."

Cassandra's reasons for no private dances were in the folder I received, and I didn't want her to think I was crossing a boundary without a reasonable payout. She was giving everything she had away. My tech guy uptown had been sending me updates on her bank account. The most recent was a Greyhound bus ticket.

At first, I thought the ticket was for her, so I had Gio go to the station and keep a low profile. When he returned, he informed me that Cassandra had dropped off a young girl named Jewel. Cassandra wore a black baseball cap, while the young girl wore a deep purple hoodie that hid her face. Still, Gio caught sight of Cassandra wiping tears from the girl's bruised eye. So I found out why Jewel had run— let's just say her father had disappeared. I quietly put enough money into Jewel's bank account for her to get by for a few months.

It only made me want to be closer to Cassandra, to help her in her mission to save these girls.

My little *topo* will never find out, not when I made sure it was all swept under the rug. I still needed to know what that little nest egg in her savings account was for. I had a feeling it meant something more than retirement.

"Yes, Boss," Gio and Dimitri said in unison.

I nodded, dismissing them with a wave. They turned back toward the club to handle the rest of the night's business, leaving me alone for the first time in hours. My eyes remained fixed on the flickering light while the sound of the city bounced around me. This city was mine, I was born here, grew up here, and it bowed its ugly head to me like a damn servant to its king. I knew Ciro was at the warehouse in the south finishing up the deal with the Russians, Nico was with a group of soldiers sending a message to our beloved Irish to stop fucking with my turf. Hopefully burning down their high earning strip club O'Malley's would make it sink the fuck into their skulls, and be a silent revenge for Cassandra.

Leaning roughly against the rough brick wall of the building, I allowed myself a rare moment of satisfaction. Control. I finally had the upper hand. My little *principessa* thought she could defy me, that she could push me away, but she was wrong. I was closer to her than she could ever possibly imagine.

The sound of a chuckle pushed past my lips before I took another slow drag of my cigarette. "What will you do next, Cassandra?" I muttered to myself, exhaling the smoke into the night. "What will you do now that I've backed you into a corner? Will you keep fighting? Or will you surrender?"

A part of me—maybe the part that had been clawing at my sanity lately—hoped she'd keep fighting. I loved the fire in her eyes, the way her defiance made her burn brighter than anyone else. Fuck, she was driving me mad, pushing me to lengths I wouldn't have considered for anyone else.

As much as I wanted to break her, I wanted to keep that fire alive, too. I needed it. She had become more than a game to me. She was an obsession, and I hated how much control she had over me even when she wasn't trying. The image of her soft, happy gaze in the restaurant made my heart flutter, my brows drawing together. What an interesting emotion.

The sound of a metal door opening broke my train of thought as Dimitri and Gio strode out. I flicked my cigarette onto the asphalt, crushing it under my heel, just like the emotions bubbling to the surface. I pushed off the wall, smoothing out my hair. "Let's go."

Sliding into the back seat, I leaned against the leather, the feeling of victory settling over me like a second skin. But as the car pulled away, something in my chest stirred—a faint, nagging sensation that I might not have as much power as I thought I did.

EPISODE 4

Cassandra

"You've got to be fucking kidding me, Vinnie!" I crossed my arms tightly over my chest, like it might shield me from the nightmare unraveling in front of me. Leo was a fucking snake, not a wolf—going behind my back and talking to Vinnie like some tattletale to his mommy.

Vinnie shifted uncomfortably in his worn-out leather chair, his hands clasped together on the scarred wooden desk in front of him. Papers and empty coffee cups cluttered the surface, telling me he had been pulling all day shifts again, probably adjusting to the new "protection" Leo had put into place—which consisted of a few of his men hovering over us and him. Vinnie was good about that, making sure our safety came first—except when it came to Leo crossing my one and only rule. "Angel, baby—"

"Don't call me baby!" I snapped, my voice sharp and raw as my chest heaved. I could feel myself spiraling, anger bubbling up with nowhere to go. My eyes flicked over the black-painted cement walls with the whiteboard he liked to scribble nonsense on and pretend like he was some genius entrepreneur. Today I noted that he added "All you can eat pasta buffet—Sundays," then he had an arrow from that to a toddler-like drawing of what I think is a table with food on it and a stick figure girl dancing on a pole. Pathetic.

Vinnie threw up his hands in surrender, the motion as pitiful as his posture. My glare met his frantic eyes, blown wide and shadowed by dirty-blonde, overgrown eyebrows.

"Sorry, I always forget." He sighed, long and slow, his head bowing like the weight of the world had finally broken him. "I didn't have a choice." When he looked back up at me, his tired eyes locked onto mine. "They had a gun to the back of my head, Angel. A goddamn gun."

I saw it then—the haunted flicker of memory darkening his face, and for a split second, I felt bad for him. Sort of. "Ugh! Fuck! Then I quit!" I barked, shoving aside whatever sympathy had almost surfaced.

Vinnie shot up so fast his chair toppled over, crashing to the floor with a clatter. He didn't even glance at it before rounding the desk toward me. His sweaty palms slid down my shoulders, trembling with desperation as he sank to his knees. "Angel, please, you can't quit." His voice cracked, his breath hot and frantic. "If you leave, he'll kill me. I swear to God, he'll kill me. Leo will get bored soon. He always does. Just hang in there." His hands came together in front of him like he was praying, his knees digging into the faded brown carpet. "I'm begging you."

I rolled my eyes and stepped back, out of reach, my stomach churning as the sour smell of his sweat hit me full force. Yellow stains spread under his collar and armpits, impossible to miss. "For fuck's sake, stand up." My tone was dripping with disdain. "Christ, Vinnie, grow some goddamn balls."

We both knew deep down I wouldn't actually leave—not with the benefits this place came with—but I sure as hell wasn't going to roll over and take Leo's demands like some kind of trained dog.

He bobbed his head like one of those cheap cereal-box toys we used to get as kids. His trembling hands gripped the edge of the desk, and he hauled himself up with so much effort I half expected him to fart in the process. Honestly, it wouldn't have surprised me.

"So…you'll stay?" he asked, panting like he'd just run a marathon. "You'll help me out?"

My glare on him was unyielding, arms tightening across my chest. I didn't want to be Leo's personal dancer, not in the slightest but Vinnie…fuck, I owed Vinnie for how well he took care of us here, especially me. "Fine. But you're paying me extra for this." My words were clipped, practically spat through gritted teeth.

"It's already been arranged. Leo's compensating you," Vinnie said, wiping his face with his sleeve like that would fix the mess he was.

I froze, the weight of his words crashing down. "What?"

Vinnie lifted his seat, sighed, then lowered himself back into it, which hissed under his bulk. "Yeah, Gio and Dimitri told me Leo's doubling your pay for nights you, uh…entertain him." His gaze darted from my face to the door, like he expected the devil himself to walk in at any moment.

"Double?" I whispered, mostly to myself. The word hung in the air as I processed it. Double would carry me a long way—enough to catch up on rent, maybe even buy fresh vegetables instead of living off frozen junk. I could even save enough to move… No, I couldn't get that hopeful. The thought made my chest tighten with something close to relief, but I quickly shook it off. No way was I letting Vinnie see me care about the money. "Alright," I grumbled, forcing a bored tone. "I'll do it."

"Thanks, Angel. You're a lifesaver. Literally." He laughed nervously, rubbing the back of his neck. "You know, Angel, I care about you girls. I wouldn't have accepted these terms if I had a choice." His voice dipped into a more somber tone, matching the haunted look on his face. "You know how I lost my wife and daughter…" He trailed off, giving me a weak half-smile that said he was holding back more emotion than he could probably handle.

I nodded. I had heard about his wife and daughter from Candy when I first started here—how they were snatched up off the streets and never found. That happens a lot in the shadows of Chicago. Rumor had it that women were being sold off like fucking cattle to the slaughter. The very thought had my heart racing with the need for justice.

Vinnie glanced at his fake Rolex, the gold finish long since chipped away. "Leonardo will be in tonight." He looked back up at me as if to say, brace yourself. "Actually… he should be here right about—"

The door burst open before Vinnie could finish, and the air in the room seemed to shift. Leonardo Romano walked in like he owned the place—hell, he did own it, along with more than half of Chicago. Shoulders squared, his tailored suit clung to him like it was made from sin itself. Confidence radiated off him, the kind that made you feel like prey before he'd even said a word.

"If you stare any longer, Cassandra," Leo purred, his voice smooth and low, "people will think you like me." He stopped in front of me, close enough to drown me in his cologne—something dark and expensive that made my stomach tighten. His hand reached out, fingers gripping my chin—not enough to hurt, but firm, like he wanted to remind me who held the power. "I'm assuming Vinnie told you about our arrangement?" His words slid through the air like melted butter.

Shit. Get it together, Cassandra.

I pinched my arm, hard enough to ground myself, and hardened my features into something unreadable. No way was I letting him see what he did to me.

"Ah, there she is," Leo murmured, tilting my chin from side to side like I was some kind of artwork he was appraising. "My feisty little *principessa.*"

I jerked my head away and took a step back, breaking the contact. "Yeah, he told me," I said coldly.

"Then why aren't you dressed and ready to work?" Leo asked, his eyes dragging slowly over my casual outfit—baggy, ripped high-waisted jeans and a fitted navy blue T-shirt with a blue Care Bear on it—Grumpy Bear, I think he was. The way his gaze lingered made my skin prickle, and I hated the heat rising under his scrutiny.

Am I ovulating? That had to be it. Why else would I be standing here imagining his strong, tanned hands curling around my neck as he pinned me to the wall?

"Cassandra," Leo growled, snapping me out of my ridiculous daydream. His dark eyes locked onto mine, and I saw something raw in them, something that matched the chaos brewing in me. "Get the fuck out of here. Now." His tone was sharp, commanding, but there was a thread of restraint under it, like he was holding something back. His jaw ticked as he waited for me to move.

My head shook and I fixed my scowl firmly in place, fighting the urge to shiver under his stare. I stomped for the door, brushing past Gio and Dimitri and gripping the worn metal handle. Before I opened the door, I glanced back at him one last time, locking eyes. "Just so we're clear, I'm leaving because I want to—not because you told me to."

That predatory grin on his face spread slowly, and I felt it crawl under my skin in the worst—and best—way. I slammed the door behind me, my pulse racing.

Yep. Definitely ovulating.

Leo

As the door slammed shut behind her, I muttered under my breath, "*Dio aiutami.*" God, help me indeed. My gaze flicked sharply to Vinnie, who was sweating through his shirt like a pig under the butcher's blade. "Don't keep me waiting, Vinnie," I warned, my voice a low growl that left no room for debate. Without another glance, I turned on my heel and strode out of the wretched office, the stench of stale desperation clinging to the air behind me.

Gio and Dimitri followed silently, their hulking shadows moving in sync with mine as we ascended the stairs to the VIP booth. The room vibrated with music and lust, the dim lights casting a golden glow over the wake of blonde flirts circling the club like vultures. They watched me with hungry, desperate stares, licking their lips and arching their backs like it might earn them a flicker of my attention. I ignored them. They were beneath me, and tonight, I had only one purpose—to claim Cassandra.

I would corner that defiance and make her confront what burned between us.

Sinking into my usual black leather chair, I leaned back, my eyes fixed on the small private stage in front of me. My body thrummed with anticipation, the memory of her earlier defiance burning through my veins like a drug. The way her dark eyes met mine tonight—wild, lustful, and rebellious—had been enough to leave me aching. She wanted me. I saw it in her flushed cheeks, the way her breath hitched when I was close.

And then there was the way she glared at me, full of venom and pride. The contradiction was maddening, intoxicating. Adjusting myself in my pants, I let out a frustrated groan, shaking my head at my lack of control. She had no idea the power she wielded over me, and that alone made me harder.

Running a rough hand through my hair, I barked, "Gio!"

"Yes, boss?" Gio appeared at my side in a fitted black dress shirt and slacks, ever dutiful. I didn't miss that he was still wearing his sunglasses, which made him look like a big, muscular *idiota*. But the reflective lens caught my distorted reflection, and I saw the way my eyes appeared with dark circles from lack of sleep and how my normally settled hair looked a bit messier than usual.

My hand roughly combed through my locks, but they seemed to have made the decision to remain unruly. "Get a bartender to bring up their best Scotch. Two glasses." I smirked as the beginnings of a plan formed in my head, one as sharp and calculated as a blade.

"You got it." He strode off, leaving me to my thoughts and the growing impatience coiled in my chest.

The sharp clicking of heels echoed only moments later over the low hum of the music, and my ears perked up. I stayed still, my expression cold and unreadable as the sound grew closer. Let her come to me. Let her walk into the trap.

When the heels stopped just short of me, I peered up. The blonde bartender with a petite frame trembled, clutching the bottle of Scotch to her chest like it might shield her from the storm brewing in my chest. My eyes hardened, making her flinch. "Set it over there," I gestured impatiently toward the mini bar across the way. She scurried to obey, practically stumbling over herself.

My eyes fell to my gold Rolex watch—a gift from my father last Christmas. It was engraved with the words Lupe Nero, a nickname he gave me when I was a teenager after making my first kill. My jaw ticked with irritation. Where the fuck was she? How long was my little *topo* going to make me wait?

"You better be careful, Leo," a familiar voice purred, dripping with amused defiance. "People might start to think you like me."

Her words hit me like a slap and a caress all at once, startling me with how deeply they affected me. For a brief moment, my heart stuttered in my chest—a feeling I hadn't experienced in years, if ever.

Rising, I turned slowly to face her, and the sight was enough to knock the breath out of me. Cassandra sauntered into the room, her dark hair swept up into a high, classy ponytail, its base glittering with diamonds. Her usual black fishnets had been replaced with ones made of sparkling gems, catching the dim light like a thousand tiny stars. The matching gemstone lingerie hugged her curves in ways that made my blood run hot. She was breathtaking, a goddess wrapped in danger and desire.

Finally finding my voice, I forced myself to speak. "Unlike you, I don't consider that a bad thing." My eyes followed her every step, like a predator tracking its prey. Her earlier frazzled demeanor was gone, replaced with a cool indifference that only made me want her more, even if her intentions had been to deter me.

"I see you found the outfit I purchased for you."

She brushed past me, ignoring my comment—on purpose, I'm sure —her perfume something floral and musky leaving a tantalizing trail in her wake.

It made me want to hit my knees and pray. She approached the blonde who still lingered awkwardly by the Scotch. Cassandra's long fingers curled around the neck of the bottle, the sight immediately sending my mind spiraling into places I shouldn't have let it go.

"Drink?" she asked, her voice a low hum that wrapped around me like a silk ribbon. With a small wave of her hand, she dismissed the blonde, who bolted for the door without hesitation.

Reaching into the inside of my jacket, I pulled my cigarettes from the pocket, needing to focus on something other than the way Cassandra's hips swayed as she poured a glass, or how she was making me lose every ounce of the control I wanted her to see. "If you're offering, *bella*," I said, flashing her a wolfish grin.

Lighting the cigarette, I inhaled deeply, the flame briefly illuminating my face before the lighter clicked shut. The scent of smoke curled around me as I watched her move, my body tense with restraint.

She poured a glass of Scotch with practiced ease, her lingerie dress clinking softly as the diamonds caught the light with each hypnotic sway of her body. When she finally turned and approached, the glass in hand, I reached for it. Our fingers brushed, soft and deliberate, the contact sending fire blazing through my veins.

"So," she began, her voice steady and calm, though her eyes betrayed the storm behind them. "What do you want me to do, now that you have me trapped?"

The Scotch burned as I downed it in one go, setting the glass onto the table with a loud clink. I leaned against the arm of the chair, letting the silence stretch between us. Finally, I spoke. "Some music would be nice…Angel." Her stage name rolled off my tongue, heavy with mockery and desire.

Her emerald eyes narrowed, and I couldn't help the wolfish smile on my lips. God, she was easy to provoke, and I enjoyed every second of it.

Black hair whipped around her head as she turned on her heel, heading for the small bar again where the remote rested. I followed, my steps slow and deliberate. When she grabbed the remote, I pressed in close, my chest brushing against her back. She froze, her body stiffening as I leaned in, close enough to inhale the warm, floral scent of her perfume.

"*Principessa*," I murmured, my lips close to her ear. My hands gripped the counter on either side of her, caging her in against the glass. "Tell me." My voice was low, rough, and dripping with unspoken promises. "What were you thinking about back in Vinnie's office? What had you looking so…out of sorts?" I shifted to her other ear, my breath hot against her skin.

She visibly shivered, and I knew I had her. The way her pulse fluttered along the column of her neck, the way goosebumps rose on her arms—it was enough to drive me mad. My hands clenched the glass tighter, my knuckles turning white with restraint.

"You really want to know?" she whispered, tilting her head to the side and exposing the smooth line of her neck. The mischievous glint in her eye told me that she had a trick up her sleeve, and I couldn't wait to see what it was.

I growled softly, pressing closer, my nose gliding up her ear and over her hair, inhaling her intoxicating scent.

And as quickly as the tension came, it was gone.

Obscene, jarring metal music blasted through the speakers, shattering the moment. I stepped back, grinding my teeth as I forced myself to reorient. When I looked back at her, she was laughing, the sound light and victorious.

"That's for me to know, and for you to go fuck yourself." Her lips tilted up into an impish smile, and hot frustration burned in my veins.

Cassandra

That was close—too close. My heart was still racing, pounding like a drum in my chest, and I couldn't ignore the embarrassing wet heat pooling between my thighs.

"Cassandra."

His sharp, dangerous tone sliced cleanly through the pounding music, freezing me in place. I turned just as Leo closed the distance again, his presence a dark, overwhelming force that made the air around us feel suffocating. Without a word, he snatched the remote from my hand and cut off the music, the relative quiet in the private space followed like a thunderclap.

"What the fuck?" he hissed, his cold, unrelenting gaze locking onto mine. That look—the one that reminded me exactly who he was and what he was capable of—made my stomach drop. The confidence I'd clung to moments ago evaporated. My face fell.

He didn't say anything else, just stared at me, his silence heavier than any insult or threat. But his anger wasn't silent—it blazed in his eyes, dark and scorching, and I found myself taking an involuntary step back. My hip bumped against the edge of the bar, rattling the glasses, and I felt the tremor of fear creep into my chest.

And then, as if he could sense my unease, his expression shifted. The tension in his jaw loosened, his eyes softened, and he stepped back, putting space between us. His hands clenched at his sides, the skin on his knuckles stretched taut, but he remained poised, controlled.

The silence stretched until it became unbearable, so I broke it first. "Sorry," I whispered, dropping my gaze to the floor. The word came out small and pathetic, dredging up old, familiar feelings I thought I'd buried long ago. If I apologized, if I stayed small enough, invisible enough, maybe he wouldn't hurt me.

The gentleness of his hands startled me. His warm fingers were firm but careful as they cupped my face, tilting it upward so I had no choice but to meet his steel-grey irises. They flicked between mine like he was trying to see into my soul, the old hurt that I must have exposed. Nice going, Cass.

"Principessa, who broke you?" His voice was quiet, almost compassionate, and it made my chest tighten with something raw and uncomfortable.

"Nobody," I blurted, my walls snapping back into place like a reflex. The vulnerable moment vanished as I forced myself to lock everything away, fortifying the fragile parts of me behind cold, unfeeling steel.

He studied me, his gaze scanning every kaleidoscope of expression I held behind my eyes, parts of me I wouldn't let him see. *"Partecipo al tuo dolore,"* he murmured, his thumbs brushing lightly over my cheekbones. His touch was soothing, but his words—I share your pain—were almost unbearable.

Because men didn't share pain. Not the men I grew up with.

My mother Ana-Marie had learned that the hard way long before I was born. She was a first-generation Italian immigrant, raised to be obedient, proper, valuable only if she married well. My father, James Bennett—an all-American veteran she met overseas during one of his tours—was never supposed to be part of her story. They barely knew each other when she got pregnant that first month. Love had nothing to do with it. Convenience did. Panic did. Shame did.

Her family kicked her out the moment they found out—she was supposed to marry some CEO in Italy she hated, but the proposal came with money her parents needed. When she sabotaged it, they bought her a one-way ticket to America and washed their hands of her. James brought her here, not out of devotion but out of obligation. And she was trapped with him from that moment on.

Abusive wasn't the only word I'd use for him. Alcoholic. Cheater. Gambling addict. My mother got her visa, became a citizen, and worked whatever jobs she could—grocery stores, diners—but none of it was enough to leave with me. So we lived poor, fast, and unfulfilling lives. She breathed for me, protected me when she could, and kept the worst of him from touching me.

And I learned early how to stay small. Quiet. Invisible. Sorry.

Which is exactly why that word had slipped out of me like muscle memory.

I felt the cracks forming in my defenses, and I couldn't let it happen. Couldn't let him in. With a sharp breath, I smacked his hands away and straightened my shoulders. "Dock my pay. I'm going home early tonight." I shoved past him, deliberately knocking into his shoulder, though I'm sure it hurt me more than him.

Before he could respond, my heels were already clicking down the stairs as I fled. If I stayed a second longer, I knew I'd break. I knew I'd let him see the parts of me no one had a right to. No one was allowed to have those broken pieces, because no one I knew was gentle enough to hold them.

WHEN I FINALLY REACHED MY building and climbed the stairs to my door, I noticed something sitting on the landing. A bouquet of burgundy anemones—my favorite flowers—wrapped in brown paper.

My heart lurched in my chest. Only one man knew these were my favorite. Picking them up, I rotated the bouquet slowly. God, dammit all to hell. Karma, God, or whomever fucking hated me and loved watching me suffer slowly.

Plucking the small card nestled between the blooms, my breath caught as I read the words scrawled across it in neat, familiar handwriting:

Grá go Deo—Love forever

-D

It was an apology, a bandage over a deep wound if I was honest. Admiring the deep crimson petals one more time, I unlocked my door and stepped inside. I chucked off my tennis shoes and strode for the kitchen. Taking out my larger glass cup and placing the flowers on the bar in the kitchen, I propped the card against the glass and stared at it for a long moment.

"Declan," I murmured softly, brushing my fingers over one of the velvety petals. "You really need to let go."

Even as I said the words, my chest tightened. My heart raced at the thought of him still thinking about me, still caring after everything. Even I cared too much; the apple never falls far from the familial tree, I suppose.

Before I realized what I was doing, I was digging through my purse for my phone. My fingers moved on their own, dialing his number, and the line barely rang once before he picked up.

His voice was warm and familiar, a smile audible in the way he answered. "Cass."

"Hey, Dec." My fingers fiddled with the card that rested against the makeshift vase. A sense of comfort settled over me, soothing my frayed nerves. "Thank you for the anemones. They're beautiful."

He chuckled, the low, familiar sound tugging at my heart. "Just like you." There was a faint rustle in the background, followed by the soft click of a door closing. "I've been thinking about you."

"Oh yeah? I couldn't tell," I teased, a laugh slipping past my lips. Talking to him was easy, like slipping into an old, worn-in sweater. Especially when he was in such a good mood. We spent a year together, learning each other's bodies, shared secrets, and accepted our demons in one another.

"Yeah, well, call me a hopeless romantic," he sighed, his tone light but edged with sincerity.

The sudden rush of emotion caught me off guard. Tears prickled at my eyes, and I walked to the couch, flopping down with a huff. "I miss you, Dec. So much," I admitted, my voice thick with everything I'd been holding back. I couldn't help it, even if yesterday's car ride ended on a bad note. I didn't think I'd ever be able to let him go.

"Are you okay, Cass?" His tone sharpened, a protective edge cutting through his warmth. "Nobody's hurt you, have they?"

He didn't need to say his name. We both knew who he meant.

"No, nobody's hurt me," I said quietly, but the way my voice trembled betrayed me.

"Then why are you crying?" he asked, his voice softening, though I caught the faintest hint of irritation beneath it.

I straightened, brushing at my cheeks to erase the evidence of my tears as if he could see them. "It's nothing," I said, forcing a lightness I didn't feel. "I just wanted to thank you for the flowers."

The pause on the other end of the line stretched too long, the weight of his growing frustration clear. Finally, he exhaled, the sound heavy with resignation. "Yeah, well...like I said, I've been thinking about you." His soft tone returned as he added, "I love you, Cass."

Biting my lip to fight off the tears threatening to roll down my cheek, I whispered, "Love you too."

I hung up quickly, the weight of his words pressing on my chest like an anvil. The way Declan swung between hot and cold—how I felt the need to please him just to coax that soft and nurturing tone in his voice, was like a drug I craved. Something I believed only I could give him.

The tears threatened to fall again, but quickly receded when a loud, insistent knock rattled my door. My head snapped toward the sound, my heart racing as I wiped my face and stood.

Leo

The old, paint-chipped door swung open, and there she was—Cassandra. Standing in front of me, in her apartment. The apartment I'd watched her retreat to countless times, always from a distance. I didn't know why I came here after the way she left the club. Maybe it was the look on her face—the hurt, the vulnerability she'd tried so hard to hide—but something told me she needed someone.

"Leo, what are you doing here?" she asked, her wide, puffy eyes betraying her surprise.

I tucked my hands into the pockets of my slacks, trying to look more composed than I felt. "You just seemed… You looked like you needed to talk." The words felt foreign coming out of my mouth, awkward and unfamiliar. Leonardo Romano didn't comfort anyone. Ever. Yet here I was, standing on Cassandra's doorstep, offering her something I didn't even know how to give.

She raised an eyebrow, clearly seeing the discomfort written all over my face. With a sigh, she stepped aside and gestured for me to come in. "I'm not even going to bother giving you a third warning," she muttered, her sarcasm cutting as always. But I understood it for what it was—a defense mechanism. She used her sharp words like armor, and it only made me more determined to peel back every layer.

Her apartment was small, cozy. The faint scent of vanilla lingered in the air, and trinkets and framed photos cluttered the shelves that seemed to barely cling to the walls. As I strolled through the space, I studied her carefully chosen belongings. They told me more about her than she'd ever admit. "You're too merciful, *principessa*." The glance I gave her from over my shoulder revealed she was still by the door, watching me like a hawk, her arms crossed tightly over her chest like she was waiting for a bigger excuse to kick me out. I scoffed. "You're also too trusting. You should know better than to open your door to a wolf."

She scoffed, rolling her eyes. "Says the man who could barely string a sentence together to explain why he's here playing my therapist."

I stopped inspecting her shelves long enough to laugh—loud and genuine. It felt strange, but good, like stretching a muscle I hadn't used in years. "Christ, no one's made me laugh that hard in a long time." I swiped at the corner of my eye as if there were an actual tear.

When I turned to look at her again, she was staring at me with a furrowed brow, like I'd glitched her system and she couldn't figure out how to respond. My lips tilted upwards on one side, and I returned to my silent exploration, eventually making my way to her kitchen. A bouquet of burgundy flowers sat on the counter, their rich color catching my eye. My gaze zeroed in on the small card propped up against the vase. I picked it up, my jaw tightening as I scanned the Gaelic writing.

Declan.

I set the card down carefully, resisting the urge to crush it in my hand. The thought of him—the Irish prince—lurking in her life still made my blood boil.

Before I could dwell on it, I forced myself to say what I came here to do. "Why did you leave so urgently? I thought we were enjoying our time together."

My eyes zeroed in on her face, watching for her reaction, but there was none. Her arms still crossed and her face stoic. I'd need to pry harder. "You looked haunted. Want to share your ghosts, or would talking about Declan be too much?" My hands remained in my pockets, fisting tightly, but I could feel my words sounded irritated when I spoke his name.

That got her attention, her eyes hardening. "Don't fucking go there." Her voice was tight, forced even as she seemed to continue to hold back. An impenetrable wall, my Cassandra. Pulling my hands from my pockets, I plucked a flower from the bouquet that rested in a glass cup. I twirled it, hoping to draw her closer.

Cassandra's jaw ticked, her shoulders tensing by her ears. "Put it back."

My smirk turned to a feral grin. I loved seeing that violence in her eyes. The anger in her always led to something more, something deeper. "Make me, my little *topo*."

Her feet stomped against the floor and I let her snatch it from my grasp, but not before I snared her in my arms. One hand gripped the back of her neck and fisted her long, luxurious strands of inky black hair firmly, and my other wrapped around her delicate but toned waist. My fingers itched to flex against her lower back.

The sound of her sucking in a breath was like a melody to my ears. Leaning in, I grazed my nose along her temple, inhaling the scent of her hair, the silky strands tickling me as I caught the vanilla and floral of her shampoo. "*Dio mio.* What are you doing to me?" My voice was huskier, revealing my need for her.

This woman made me weak. A part of me despised it, but the other part—the one that I was discovering only came out for her—wanted to drown in it. Cassandra filled me with passion, fire, and determination. I wanted all of her as much as I needed her to consume all of me. I knew she could handle it; she was the reincarnation of Minerva—goddess of strength, courage, and warfare.

Just a single burning look in her emerald eyes had my heart clenched in her nails, bleeding eternally. Maybe it made me weak. This moment with her in my arms, glaring at me like I was Pluto himself, but Pluto was more than just the god of the underworld and the dead; he was also the god of wealth, specifically precious gems— and she was my emerald, divine beauty and eternal glory.

She was making me break every rule I'd ever lived by. I'd never gone to a woman's home before; I only ever went where blood or business demanded. But she was no business—she was a treasure I couldn't walk away from.

"Leo." Her voice was a warm whisper against my cheek, like the touch of an angel's hands before a miracle.

"Yes, *principessa?*"

Before the conversation could go further, my phone buzzed in my pocket. I didn't know if my ears played tricks on me, but I swear on my mother's life I heard a disappointed sigh when I released her and retrieved the cold metal from my pocket. Peeling my eyes from hers, I glanced at the screen. Ciro.

"What is it?" I barked, my tone cold and clipped, slipping back into the role I knew best.

"We've got a problem down at the warehouse," Ciro said, his voice grim. A huge problem, then.

My grip on the phone tightened, my knuckles whitening. "I'll be there in thirty minutes." I hung up and slipped the phone back into my pocket, my thoughts snapping from Cassandra to business.

But not before I reached for her again. She was rooted to her spot in front of me. Her eyes followed my every movement, wary and guarded. Without a word, I reached for the back of her neck, my fingers curling around it firmly but gently. Her breath caught as I pulled her closer once more, my eyes locking onto hers—red-rimmed emeralds that still managed to burn.

"If I find out that Irish prince of yours was the one who broke you…" My voice dropped to a dangerous whisper. "He's dead."

Releasing her reluctantly, I stepped back, my body moving of its own accord as I gripped the door handle. Every instinct in me wanted to rip the door off its hinges just to release the frustration burning inside, but I held back. I wouldn't do anything to cause her more distress. "Cassandra," I said, my voice softening, "if you ever need help, I'll come for you. Always."

With that, I opened the door and closed it quietly behind me, leaving her alone.

THE CAR RIDE to the warehouse was tense, my mind torn between thoughts of Cassandra and whatever disaster awaited me at the docks. My jaw set, frustration sharpening my focus. "Gio," I snapped, my voice cutting through the silence. "Brief me."

Gio turned in the passenger seat, his face serious. "Ciro says the latest shipment was tampered with. He caught two of the men involved. They're waiting for interrogation now."

I nodded, my jaw tightening. This was going to be an ugly night, but part of me welcomed the violence. I needed an outlet for the storm raging inside me, and those men had just volunteered to be my punching bags.

The car pulled up to the warehouse, the stench of fish and mildew hanging thick in the air. My Armani shoes crunched against the gravel as I strode toward the entrance, Gio and Dimitri flanking me. Inside, Ciro was waiting, a twisted excitement shining in his eyes. The sick bastard loved this part of the job.

"Took you long enough, cousin," he said, clapping my hand in a rough shake before pulling me into a quick hug.

I smirked. "Calm down, boy. You'll get your fix."

He led me to where the two men were bound to chairs, burlap sacks over their heads. My eyes swept over them, and I gave a sharp nod to the guards. They yanked the bags off, revealing two terrified faces—one blonde and scruffy, the other dark-haired and already bleeding from Ciro's handiwork.

Grabbing a fistful of the blonde's greasy hair, I yanked his head back, forcing him to look at me. His bloodshot blue eyes darted around the room, frantic.

"Good evening, gentlemen," I drawled, my voice dripping with menace. "Or should I say, *ratti*."

The blonde grimaced as I pulled his head back further, pressing the cold barrel of my gun under his chin. "Now, you're going to tell me exactly what I want to know, or I'll make this as slow and painful as possible."

Ciro stepped forward, his fist cocking back before smashing into the dark-haired man's nose with a sickening crack. Blood sprayed everywhere as the man howled in pain, his head lolling forward as he tried to recover.

I smiled coldly. "See? I'm a fair man. You get one chance to talk. Just one."

The blonde hesitated, his wide eyes darting to his partner. I shook my head. "Wrong answer."

In perfect sync, Ciro and I both fired, the gunshots ringing out as we shot each man in the foot. Their screams filled the air, echoing through the warehouse as they squirmed in agony against the restraints. The warm metallic scent filled the air, mixing perfectly with the acrid smell of gunpowder.

"Start talking," I growled.

It didn't take long for the two Irish pricks to spill their guts. It was pathetic. One thing was clear, though—the Irish were pushing for a war, not just with us but the Russians too. A war I felt I might be too distracted for, whether Cassandra knew it or not she was a cast member in this play the Irish were putting on and it only made me want to protect her more from them but also herself.

Even so, the world didn't pause for my unraveling, business was business. The two *ratti* couldn't stop their tongues from moving, giving us their job details—the main one being to make the tampering look like the Russians' doing.

Fools believed they'd live. Obviously they were new and stupid and hadn't been tortured long enough by Finnegan and his Mcbastards.

The Irish only held a small turf on the west side of Chicago, and they had been trying to get the Russians and Italians to wage war with each other for years, hoping to scavenge what might remain from the aftermath. They were stupid, and our relationship with the Russians was too strong—something my father and Aleksander's father had been cultivating and nurturing for quite some time very discreetly. They knew keeping the strong ties quiet would be more of a benefit when gathering information, and Aleksander and I felt the same way.

Alone, Ciro and I cleaned our guns with dirty rags that we found near a crate, rubbing the heated metal with silent praise.

"The little vixen still giving you a hard time?" Ciro asked, his tone light and teasing, though his smile was razor-sharp.

My glare was menacing, the kind that would've sent most men running. "Don't start with me." The edge in my voice softened as I sighed and ran a hand through my hair, the gritty sweat and grime from the warehouse clinging to my skin. "But yes, Cassandra is weighing on me."

Ciro's self-satisfied grin widened as he nudged my arm with his elbow. "You need a wingman?" He winked, his words deliberately provocative. "Or are you just scared I'll steal your girl away?"

I didn't hesitate. Whirling on him, I grabbed the front of his jacket, yanking him close until our faces were inches apart. My grip was iron-tight, my voice low and deadly. "That's not something to joke about, Ciro."

He raised his hands in mock surrender, his grin faltering but never fully fading. "Christ, alright. I won't be your wingman." His tone was placating, but the humor still glinted in his eyes.

I shoved him roughly, my fingers smoothing out the lapels of my jacket after pulling it on over my blood-stained white button-down. "Besides, that Irish bastard is already in my way. And I think he's the one who wounded Cassandra."

Ciro's smirk returned, his eyes alight with wicked anticipation. "You know I'm always up for a hunt."

My chuckle was low, the sound rumbling from deep in my chest. "Yeah, I know you are. That's why you're *L'Uccisore.*" I pounded my fist lightly against his chest, a playful gesture, though the bond between us ran deeper than words. Ciro returned it with a wide grin, pounding his own fist against my chest like we used to do as teens.

He wasn't just my cousin. He was my brother in every way that mattered. Since the deaths of his parents, he'd been my shadow, and we'd been inseparable. People often mistook us for actual brothers—our similar builds, grey eyes, and sharp features lending themselves to the illusion. He was the only person I trusted, the only real friend I had.

"Gio!"

His footsteps crunched against the gravel as he came to an abrupt halt in front of me. "Boss?"

I didn't waste a second. "Find out if Cassandra's precious prince ever laid a hand on her." My jaw clenched as the words left my mouth, my hands already curling into fists at the mere thought.

Gio nodded, his expression stoic. "You got it."

As he turned to carry out my orders, my knuckles flexed, aching for something—or someone—to break. If Declan had hurt her like all the other girls I'd heard about, it would be the last thing he ever did.

Cassandra

Last night was a whirlwind. Between ovulation-induced insanity, Declan's flowers and call, and Leo showing up at my apartment to offer his warning—and his protection—I was emotionally drained. Completely overwhelmed.

I didn't know how much more of this endless, testosterone-fueled tug-of-war between the two of them I could take.

But one thing was for sure: Leo was everywhere in my head. Not just when I left my house. Every time I saw a picture of my mother. Every shift at Inferno. Hell, even when I made something as simple as spaghetti. It was infuriating. I couldn't let him claw any deeper. I had to focus on my goal—leave. Go anywhere. Leave my problems behind.

The search I made last night after Leo left had me landing on Florida, somewhere far away and warm. At least there I'd have beaches and palm trees—not asphalt and gunshots. But a move like that would push my escape plan back another six months.

My thoughts played an exhausting game of mental gymnastics while I washed the last of tonight's dishes. My grip tightened on the plate, and I barely registered the sound of the door opening until it was too late.

The plate slipped from my soapy hands, shattering as it hit the sink. Instinctively, I snatched the knife from the drying rack and spun around, holding it up defensively. My breath hitched, my heart pounding.

When Declan's face appeared in the doorway, I exhaled a shaky breath, lowering the knife. My shoulders sagged, but my pulse remained erratic.

Declan noticed my fighting stance and smirked, stepping inside as though he owned the place. "Oh yeah, Cass? You bringing a knife to a gunfight?"

"Shut up, Dec." My words came out sharp as I set the knife back down and reached for a towel, drying the soap and water from my hands. "I told you to knock or at least give me a heads-up before you show up at my apartment." A glimpse of him tucking a small metal object into his jeans pocket had irritation flaring in my chest. I knew he'd had another key made.

"I know," he said with a lazy shrug, approaching with a predator's version of patience. "But this is an emergency." His eyes flicked to the bouquet of flowers on the counter, and a smug grin spread across his face. The dimple in his cheek deepened as he closed the distance between us.

Before I could respond, his hand slid around my waist, pulling me against him, while the other tangled in my hair, gripping harder than Leo did last night. He tilted his head, brushing his nose lightly against mine. The featherlight touch melted my defenses, and suddenly, I couldn't remember why I was upset.

"Hi," I whispered, my voice barely audible.

"Hey." His voice was low, a sultry purr that sent a shiver down my spine. "I've been thinking about you."

He pressed closer, the evidence of his desire hard against me. My hands slid around his neck on their own, my fingers toying with the soft, dark curls at the nape. "Oh really? I couldn't tell." My laugh was breathy, almost shy.

Declan didn't waste another second. His lips crashed against mine, hard and messy, and I didn't stop him. My heart had been missing him, my body craving touch. He walked me backward until the counter pressed into my lower back, his hands sliding down to grip the backs of my thighs. Without effort, he lifted me onto the counter, and I let out a soft gasp.

A low, primal growl rumbled in his chest. "Fuck, Cass. I've been craving you."

"And you should feel how wet I am for you," I whispered, my voice dripping with desire. Pulling him closer, I pressed kisses along his jaw, trailing up to nibble on his earlobe.

"You have no idea what you do to me, baby." His lips brushed against my neck. His hands slid under my thighs, pulling me closer to the edge of the counter. My legs dangled as he ground his hardness against me, making me whimper shamelessly.

His teasing smile brushed against my lips as his calloused hands glided up my thighs, his thumbs pressing firmly against the sensitive skin of my inner legs. "Tell me how wet you are, Cass. I need to know how badly you want this."

"Dec," I coaxed, my voice husky, "if you just move your thumb a little closer, you'll feel for yourself."

His thumb slid up and beneath my loose grey pajama shorts, brushing over my clothed entrance with deliberate pressure. The friction sent a moan tumbling from my lips, and he grinned against my mouth, nipping at my lower lip.

"Such a needy little thing," he rasped, teasing the seam of my panties with his thumb. "So desperate for me."

"Bedroom," I murmured, my voice a breathy demand. "Now."

Without hesitation, Declan lifted me into his arms, carrying me through the apartment with hurried, purposeful steps. He pushed the door to the bedroom open with his foot and threw me down onto the bed, my body bouncing slightly against the mattress.

We didn't waste any time. Clothes were stripped away in a rush, his shirt first, then mine. My shorts were next, and I shimmied out of them as I scooted backward until my head hit the pillows. I spread my legs wide, showing him exactly how much I needed him. I needed someone to distract me, even if it was one of the men who already complicated my life.

Declan's eyes darkened as his gaze devoured me. He unbuckled his belt and shoved his pants down with an urgency that sent heat pooling low in my belly. When his boxers came off, I couldn't help the way my tongue flicked over my bottom lip, my eyes fixed on him.

"Fuck, Cass," he growled, his voice strained with desire. "I missed the way you look at my cock."

He climbed over me, his lips crashing against mine as he pressed the head of his cock against my entrance through my soaked panties. My hips bucked instinctively, chasing the friction.

"Dec, I missed this," I murmured, my hand reaching between us to wrap around him. His velvety hardness was hot and familiar against my palm, and I stroked him slowly, savoring the way he shuddered under my touch. I couldn't help it; everything bad between us seemed to have disappeared in the frivolous moment. I felt like a shaken champagne bottle, ready to pop at any second—especially after Leo's encounter with me last night at Inferno. It had me more worked up than I'd like to admit, but Declan was the one uncorking me.

"Baby, you're driving me insane," he groaned, biting my lip hard enough to make me gasp. The sharp sting sent sparks of pleasure racing through me.

But then, just as quickly as the heat built between us, it shifted. Declan's movements slowed, his grip on my thigh tightening. His eyes darkened, but not with lust—with something colder. Harder.

His hand wrapped around my throat, firm but not yet threatening, and he leaned in close, his lips brushing against my ear. "Especially with this Leonardo Romano shit," he whispered, the name dripping with venom.

My eyes snapped open wide, but before I could process his words, his grip tightened.

"Declan, stop—" I managed to rasp, clawing at his wrist as my breath caught in my throat.

"You think I wouldn't find out?" His voice was low and dangerous, a menacing hiss. "That fucking wop came here last night, didn't he?" His ice-blue eyes burned with fury as he tightened his grip further. "He knew Séamus and Bran weren't watching the post last night."

My legs thrashed under him, panic rising as my eyes felt like they were bulging from the sockets. My nails dug into his arms as I tried and failed to push him off me. My nudity and our vulnerability felt suffocating instead of romantic and passionate.

"You're mine, Cassandra. Do you understand?" he snarled, his other hand slapping me hard across the face. The sting exploded across my cheek, and tears blurred my vision as I choked on my words.

"Nothing happened, Declan," my voice was weak and raspy. "I swear."

Another slap. My head snapped to the other side, my teeth

clacking together painfully. Fuck, not again. If I don't get away he might kill me this time, just like my dad killed my mom.

"I said, do you understand?" His voice was quiet, eerily calm, as his hollow gaze pinned me in place.

My chin dipped, the ringing in my ears blaring as the fight left my body entirely. "Yes, I understand." I pushed my fear, humiliation, and pain deep, deep down into the darkest pits of my mind.

A wicked smile spread across his face, his tone softening as if we were sharing a tender moment. "Good. I'm glad we're on the same page."

He released me, rolling off me with casual ease. My body stayed frozen in place, my face felt too hot, and the rush of blood to my head made me woozy. I couldn't let him see; I had to protect myself, again.

Declan planted a gentle kiss on my forehead, his words soft and sickly sweet. "I'm sorry about the slap, but I need you to understand that you're mine. I love you, Cass. You know that, right?"

I stared at the ceiling, numb. "Of course I know that." The words on my tongue felt foreign and distant, that shaky feeling in my chest telling me I was doing a poor job of holding back my emotions.

"Good," he said, standing and dressing quickly, as if nothing had happened. "You're absolutely beautiful."

He planted another cold kiss on my forehead, then turned and strode out of the room.

And just like that, he was gone, leaving me alone in the silence of my bedroom, naked, shivering, and completely and utterly alone.

My trembling fingers brushed over my cheek, the sting still sharp. It was already starting to swell. I needed to get this under control—or I wouldn't be able to go to work tomorrow.

Or worse…Leo was going to kill Declan.

Leo

Walking into my family home usually made my troubles melt away. The smell of Italian cooking, the echo of laughter, the warmth of familiarity—it was always enough to lift my spirits. But not today. Not when one issue clung to me like a tumor, refusing to be ignored. Cassandra Bennett.

Even the intoxicating aroma of simmering sauce and garlic couldn't shake the weight pressing down on me.

"Leo, let's get you a drink. It'll help get your mind off her," Ciro said, clapping me on the back. His tone was light, but his smirk told me he wasn't done stirring the pot.

I let him steer me toward the kitchen, where the rest of the family waited. My jaw clenched, and I tucked my hands deep into my pockets to hide the tension from my mother. The last thing I wanted was for her to pick up on my mood.

When we entered, the room erupted into affectionate chaos. My mother and sister cooed loudly, rushing over to pull me and Ciro into tight hugs. I did my best to return their enthusiasm, careful to mask just how distracted I really was.

My father was next, his usual stoic expression softening just enough as he clasped my hand and pulled me in for a firm hug. His voice lowered as he whispered in my ear, "You need to do a better job of hiding your discomfort around your mother."

He pulled back, giving me a pointed look before a tight smile softened his words. "Missed you, son."

"Missed you too." I nodded and stepped back, giving him and Ciro space for their usual greeting. It was the perfect excuse to pour myself a glass of vintage Italian merlot—and one for Ciro while I was at it.

"So, you failed at fooling your father," Ciro commented when he joined me in the corner of the kitchen not being used by my mother as she flitted around the boiling pots and steaming pans, the teasing lilt in his voice impossible to miss.

He accepted the glass I handed him, swirling the wine before inhaling its aroma like some self-proclaimed sommelier. Turning toward my mother, he raised his voice just enough to get her attention. "This is a good year, Antonia. *Brava.*"

She turned to him with a smile so wide her eyes crinkled at the corners. "Thank you, *caro!*"

I muttered into my glass, "Kiss ass."

Ciro chuckled, taking a sip of the wine. "Someone has to make up for your sourpuss attitude today."

"Don't expect a thank you," I shot back, the corner of my mouth twitching despite myself.

"What's new, boys?" Alessia asked as she grabbed an empty glass and poured herself a generous serving of wine, her elbows resting on the kitchen bar beside Ciro.

Ciro grinned impishly, leaning casually against the counter. "Oh, you know. Same ol', same ol'. Taxes, working..." His grin widened. "Leo getting flustered over a girl."

Alessia nearly choked on her wine, sputtering into her glass. Meanwhile, I coughed so hard I felt like the wine might kill me on the spot.

Ciro clapped me on the back, laughing deviously. "Easy now, no need to get all worked up."

"Fuck you, Ciro," I muttered between gasps, glaring at him.

"A girl?" Alessia leaned in closer, her dark hazel eyes glittering with interest. "What's she like? Gloomy and boring, just like him?" She gestured toward me with her glass, her smirk as cutting as ever. She pushed back her thick dark brown shoulder-length hair with her fingers, the straight pieces falling back into her face.

I placed a hand over my chest, feigning mock offense. "You really know how to wound a guy, *sorella*."

Ciro barked out a laugh, clearly delighted by the banter. "I haven't met her yet," he said, leaning conspiratorially toward Alessia. "But any woman who can ruffle tall, dark, and gloomy's feathers is alright in my book."

"Alright, you two," my mother's voice cut through the laughter like a knife, her Italian accent equal parts stern and affectionate. "Leave *mio caro figlio* alone."

Striding over to her, I slipped an arm around her shoulders, pulling her into my side and pressing a kiss to her forehead. "Thanks, Mama."

She reached up, cupping my cheek with her warm hand, the strong scent of garlic and basil on her skin. "Any woman would be lucky to have you as her *amante*," she said, her voice full of maternal pride. She patted my cheek gently. "I love you, *caro*."

"I love you too, Mama." I released her, leaning against the counter beside the stove as she returned to stirring the sauce. The kitchen had cleared out, leaving the two of us alone.

"Mama, can I ask you something?"

She looked up from the bubbling pot, her soft gray eyes meeting mine. "Of course, *caro*. Anything."

Her beauty struck me in that moment, as it always did. Her dark brown hair, streaked with silver, was pulled back by a white head-band. Her olive skin was radiant, and her graceful presence filled the room. She wore her favorite black skirt that hit her ankles and a complementing black tank, her favorite white apron my father bought her three Christmases ago protecting the cherished garment.

Being home, I always felt like I could put down my tough exterior and just be me. Something I appreciated about my family more than anything in this world. Even my father was more human here. I swallowed hard, feeling the weight of my question settle in my chest. When the lump in my throat refused to budge, I took another sip of wine for courage. "When you and Dad met…did you two instantly fall for each other?"

She paused, setting the well-worn wooden spoon down with care before turning to face me fully.

"Absolutely not." Her hands settled on her hips, her Italian accent thickening with her conviction. "I despised your father. He was a… how do you say it in English?" She tapped her chin thoughtfully. "Ah, yes. An asshole." She spat the word with a flourish.

From the other room, my father's voice rang out, full of amusement. "She wasn't a ray of sunshine either!"

The sound of muffled laughter—from both Ciro and Alessia—followed, making me roll my eyes. My family's nosiness knew no bounds.

My mother turned toward the sound, raising her arm to make a crude Italian gesture even though my father couldn't see it.

"I love you too!" he shouted, his laughter echoing through the house. My parents knew each other better than they knew themselves, they had always been like that. My mother was always able to bring out my father's softness, while my father always cherished my mother like the goddess Venus herself.

She huffed, muttering under her breath, and turned back to me. "Anyway," she continued, waving her hand dismissively, "it took him a year to convince me to go out on a first date. And even then, I didn't like the bastard."

I chuckled, shaking my head. "So, what made you fall for him?"

Her expression softened, her eyes growing distant with the now fond memory. "Eventually, I started to see the man he truly was," she said, her voice turning to a softer tone. "Behind all his bravado, there was a gentle and loving man." She stepped closer, placing a hand over my heart. I covered her hand with mine, the gesture full of unspoken affection. "Just like you, *amore*."

A warm smile spread across my face, but it didn't last long.

"She's lying to you, Leo!" Ciro shouted from the other room, his voice dripping with mischief. "She's just trying to make you feel better about your caveman-like tendencies!"

Alessia's cackling followed, and my mother stormed out of the kitchen, wooden spoon in hand, cursing at them in rapid-fire Italian. I heard the shriek from my sister and the screeching of chairs as Ciro laughed wildly. The sound of rushed footsteps, Italian curses, and my sister cussing out Ciro was all too welcome and heartwarming.

I laughed, shaking my head at the chaos. Whether it took a month, a year, or a lifetime, I'd find a way to break through Cassandra's walls.

She would be mine.

EPISODE 5

Cassandra

What the hell was wrong with me?

I pressed cold fingertips to my swollen face, wincing as pain flared beneath my skin. My reflection was hideous. I looked like a slightly less deformed version of Harry Potter after Hermione cast a spell on his face to prevent the Snatchers from recognizing him.

Christ. I hadn't realized how hard he had hit me the night before. Or maybe I had—maybe I just didn't want to admit it. The whole thing blurred together, disjointed and surreal. One minute, he had been loving and completely sexy, and the next, he was a goddamn monster.

I ran a hand through my long black hair, my fingers trembling slightly as I gave myself one last, lingering stare in the mirror. A bitter laugh bubbled up, but I swallowed it down. *Get over it, Cass.*

I shook my head, but the motion sent sharp pain ricocheting through my skull. A pounding headache throbbed behind my eyes, and my stomach turned. I needed to call out of work. I'd just tell Vinnie I had come down with something and that I'd work doubles next week.

Giving myself my best you'll-be-fine nod, I stepped out of the cramped bathroom. My footsteps felt heavy, but my body thrummed with restless energy, like I needed to move or run—but from what? The living room was quiet, but my chest still tightened as my gaze darted toward the door.

He's not coming back.

"Calm down, Cassandra. He won't come back." I whispered it like a prayer, like if I said it enough times, it would become true. But my body didn't believe me.

I searched for my phone, flipping couch cushions onto the floor. My fingers dug into the fabric, frustration heating my skin. Why couldn't things just be easy?

With a defeated sigh, I dropped onto the couch, exhaling through my nose in slow, measured breaths. My heart was still beating too fast. My temples ached.

Fuck me. Fuck this bitch Karma for cursing me at every turn. And fuck everyone around me.

I threw an arm over my eyes, wincing at the pain it inflicted on my swollen face, and let myself breathe, just for a second. If I didn't, I was pretty sure I'd cry—and I was so goddamn tired of crying.

But then, the silence shifted. The tension in my muscles had nothing to do with last night's fight anymore. It was older.

It had been 21 years, but some things never left you. Some things weren't memories. They were stitched into the fabric of your body, buried under your skin, waiting for the right moment to claw their way back to the surface.

I had been six years old the night I first learned what it meant to survive. Hiding in the deepest part of my parents' closet, I pressed my small body into the shadows where Mama kept our go bag. It was just big enough for the essentials—some cash, a burner phone, a change of clothes. We had packed it together, rehearsed where to find it, what to do if things got bad.

They had gotten bad.

"You fucking bitch!"

Papa's voice rattled the walls, and I flinched so hard I bit my tongue. The coppery taste of blood filled my mouth, but I barely noticed. Curled tight in the dark, I listened.

"How dare you overcook the pot roast! How many times have I told you—if it's not perfect, don't fucking serve it!"

Mama didn't argue. She never did. The sickening crack of a fist against flesh sent a jolt of terror through me. Then her body hit the floor.

She never screamed. Never cried. She just took it. Like she believed enduring one more blow would somehow save her from something worse.

Through the closet slits, Mama's eyes found mine.

"*Aiuto.*"

Her lips barely moved as she mouthed the word. At the time, I didn't realize it meant help in Italian. But I knew what it meant by the look in her eyes.

My small hands fumbled through the bag, frantic as I searched for the phone. My heart pounded so hard I thought it might shake my ribs apart. Another crunch. Another grunt. Mama's body jerked against the floorboards.

I moved faster.

When I finally found the phone, my fingers trembled so badly I could barely press the buttons.

"911, what's your emergency?"

I stuttered so hard I didn't think they could even understand me. But I kept my eyes on the slits of light between the doors, watching as Mama's face blurred into something unrecognizable.

If the police didn't hurry, she was going to die.

The wait felt like an eternity.

My silent sobs, my hands clamped over my ears, my eyes squeezed shut—these were my only shields from the horror happening outside that door.

Then—sirens.

I had never felt such violent relief in my life.

But what if Papa sent them away? What if they knocked, and he smoothed his voice over, convinced them nothing was wrong? Mama would want me to stay hidden. But I couldn't. I had to save her.

Slowly, I stood, waiting for the perfect moment. Then, I ran. Papa only caught sight of me as I dashed through their bedroom door.

"Get back here, you little bitch!" His voice was thunder, his pounding footsteps rolling in like an oncoming storm.

My little feet flew across the house. I reached for the front door handle, wrenched it open—just in time for the police to see Papa's face contorted with rage. My fear-stricken expression must have said it all because they immediately grabbed me, shielding me from the monster I knew would have ended both our lives if I hadn't taken action that day.

A HEAVY, shaky sigh left my lips.

I hadn't thought about that night in years. Not in full detail. It had always been a shadow lurking at the edges of my mind, surfacing in nightmares, in tense shoulders, in the way I sometimes flinched when voices rose too loud.

It felt fresh. It felt here.

I ran a hand down my face, letting my fingers linger on the swelling along my cheekbone.

It was funny, in a sick, twisted way. After everything I had survived, after swearing I'd never let anyone make me feel like that little girl again…I had ended up here.

A bruised face. A racing heart. A mind that knew better—but a body that had never stopped bracing for impact.

My eyes drifted toward the shelf, to Mama's photo surrounded by the last few trinkets I had of hers.

"*Sempre e per sempre,*" I murmured. She had told me it meant forever and always. A warm tear traced a slow path down my swollen cheek. I swiped it away.

Mama, I wish you could be here with me. To tell me how stupid I am.

Or maybe…to tell me I wasn't stupid at all. That it wasn't my fault. That I wasn't turning into her.

Shaking my head, I pushed up from the couch and continued searching for my phone.

Leo

Ciro and I sat in the back of the black SUV, waiting. The engine idled, a steady, low rumble beneath us as we waited for Nico, my *caporegime*, to give us the green light. Inside that dump of an apartment, three *idiotas* from the Irish mob thought they could hide from my wrath. They were about to learn how wrong they were.

I stretched my neck from side to side, feeling the pull all the way to my shoulders, tension sinking deep into the muscle.

Besides this fucking mess, Cassandra had been taking up way too much room in my head. I'd been giving her space on purpose. When I showed up at her apartment, she had been overwhelmed—I could see it in the way she kept her body tense, her eyes darting like a frightened little *topo*. That wasn't what I wanted. I didn't want her skittish around me. But the scent of her had lingered on me long after I left.

Floral, but not the overpowering, artificial kind. Sweet, citrusy, with undertones of earth and vanilla beans. It was fucking intoxicating. Even if I closed my eyes, I could almost smell her.

A sharp nudge to my ribs yanked me out of my thoughts.

"Get your head on straight," Ciro muttered, irritation clear in his voice.

He had every right to be pissed. I hated it too—hated that my mind kept drifting back to her. I growled, rolling my shoulders before shrugging off my slate grey suit jacket. "Yeah, yeah."

Straightening in my seat, I rolled up my sleeves. I needed to focus.

A tap on my window pulled my attention. I rolled it down, locking eyes with one of my soldiers—a tall, lean man with jet-black hair and eyes to match. He wore a simple white Hanes V-neck and dark-wash jeans, standing out in contrast to the rest of us.

The whirl of the window sounded louder than necessary against my swirling thoughts. "What is it?"

Unfazed, he met my gaze. "Nico says it's a go."

I nodded, a silent dismissal. He got the message and stepped back.

As I rolled the tinted window up, I turned to Gio, who sat in the front. "Get that guy's name."

Then, I turned to Ciro. "You ready?"

Ciro let out a low, dark chuckle—the kind of laugh you'd hear from a villain in a movie. "Born ready." The humor in his voice faded fast, his dark gray eyes locking onto mine, filled with the same unrelenting darkness that simmered inside me.

Pushing open the door and stepping into the thick, humid air, city sounds echoed around us—horns blaring, distant sirens—but they faded into the background as I set my mind for battle.

We were about to find out what the Irish were up to—since the last ratti motherfuckers didn't give up the full details. Ciro moved beside me, close but not crowding. The distinct click of his gun cocking made my pulse quicken with adrenaline, but I wasn't so antsy as to pull mine out yet. No, I liked to let them think they had a chance.

Ciro? He was the bad cop.

Me? I was the bad cop who liked to pretend he was a good cop. It made breaking them all the more interesting.

As we climbed the last steps to the apartment, the thick, metallic scent of blood filled my nose—a telltale sign that Nico and his boys had already put in some work. A scrawny, bald man stood outside the door, leaning against the frame and staring at his phone. The moment he spotted us, he snapped to attention.

"Boss. Ciro." He dipped his chin. I didn't acknowledge him. I twisted the cool metal of the doorknob and stepped inside.

The room was plastic-wrapped—a crime scene before the crime. Blood spattered across the plastic like some fucked-up abstract painting. Nico stood in the center, his fist tangled in a man's dark brown ponytail, forcing his head back before releasing it. The man sagged forward, his body limp, head hanging like a broken marionette.

Nico glanced up, his voice light—like we had just arrived for dinner. "Boss. Ciro. Just in time." Ciro was already scanning the scene, gun in hand, the barrel pointed lazily at the floor. But I knew that tell—the way his free hand raked through his hair. He was getting too excited.

"What have you gotten so far?" he asked.

Nico sighed, glancing at the three men tied to metal chairs. "Just that they won't talk. Nothing else." His jaw clenched. "Fuckers have tight lips."

I let out a slow breath through my nose, irritation settling deep in my gut. "Leave it to us." My voice was flat, controlled—but my hands had already curled into fists.

Nico nodded, motioning for his men to clear out. Just as he was about to shut the door, I spoke.

"Wait outside," I said. "I don't trust that Mr. Clean knockoff motherfucker to do his job."

Nico scowled, glancing left—no doubt at the man I was talking about. But he didn't argue. The door clicked shut behind him, leaving just me, Ciro, and the three soon-to-be-dead men sitting before us.

Ciro and I stepped forward, taking in the damage. Two were redheads—twins, judging by their matching noses. They were missing fingernails, their shirts soaked in blood. The third—ponytail guy—had deep stab wounds in both thighs. Thick, dark red blood still oozed from the wounds in his dark denim, pooling beneath the chair.

"Look at me." My voice came out low and sharp.

Ciro pressed the barrel of his gun against ponytail guy's temple, tapping it once. His head lolled before centering again. I grabbed his throat, tilting his chin up before slapping him hard across the face.

"Wake the fuck up," I growled. His shit-brown eyes snapped open. The twins stiffened, their swollen faces fully alert. I let the silence stretch, watching them. "Do you know who I am?" My tone was quiet. Dangerous.

Their gazes flicked between each other, then back to me. No one spoke. Wrong move.

My grip tightened around his throat. His bugged-out eyes stared back at me, panic creeping in. "Talk," I demanded, voice deadly calm, "or all that money you did this for? It'll be for nothing."

Ciro tapped the gun against his head again, reinforcing the threat. And if these idiots thought we were bluffing, they were about to get a very painful reality check.

A lot of Ciro's and my torture techniques came from my father. We had shadowed him since we were twelve, watching, learning, absorbing every brutal lesson like it was gospel. By fourteen, we had already tortured and killed our first man—a rogue gang bastard we'd finally tracked down, one of the scum responsible for Ciro's parents' deaths.

That one felt good. And we had no regrets.

After that, we hunted down every last one of them, one by one, fulfilling a vow we had made the moment Ciro came to live with us at five years old. To this day Ciro was still hunting them down.

Though Ciro and I were the same age, trained the same way, and could both easily lead, I had been chosen as Don for one reason alone —I was the Don's son. Ciro accepted his position as second with a similar pride.

Ciro suited as my second, where he could unleash his rage and sadism without dealing with the daily bullshit that came with running an empire.

And at that moment? That rage was on full display.

AN HOUR IN, Ciro was twisting on the silencer, making sure the three bloodied men in front of us knew he wasn't fucking around anymore. We had already put in some work, but so far, they had given us nothing.

I sighed, running my free hand over my face, smearing blood over it like war paint. My other hand gripped the torn shirt I had ripped from one of the twins earlier, repurposed as a personal hand towel. Sweat, blood, and fear filled the air, thick enough to choke on.

Ciro let out a low, amused chuckle, his gaze flicking between them like a predator choosing its next meal. "Either you tell us what the Irish are up to, or you die," he said simply, raising his gun and aiming it at ponytail asshole's head. "This is your last warning."

The man spat onto the plastic-covered floor, blood streaking the saliva. A silent act of defiance.

Ciro didn't hesitate. The sharp, suppressed snap of the Glock 19 firing echoed through the room, followed by the sickening splatter of flesh and brain matter against the plastic-covered wall. The man's head snapped back, blood pouring from the large exit wound in the back of his skull.

His lifeless body sagged, and for a moment, there was nothing but silence—just the sound of blood dripping onto the floor. Ciro sneered, already pointing the gun at the next man. The twin on the left tensed, his fingers twitching against the zip ties that bound his wrists. He stared at the guy's body slumped beside him, the head still tilted at an unnatural angle.

My fingers flexed, the torn shirt crumpling slightly in my grip. Ciro's grin widened, and I already knew what he was about to do. He began flicking the gun between the two brothers.

"Eeny, meeny, miny, moe."

The twins' chests heaved in unison, blood and sweat mixing on their skin.

"Do you want to have him continue?" I asked roughly, my voice low, sharp.

They didn't answer.

Ciro continued, his voice mocking as he recited the next line. "Catch a tiger by his toe."

The gun flicked between the two of them again, quicker this time, the cold barrel softly tapping their foreheads.

"If he hollers, let him go."

They looked at each other, a silent desperation passing between them. I could see it—the moment it clicked. One of them was going to break.

"Last chance," I said through clenched teeth, my headache pulsing behind my eyes. Not that I gave a fuck whether they lived or died. I just needed one of them to tell me what I needed to know.

"You can spill your guts…" I tilted my head slightly. "Or watch your brother die."

Ciro pressed the barrel harder against one of their foreheads, adding weight to my words. "Eeny. Meeny. Miny—"

"Okay, okay!" The twin on the left gasped, his voice raw and desperate.

Ciro and I both stilled, exchanging a quick glance. I scoffed. Knew it.

"Go on," I encouraged.

Ciro didn't move the gun. His stare remained locked on the twin, adding to the pressure, the weight. The man hesitated, his chest rising and falling rapidly, his pupils blown wide with fear and adrenaline. Slowly, he turned to his brother, a silent conversation evident by the way they locked eyes.

A mute accusation. A betrayal. He inhaled deeply, his breath wavering. "Finnegan McCalister," he finally rasped. "They're planning to raid the Russians' warehouse next month and steal their entire shipment of guns. They plan on blaming it on you."

Ciro let out a low whistle, tapping the gun against the twin's blood-matted hair like a pat on the head. "See? That wasn't so hard."

The brother on the right turned his head slightly, his swollen eye narrowing at his twin. Then, without hesitation, he spat blood onto the floor. I could see the fire behind his eyes, the rage bubbling beneath the surface. Three of us knew what was about to happen.

Ciro pulled the trigger.

The shot was clean, straight through the right twin's good eye. His body jerked, blood splattering in a thick spray against the plastic. The remaining twin flinched violently, his chest heaving, his face pale.

He didn't even scream. Just stared at his dead brother, shock creeping in, slow and suffocating.

Ciro and I watched in silence, letting him absorb the reality of his situation.

"You're free to go," I finally said, voice flat and indifferent. I shoved my dirty hands into my pockets, knowing I was going to have to burn this suit anyway. "I'll let the Irish mob finish you off."

The last remaining ratti twitched, his fingers flexing against the blood-slicked zip ties. He didn't move. Didn't breathe. His brain was still catching up, still trying to process what I had just said.

Ciro laughed, loud and amused, like I had just cracked the funniest joke he'd ever heard.

I didn't stay to watch. My stiff body turned, already stepping over the blood-smeared floor, my mind moving past the mess, past the bodies, leaving the useless fucker sitting in that chair.

Cassandra

Tugging the old, worn-out baseball cap further down my face to conceal the remaining bruises, my hand gripped the handle and yanked the back door to the club open. I had been absent for almost four days—the longest I had ever been out of work.

Time I didn't have. I was still behind on rent, and I refused to touch my savings account. More than anything, I wanted to get out of here. If Leo came in tonight, I would have to come up with an excuse for why I still had these lingering bruises. The last thing I needed was for him to think he was saving me by killing Declan. The knot in my stomach loosened slightly—a reaction I refused to examine.

A blast of A/C hit me first, followed by a wave of perfume—most of it cheap—that burned the inside of my nose. It wasn't the first time I had walked into a job with bruises, but it was the first time here, and the last thing I needed was for the girls to fuss over me. My sneakers squeaked against the floor as I made my way to my station, the clutter of my workspace reminding me of how fast I had left almost a week ago.

I started organizing, avoiding my own reflection in the vanity mirror. The bulbs burned too bright, their glow a silent threat to expose me. A delicate hand on my shoulder made me jump.

"Jeez, you're skittish today, Angel." Candy's high-pitched voice cut through the distant club noise, sharp as ever.

I kept my eyes down, fumbling with my makeup containers. "Yeah, sorry. I didn't sleep well last night."

Candy snorted. "What, Mr. Romano fucking your brains out for the past four days?" Her tone dripped with a mix of envy and sarcasm —a characteristic she had that I'd never appreciated. "Must be awful." She rolled her eyes, and I caught it without revealing too much of my face. I've been gone for almost a week 'out sick' and this bitch had the audacity to say I was fucking Leo?

"Candy, fuck off," I warned. "Nobody likes a jealous bitch."

She shoved me, sending my hip into the vanity. A few of my things rattled together from the impact.

"I'm not jealous of you," she scoffed, flipping her long, bleach-blonde hair over her fake-tanned shoulder.

Without thinking, I whirled and shoved her back. The moment she caught sight of the faint bruises on my cheeks and neck, her eyes went wide. Before I could react, she pulled me into a hug. "Shit, Angel," she whispered into my hair. I felt one of her hands waving behind my back, and a second later, I heard the murmurs of the other girls gathering.

"What happened?" someone asked.

Candy's voice hardened. "Girls, Romano beat the shit out of her."

A chorus of gasps and hisses spread through the room. I pulled back, shaking my head, my eyes stinging. "No, it wasn't Romano." My fingers fiddled with the brim of my hat, my hair, anything to keep busy.

Candy's soft fingers tilted my chin up, her other hand pulling off my cap. "Jesus Christ," she murmured, inspecting the damage. "Then who did this to you?"

I couldn't look at them. My gaze stayed glued to the ceiling, my hands still fidgeting. Their stares burned into me. When Candy finally released me, she wiped at the tears I hadn't even realized had fallen.

"Never mind, sweetheart," she said softly. "If you don't want to talk about it, I understand." She nodded at me, then gave the rest of the girls a knowing look. "I'm sure I can speak for most of us when I say we know what it feels like to be in your shoes right now."

An echo of agreement rippled through the room, and before I knew it, I was engulfed in a group hug—fifteen girls pressed into me, their blonde hair in every shade poking at my face, tangling in my mouth. But I didn't pull away. I just sank into it. I hadn't realized how badly I needed this.

By the time we hit the floor, my bruises were concealed thanks to the girls using every trick they'd learned over the years, and my heart was wrapped in something warm and fragile. We moved as a unit, stepping into the club like a pack of lionesses. The feeling was intoxicating. Empowering. Something I was desperately trying to cling to, especially since I was known for my defiant and tough personality here.

A tall man with mocha skin prowled toward me, but Sapphire intercepted him with ease. Before I could react, Candy grabbed my hand and dragged me toward Vinnie's office.

"You're not dancing tonight," she said, her grip firm. "You should bartend."

It caught me off guard—Candy and I had always had a competitive streak, bantering like sisters about everything. But this? This was something different. This was protective. She kicked open Vinnie's door with her eight-inch platform heels. He flinched, startled, but when he saw us, he relaxed. Well, as much as Vinnie ever could. Sweat pooled at his thin hairline, dripping down the side of his face.

"What can I do for you ladies?" His brown eyes darted between us, trying to gauge if this was a casual request or something more dangerous.

"Vinnie, Cassandra is going to bartend tonight," Candy declared.

Vinnie's gaze landed on me, his expression shifting. I felt see-through, like if he looked any closer, he'd be able to read every secret, every wound, every demon lurking just beneath the surface.

"Sure, Candy." He grabbed a hanky from his desk and blotted his forehead. "But you'll have to coordinate with the girls to cover Angel's dance rotations." His worry was obvious as he glanced back at me. "You okay?"

I bit my bottom lip, hesitating. "Yeah," I murmured, not wanting to go through this again. I changed the subject. "Is Romano coming in?"

The second his name left my lips, my pulse spiked. Leo had seemed to crawl into my thoughts these past four days, especially when I watched my bruises change colors. A part of me wanted to tell Leo so Declan could get what he deserved, but the other piece of me—the piece that still held onto the softer side of Declan—couldn't. He was a disease I both clung to and wanted carved out of me.

Vinnie leaned back in his old leather chair, the tight buttons of his shirt barely containing his hairy chest and stomach. "No, he won't be in for a while." Relief softened his voice.

I wished I felt the same. The butterflies that had been stirring in my stomach turned to lead. My heartbeat stuttered. I bit the inside of my cheek as I gathered myself. Come on, Cassandra—you're trying to leave. You don't get to fall for another man.

"Angel, you work the bar, and Candy, you handle rotations," Vinnie confirmed. "Let me know if you need anything else." He gave us an uncertain smile, but that was just Vinnie—not a bone of confidence in his body. But probably the nicest man I knew.

Candy's grip tightened around my hand as she pulled me toward the door. My legs felt unsteady, like a baby fawn tripping over itself, but she kept me moving.

I ran the bar instinctively, falling into the rhythm of it with Grace and Fiona. But my mind was elsewhere. Every man who looked even remotely like Leo caught my attention. Every so often, I swore I heard his deep, breathy voice drifting through the bar, sending my stomach plummeting.

Cassandra, you literally just had the shit beaten out of you, and here you are, craving another possessive, controlling asshole.

A quieter voice whispered back. Yeah, but he's different.

Is he different?

Maybe.

Leo

My eyes zeroed in on Finnegan the second Ciro and I stepped into the private office space we had rented out in New City—neutral turf. A long redwood desk split the room in half, much like the invisible line that divided the territories we both claimed. The cheap gray carpet had silver threads woven through it, shimmering in the daylight from the large dusty windows.

Renting this space had been one of the conditions of the meeting. I had set it up, though Ciro had nearly convinced me to skip the niceties altogether. But I knew that declaring war took more than just anger—it took coordination. I'd have to inform my crooked cops, rally my men, and spend the money to arm them properly. A fucking headache.

Still, if I had to do it, I would.

Finnegan sat across from me, posture relaxed, his expression almost gentle. To anyone else, he looked like someone's sweet old grandpa. A man who handed out candy to kids and told bad jokes at family barbecues. But I knew better. He was more diabolical than I was, ruthless in ways that still made my skin crawl. Whether it was hunting down men or breaking in henchmen, Finnegan had no fucking limits.

He had to know we were onto him, but I wanted to hear why. My gaze flicked to his favorite attack dog, Séamus—also known as Scál, which translated to phantom in Gaelic. A big Irish brute, infamous for making people disappear without a trace. Séamus held my stare, giving me a look of both respect and warning. I returned the sentiment.

Ciro pulled out a rolling chair and plopped into it effortlessly. On the surface, he looked playful—casual, even. But I knew better. The man was a lit fuse, ready to explode at the slightest provocation. The squeak of the pleather seat echoed through the room, amplifying the silence.

I lowered myself into my chair with slow, deliberate movements, resting my head back as I propped an ankle on my knee. My ring-clad fingers laced together and settled against my stomach.

Finnegan smirked.

It took everything in me not to grind my teeth. I couldn't show irritation. Couldn't show weakness.

His Irish accent came out thick. "You handled most of our rat problem." His tone was casual, as if we were discussing the fucking weather. "The last pest is in our basement, living out the rest of his moments."

Christ. I didn't even want to know what kind of medieval torture Finnegan had lined up, but I bet that poor bastard was wishing Ciro had just put a bullet in his skull. I exhaled slowly. "Let's get to the point, Finnegan." My eyes remained locked on his, my posture still easy, casual.

Ciro chuckled beside me, then reached into his waistband, pulling out his Glock 19 and placing it on the table with a solid thunk. He leaned forward slightly, his scarred olive forearms resting on the polished wood. His usual casual outfit—maroon V-neck and light-wash jeans—only added to the illusion of indifference.

"Yeah," he drawled. "I wanna know when you grew such big—"

The door flung open. I didn't even need to look. The arrogant energy that came with the entrance told me exactly who it was.

Declan McCalister.

"You mean compared to your shriveled walnuts?" Declan grinned, wide and sharp, like the fucking Cheshire Cat.

A low growl rumbled in my chest. I kept it caged, but Ciro saw it— the tension coiled in my frame, the death stare I leveled at the bastard. Declan's slow, deliberate steps were a taunt. A test. He knew I hadn't been expecting him.

"Declan," I said, my tone tight.

"My son's learning the ropes," Finnegan said, sneering. "I'm sure you can understand that." That crooked smile widening. "How's your father doing, anyway?"

Ciro exhaled sharply, his patience thinning. "Enough of the pleas- antries."

Declan spun a chair around and flopped into it, leaning back, spreading his legs wide. A blatant power play.

What a fucking joke. I wasn't some rookie he could rattle.

I ignored him, my gaze locked back on Finnegan. "Talk."

The old man's smug expression faded, replaced by something colder. His hands clasped together on the desk. "The shipment. Is that what you're referring to?"

"You know damn well why we're here." My hands itched to reach across the table and end it right then and there. "Don't play stupid."

Finnegan's knuckles turned white, but it was Declan who spoke. "Don't speak to my father like that, you fucking wop bastard."

My stare didn't shift. Didn't flinch. I was getting to him.

"Tell me now, Finnegan."

Declan's glare was searing, his entire body rigid with tension. If looks could kill, I'd be nothing but ash.

Finnegan sighed. "You had something I needed." He said it so matter-of-factly, as if age entitled him to my shit. But it was all lies, this fucking guy wasn't going to admit that we'd caught him, which made me believe that he had something else up his sleeve.

Ciro's fists slammed into the table, the sound reverberating through the room. I didn't blink, Finnegan and I were still locked in a stare-off.

"So you thought you could hire some fucking idiots to steal from me instead of negotiating?" My voice was calm, even. A stark contrast to the fury coiling in my chest. I leaned forward, mirroring Finnegan's posture. I wasn't going to tell him what we actually knew, that his men had told us about his plans to frame us next month. "Those guns were mine. I paid good money for them. And now, you're going to return them."

Silence.

Then Declan shot up from his chair, snapping.

No control. No restraint. Pathetic.

I barely resisted the urge to shake my head. He'd make a terrible mob boss. Emotions made people easy to manipulate. And at that moment, he was handing me leverage.

"We won't return shit," he spat, his face going red.

I didn't even acknowledge him.

"Look at me!"

Finnegan's teeth clenched—the only sign of his displeasure, his embarrassment.

Then Declan's voice turned mocking. "Look at the fucking face that owns that sweet little pussy you keep chasing after. You know the one. The one you're so interested in."

Ciro sucked in a sharp breath. I forced myself to move slowly, turning my head at a controlled pace.

"What the fuck did you just say?"

Declan's posture shifted, the rigidness bleeding into something looser. Cocky. His father, though—his father had gone stiff beside him.

I rose to my full height, towering over Declan by a solid five inches.

Declan squared his shoulders, his ice-blue eyes drilling into mine. "You heard me," he said through gritted teeth. "Cassandra's mine."

My fingers curled against the desk. Control yourself.

I fought the urge to lunge across the table and choke the life out of him. "Last I heard, she left you."

"That's not what she said a few nights ago when I had her pinned underneath me." Declan's lips tilted into a cruel smile that told me he wasn't lying about some of what he was saying.

Séamus coughed, like he was calling Declan's bluff.

I'll have to ask my little *topo* later about what he had said.

"Well, you know she only dances for me at Inferno."

Declan took the bait instantly. Whipping out his gun, he cocked it and aimed it at my face. Ciro moved before I even had to, his own weapon drawn. Séamus flicked his gun between my cousin and I.

Shaking my head, I chuckled, tucking my hands into my pockets. "Finnegan, call off your rabid dog."

Finnegan's glare could have cut through steel. "Sit the fuck down," he snapped at Declan.

And that was all the evidence I needed. Declan was the one who broke Cassandra.

Declan slowly lowered his gun and tucked it into his waistband, his chest rising and falling with barely controlled, angry breaths. With a sharp exhale, he collapsed back into his chair, running a hand through his dark hair. The agitation still burned in his icy glare, his jaw clenched so tight it looked like it might crack.

Séamus didn't lower his weapon until Ciro did.

Only once the room settled did I move, lowering myself into my chair with deliberate ease. I made sure they saw it. That I wasn't rattled. That I owned this moment.

The silence stretched.

Then Finnegan finally spoke.

"I won't be returning shit to you, Romano." His voice was even, but the edge was there. A warning. His fingers pressed against the table as he pushed himself to his feet, slow and steady. "And if you so much as have anyone step foot in my territory to retrieve it…" His gaze locked onto mine, piercing and unyielding. "I'll be sure Cassandra is given a special visit."

That last line—I had handed him ammunition the moment I mentioned Cassandra. I had exposed a fault line. Every muscle in my body went rigid.

A low warning vibrated from Ciro's chest.

Declan smirked—one last attempt to get under my skin. Then, like the fucking coward he was, he turned and followed his father out the door, flipping me off on his way out.

Séamus lingered. He shook his head once—whether in amusement or disapproval, I wasn't sure—then gave me a respectful nod before exiting.

Ciro and I waited. Listened. Only when we were certain they were out of earshot did I speak. I leaned back in my chair, exhaling slowly. "Let our men know."

"The Irish have declared war."

Nobody threatens me. And Cassandra Bennett—she was my little *topo*, my *principessa*—which meant I'd protect her at all costs, even if it meant she hated me for what I was about to do.

Cassandra

My onyx hair whipped around me like a ribbon dancer, following the slow, deliberate arch of my body. The faces in my upside down vision blurred as I spun. Yellow, orange, and red lights flashed in time with the music, the colors swirling like fire above me.

The bass vibrated through me, my favorite song blasting through the club's surround sound. Cash rained down like soft paper kisses against my skin. My wide smile mirrored the satisfaction curling in my chest.

They always paid well when I danced like this. And when I was back to my normal self—well, as normal as one could be—my regulars were frenzied for my attention.

I slid my hands up my ribs, hooking my fingers beneath my bra straps. The energy in the room was thick with anticipation. But just as I was about to peel the lace from my skin, my eyes caught a pair of steel-gray ones in the crowd.

The world kept spinning. I wasn't sure if I had seen correctly. My movements had me dragging my body down the pole in a slow, sinuous descent. Encouraging whistles and catcalls rang out around me, but they barely registered—I was too busy searching.

Where were those wolf's eyes?

My feet hit the stage. Rolling my hips, I kept up my performance, gaze flicking from face to face.

And then I saw him.

Leo sat at the end of the stage, front row. He had forcefully moved one of my regulars for the spot—I could tell by the way the poor bastard was sulking a few seats away. Leo's gaze roamed over me, slow and possessive. And even though I was practically undressed, it felt like he was peeling the rest of my clothes off with just his stare.

My breath caught, and I felt the flutter of excitement that only a school girl crush could induce. I hadn't seen him in over a week.

Calm yourself Cassandra.

Even as I forced my secret emotions down, I didn't falter. Instead, I eased into my usual routine, settling onto my heels, keeping my body moving just enough to keep the money flowing. Technically, I was his personal dancer and waitress whenever he came to the club.

But the way he was looking at me? It felt different.

Our eyes locked. A heated staring contest.

My body moved on instinct, hips undulating as I crawled toward the edge of the stage. Bills slid beneath the thin fabric of my G-string, fingers grazing my skin as I passed, but I barely felt them. All I felt was his eyes dragging over me, unhurried and deliberate.

Easing toward him, I settled onto his lap, my hands bracing against his firm, broad shoulders.

A wave of groans filled the club—disappointed customers who had lost my attention—but I barely heard them.

Leo and I were locked in a silent battle.

Who would break first?

His hands hovered over my skin as they trailed up my arms and down my back, never quite touching. The heat from them sent shivers cascading down my spine, goosebumps rising in their wake.

The scent of him wrapped around me—dark spice, something rich and clean like cognac with the smell of tobacco. My lips parted slightly, my breath coming a little faster, and fuck, I could feel my thin G-string dampening by the second.

Leo was dangerous. A stunning, untouchable Italian Don who radiated power and control.

His voice was a low, dark rumble, vibrating through my chest. "*Principessa*, if you don't get off my fucking cock right now, I'll have to fuck you in front of all these men."

He leaned in, his lips brushing against the shell of my ear. "And I don't want these men hearing the noises I'd make you scream, otherwise I'd have to kill each and every one of them."

A sharp pulse of heat shot through me. My thighs clenched. A soft whimper escaped before I could stop it.

Fuck.

I couldn't even blame ovulation this time. I had gone nearly a week without seeing him, and yet the second he was near me again, my body reacted like this. I forced myself to still, exhaling slowly as I slid off him. My long hair spilled over my shoulder as I moved.

Leo's gaze followed, his expression dark with barely restrained need when I looked over my shoulder one last time.

Thank fuck I was wearing black panties. But judging by the look he had in his eyes, I knew he had felt the wet spot I'd left behind on his slacks. My music stopped and the DJ's voice came over the speakers, introducing the next girl to the stage. I took a moment to scan the room. That's when I saw them.

A second pair of steel-gray eyes.

My brows furrowed, and my head snapped between the two men, trying to make sense of what I was seeing.

They looked so similar.

My shocked stare finally settled on Leo, who was smiling like a predator. Standing, his strides ate up the short distance between us. He towered over me, his presence suffocating but still welcome. He leaned down from behind me, his hand sweeping my hair away from my ear and down my back, lips grazing the shell. A heated shiver ran down my spine and I felt my breath catch in my throat.

This crush—or whatever this was—was drifting into dangerous territory. I couldn't fall for Leo. Not then. Not ever.

"I'll meet you upstairs, *bella.*"

Then he strode past me, adjusting himself as he went. The lookalike clapped him on the back, laughing, only to earn a hard hit to the gut. He howled again, his laughter eerily similar to Leo's.

I tilted my head, confused.

The other man gave me a quick glance over his shoulder, caught my stare, and winked.

What the fuck?***

Leo and his almost-twin were huddled by the small bar in the VIP lounge when I arrived. Gio and Dimitri acknowledged me with a curt nod. I had taken the time to get dressed—slipping into my usual black fishnet dress over matching lingerie—but the moment I stepped into the room, I felt the weight of both their stares.

It rooted me in place. Holy shit.

They were almost identical. The only difference was lighter brown hair, a softer gaze with something unnerving beneath it, and features less sharp than Leo's—but the resemblance was undeniable.

I blinked rapidly.

The man chuckled.

"Seems like we broke her." His voice was deep, raspier. Leo's tone had a smooth, velvety quality—like warm cognac sliding over your tongue. Leo took a slow sip of amber liquor, watching me carefully.

I crossed my arms, schooling my expression as I turned to the stranger. "And who exactly are you? We didn't agree that I'd be entertaining the riff-raff you dragged in off the street." My gaze flicked over his casual outfit—maroon V-neck tee, dark jeans, combat boots.

Leo coughed into his drink. Gio and Dimitri—men I'd gotten used to seeing more than Leo himself and had grown familiar with. The new guy slapped Leo on the back, laughing harder.

"Ah. I see now why you're obsessed," he said, grinning. His smile was bright, almost infectious. "She's as beautiful as you said she was, brother."

"Brother?" I repeated, my eyes snapping back to Leo. It made sense. The similarities, the shared mannerisms.

Leo finally set his glass down, running a hand through his disheveled dark hair. "Cousin, actually." Then, his gaze locked onto mine. Serious. Intense. "Come, *principessa*. I'll introduce you."

Something in his tone made my stomach knot, and I felt weirdly warm and fuzzy, like I was cherished. Still, I played along. Cautiously approaching the two large, intimidating men, I kept a safe distance, skeptical of the new guy.

Leo gestured toward him. "This is Ciro. My cousin and *consigliere*. Second-in-command."

Ciro gave me a slow once-over, then smirked.

"We grew up together," Leo added. "We're practically brothers."

My lips parted slightly. Leo stepped closer, his voice dropping. "We need to speak with you. It's important." The shift in his energy sent a warning bell ringing in my head.

I nodded slowly and led them toward the seating area, letting them settle before I hopped onto the small stage, which sat slightly higher than them.

I smirked to myself. That would bother Leo.

Sure enough, his expression darkened slightly, and he ran a hand over his face. "I'll be blunt, Cassandra." His voice cut through the moment.

My stomach tightened. "No." I stood abruptly.

Leo and Ciro both gave me matching glares and simultaneously commanded, "Sit."

Instantly, I sat back on the stage, crossing both my legs and arms, exhaling sharply in frustration. The bossiness from one was annoying. But two? That was obnoxious.

Ciro tsked, shaking his head playfully. "Such a brat."

Leo shot him a scowl. "Not now, Ciro."

My eyes narrowed and my crossed arms hid my shaky hands. "What do you want?" My voice came out sharp, defensive. I hated not having a choice, and I could already tell this wasn't going to be some 'I'm giving you a raise' or 'you're fired' conversation. No, this was something more that involved danger, and danger mixed with being a stripper only spelled out D.E.A.D.

Leo ignored my tone. His jaw ticked, his gaze sharpening like a blade. "We need information on Finnegan and Declan."

My stomach twisted and all the warm, fuzzy feeling dried up, replaced with panic.

"You're going to tell us everything you know about the Irish mob."

The blood drained from my face. My fingers instinctively went to my chest, rubbing the spot where my pulse pounded too hard beneath my skin, then my hand drifted up to my throat.

Did Leo know?

The memory of Declan's hands on me resurfaced, an unwanted phantom touch.

Fuck. I couldn't let Leo kill him. No matter what Declan had done —no matter how much of a monster he was—there was still a part of me that would always care. I swallowed hard. "Why?"

Ciro cut in smoothly. "The less you know, the better, sweetheart."

My head snapped toward him, my glare ice-cold. "Don't call me that."

Ciro only chuckled. "Apologies, *piccola strega*."

My eyes narrowed further, but I didn't take the bait. Instead, I squared my shoulders, my focus shifting back to Leo. "Tell me why, and maybe I'll give you what you want."

Leo pinched the bridge of his nose, exhaling heavily. "I've got a fucking headache, Cassandra. I don't have time for your games tonight." His voice was low, laced with exhaustion, but his frustration was razor-sharp.

My fists clenched at my sides, sweaty and shaking so bad it would look like I had endured a blizzard. "I don't give a fuck how you feel." My voice cut through the room, unwavering. "I won't betray the people who cared for me when I couldn't care for myself." My mind spun with worst-case scenarios. What would happen to Finnegan? To Declan? His entire family? I didn't want their blood on my hands.

The sound of metal scraping against leather pulled me from my thoughts. Ciro pulled out his gun, settling it in his lap. A silent warning. "Eyes up here, *piccola strega*." He tapped two fingers against his temple, his steel-gray eyes glinting with something dark and dangerous.

A shiver crawled down my spine and I couldn't sit still any longer.

I started to pace, feeling like a trapped animal. "Leo, I can't." My hands flew as I spoke, the words rushing out. "They're like my family. Please—I don't want to be a part of this."

Leo rose from his seat in one fluid motion, cutting off my pacing as his hands gripped my shoulders, stilling me. His touch was firm, grounding, but most of all it was gentle. When I peered up at him to scowl, I saw the brief concern there, understanding.

"You will be a part of this." His voice was calm, but the storm beneath it that replaced his softness was barely contained. "And I'll tell you just enough to help you make the right decision. But if I hear that you ran your mouth to the Irish, don't think that pretty face will stop me from putting a bullet in it."

I swallowed. Hard. Then nodded. My arms wrapped around

myself. I couldn't believe I had put myself in this situation. I'd avoided being involved in the mob wars for so long, and in that situation not only my life but also those who I cared about were in harm's way.

Leo's grip loosened, but his eyes stayed locked on mine. "They stole from me," he continued. "Finnegan refuses to be reasonable. He's declared war."

Ciro snorted from behind him, leaning back in his chair like this was all some casual hangout, but he didn't say anything—keeping his opinions to himself. However, I could see he thought I wasn't trustworthy yet, and that stung more than I'd like to admit.

Leo ignored him.

Before I could react, he cupped my face in his hands, forcing my attention back to him.

"*Principessa*," he murmured, his voice softend. "I know this might be hard. But whatever claim Declan thinks he has on you?" His thumbs brushed against my cheekbones. "That means jack shit to me."

What did he just say? I jerked back from his touch.

"Claim?" I scowled, my anger flaring. "Declan might say I'm his, but that's not true." I crossed my arms, lifting my chin defiantly. "I'm nobody's."

Ciro's laughter filled the small VIP lounge, loud and booming. "Sure," he mused, arching his brow mockingly. "And I'm a fucking priest."

Leo shot him a warning look. "Ciro, I swear to God." His gaze returned to mine. "Cassandra." His thumbs brushed delicately over my cheekbones, and it took everything in me not to lean into it. "Either you give me what I want, or I take it from you." His expression was both a warning and a plea, and that combination made my stomach twist into a pretzel.

I knew Leo well enough to understand what he meant. If I didn't cooperate, he'd find a way to make me. I gnawed at my lower lip, the sharp taste of iron touching my tongue before I even realized I had bitten down too hard.

Leo's eyes flicked to my mouth. A self-satisfied smile curled at the corner of his lips. Then, before I could pull away, his thumb swiped across my lip, collecting the blood, and he brought it to his mouth.

Licked it clean.

I sucked in a sharp breath, my pulse stuttering. "Christ," I whispered.

His smirk deepened. Leo leaned in, voice smooth, dark, and intoxicating. "What will it be, *principessa?*"

EPISODE 6

Cassandra

Fuck. I really didn't have much of a choice.

Leo stood in front of me, imposing, unshakable. My gaze flicked over him, running up and down the broad expanse of his frame, heat curling deep in my core. I forced myself to look away, settling on Ciro instead—lounging in his seat like this was just another night, another conversation, another game to be won.

The club's music thrummed just beyond the two-way glass, while the muffled sounds of whistles and catcalls followed by drunken laughter carried on like I wasn't in a possible life or death situation, like I wasn't about to be forced to spill my guts about any personal information I had on the McCalisters. It made me feel resentful. I gave this club my all and nobody seemed to give two shits. I was up here with two of the most dangerous men on the east side of Chicago, feeling like I was snared in an invisible net cast by poachers.

The red glow of a ceiling light crossed over my vision, almost mimicking the anger that simmered in my heart. Not just at the current situation I was in, but at the fact that this was the life I lived, the life I felt forced to play out like some fucked up version of the Sims, and I was fully expecting for the doors to be deleted and a full blown fire to break out and consume my entire life. Not that my insignificant life meant anything to anyone, it barely meant anything to me.

Leo's calloused thumb skimmed over my right cheek then my bottom lip, each slow stroke sending fire through my veins, scrambling my thoughts like a siren's song. *I was absolutely fucked.* If I ratted out Declan's family, they'd hate me forever—probably kill me. I wouldn't blame them, I'd hate myself more than they ever could.

Declan's mother Abigail and twin sisters Maeve and Rowan were tough women, each of them having their own ways of surviving. Abigail with her take-no-shit attitude, Maeve with her ability to hack and manipulate, and Rowan, petite sweet Rowan. She was the one that I respected most, she was graduating med school soon to be a surgeon, she found a way to survive and live a life outside of crime. And then there was his father… Even if what Leo was saying was true, Finnegan had cared for me. Treated me like his own. I could still picture those family dinners—gathered around their old, worn-out dining table, the one that had been shipped all the way from Ireland because it had belonged to Finnegan's great-grandmother. The smell of bangers and mash filling the air, wrapping me in warmth. Even Declan managed to be on his best behavior at dinner.

"Cassandra, answer me."

Leo's tone sharpened, insistent. My pulse stuttered, sweat pricking at my hairline. I flicked my gaze up to the stage lights, searching for an excuse, but they were dim, barely an excuse at all. My nails found the holes in my fishnet dress, fingers worrying the fabric as my mind raced.

"I…" I hesitated, meeting his steel-gray gaze again. There was patience there—thin, strained, but patience nonetheless and it surprised me. I knew he didn't offer that to just anyone. I also knew that if I gave him the wrong answer, I wouldn't be walking out of Inferno.

The low thump of the bass matched the pounding in my ears. Everything felt too close and too far away all at once. My chest rose and fell in quick bursts, and then—his arms came around me.

I froze.

Wait—Leo was hugging me?

I tipped my head back, barely getting the chance to look up at him before one of his strong hands guided the side of my face against his chest where the sound of his steady heart beat pumped. My fingers curled instinctively into his jacket, my senses flooded by the scent of dark spice and cigarettes. It should have set me on edge. It should have reminded me of exactly who he was. Instead, I felt safe, secure, and oddly not alone.

What an odd sensation to have in the arms of a killer. A man asking me to choose a side. A man demanding I help murder people I loved. It was fucked up, like being hugged by the angel of death just before they took your soul.

But maybe...maybe I could save some of them. If Declan and Finnegan were his only targets, maybe I could keep his mother and sisters out of it. They at the very least deserved a chance, a life better than the one they were brought into and the nightmare I was forced to participate in.

I swallowed around the lump in my throat, voice barely above a whisper. "Let's make a deal."

Leo pulled back instantly, hands gripping my shoulders. "A deal? With the devil? Are you sure, *Principessa?*"

"Deal?" Ciro laughed, the sound sharp with disbelief. "Leo, you're going to let her make conditions?"

Without missing a beat, Leo and I turned on him at the same time.

"Shut the fuck up, Ciro."

Ciro only laughed harder. "*Dio mio.*" I heard the shift of metal on leather, followed by the rustling of fabric. I exhaled slowly, knowing he had just put his gun away. I would never forget that these men were dangerous—but I'd been around dangerous men my whole life.

Leo tilted his head, studying me with a knowing grin. "When I make deals, I always collect, Cassandra." His voice was smooth, edged with dark amusement. "So, I'll ask again. Are you sure you want to sell your soul?"

Electricity crackled between us, the lump in my throat thickening, turning into something dry and suffocating. I squared my shoulders, gathering every ounce of bravado I had left.

"Good luck finding one." My lips curled into a feline smile of my own, if I wanted to be taken seriously I needed to seem like I had something to offer.

His gaze darkened, something wicked flickering in his steel-gray eyes. "Then let's make a deal, *Principessa.*" His voice dipped into a deep, gravelly growl, his body unmoving, so close still that I could feel the heat radiating off him. My neck ached from looking up at him, but I refused to back down.

Then—after a long, drawn-out moment. And when I say long, I mean it felt like eternity—he finally moved.

Carefully, as if handling the most precious doll, he released me and sank back into his black leather chair, stretching out with a slow, deliberate ease. He propped an ankle on his knee, then reached inside his jacket, pulling out a pack of cigarettes. The gleam of steel caught my eye, heat curling through me for an entirely different reason, before I forced myself to step back toward the stage, perching on the edge.

Both men watched me expectantly.

I understood their silence, but I needed a moment to gather my words. I couldn't afford to falter. Not when I had an opportunity to save three women caught in the middle just like me.

Licking my lips, I finally spoke. "I want Abigail and her twin daughters Maeve and Rowan left alive. In exchange, I'll give you information about the Irish." I needed to be strong. To hold my ground. So I lifted my chin ever so slightly, exuding confidence I wasn't sure I actually had.

Neither of them reacted right away. Instead, they exchanged a glance—a silent conversation passing between them, unreadable and unnerving. The longer they took to respond, the more anxious I became, but I refused to let it show.

What if they refused my deal? I knew I wasn't in a position to request anything—they could easily torture me and take what they wanted. I wish I could say I was tough like those female heroes in war or spy movies, but I wasn't, and that was the truth. If they so much as pulled out a stereotypical pair of pliers and threatened to peel off my fingernails one by one, I would squeal like a damn shameless pig. And that's reality. This world isn't a fucking movie—it's ruthless, cruel, and unforgiving to those caught in the chains of the streets of Chicago.

Ciro's gaze met mine again, and I saw it—that dangerous glint, the barely concealed thrill lurking just beneath the surface. Leo, on the other hand, studied me with something darker. Something unreadable. Something that sent heat licking over my skin all over again.

I held my breath, waiting.

Leo

I kept my fucking excitement in check, adjusting slightly in my seat. What I was about to counter-offer was already making all the blood in my body rush south, and the fact that I knew my deal would piss Cassandra off? Even better. My little *topo* always looked so damn good when she was angry.

Inhaling deeply, I took a long drag of my cigarette, watching as the ember brightened before fading into the haze of smoke curling through the air. It twisted and mingled with the multicolored lights of the small stripper stage Cassandra was perched on, a contrast that only made her look more untouchable.

Steady your heart.

I was the fucking Don—I needed to act like it.

Narrowing my eyes, I finally spoke, my voice low and smooth. "Alright. I'll coordinate that with Ciro and Nico."

I studied her carefully. The tension in her shoulders eased, her posture softening in a way that sent a rush of something dark and primal through me.

Fuck, I can't wait to see that turn into rage. Here we go.

"However," I continued, watching her sagged relief snap back into taut fury, "I want to make a condition. In exchange for their lives."

After speaking with Finnegan today, his threat toward Cassandra sat heavy on my shoulders. This counteroffer wasn't negotiable, but her conditions gave me room to slip it in without appearing territorial.

Her reprieve was short-lived. Cassandra's hands balled into fists on her lap, her glare cutting through the dim lighting like a blade. "Is this an offer I can refuse?" Her voice was tight, barely restrained, and I wanted—no, needed—her to explode. I wanted that fire, that passion.

I'm positive my little *topo* knew that I didn't need to make deals, I rarely ever did. But for Cassandra—my *principessa*—I would give her anything. She was mine and I always took care of my possessions.

Before I could respond, Ciro fucking laughed.

"We're not a cliché, *piccola strega*."

My jaw ticked. The fact that he already had a nickname for her made my blood boil. He was intrigued by her. I saw it. And that was a problem. Because Cassandra? Was mine. Only mine.

"You can refuse," I growled, shooting daggers at Ciro, "but you won't like the consequences."

Cassandra didn't even flinch. "Or what? I'll be sleeping with the fishes?"

Ciro let out a howling laugh, and I fought back my own smirk, though the amusement tugged at my lips. "Always a smartass, *bella*."

That's what I loved most about my little *topo*, she used her sharp tongue as a blade, and she was good at it, but over the past few weeks of observing her I knew it was a deflection from when she was feeling vulnerable. And by the way her chest heaved, and the subtle way her fingers traced the small holes on her dress she was anxious.

Her glare sharpened. "Stop calling me beautiful. Or your princess. I understand Italian, asshole."

Holy fuck.

My cock twitched at that. Not just because she was being a brat—though that certainly wasn't hurting—but because she understood *Italiano*. I uncrossed my legs, shifting just enough to spread them wider. "*Principessa*," I purred, "if you don't stop that filthy mouth of yours, I'll have to make you." And I knew plenty of ways to punish her, and she would enjoy every single filthy thing I wanted to do to her.

Her eyes flickered down, exactly where I wanted them to, and I felt the small hitch in her breath.

We'd been playing this game of 'fuck me eyes' for too long. I wasn't about to lose.

"Christ, Leo." Ciro chuckled, running a hand through his hair. "That is not how you seduce a woman properly. Mama would wash your mouth out if she heard you."

I ignored him, keeping my gaze locked onto Cassandra's, a silent challenge crackling between us.

Her emotions were always so easy to read—wide, expressive emerald eyes, flushed cheeks, the slight tremble in her breath. And in that moment? I had her. The red light flashed overhead sharpening her angles and fuck she looked like a wounded angel ready to seek her revenge—breathtaking. I wanted to run my fingers over her smooth skin, trace every line of her features until I memorized them.

But then—just as quickly as she let me in, she slammed the door shut.

Disappointment furrowed my brow as she crossed her arms over her chest, no doubt to hide her hard nipples, her jaw tightening in a poor attempt to sell her act. "Well, I guess I don't have many choices," she grumbled, voice dripping with reluctance. Then, after a pause, she exhaled sharply. "Tell me your condition. Let's get this over with."

There she was.

I shook my head, extinguishing my cigarette in the glass ashtray on the small gold table between our chairs. Then I stood, tucking my hands into my pockets to keep myself from touching her again.

Ciro rose beside me, but I had the last word.

"You'll live at my estate until further notice. That is my condition." I tilted my head slightly, watching the way her breath hitched, her pupils dilating. "And as it was stated, you don't have many options to choose from."

Cassandra went pale. Slack-jawed. Frozen.

Fucking stunning.

Little did she know that I already had my men at her apartment gathering her things. I made sure to create a distraction to have Séamus and Bran leave their posts out front of her building long enough to collect all the essentials and put the rest in storage. I'd save this piece of information for when she came asking later—I was already anticipating that moment.

She didn't say anything—not yet—so I stepped forward, closing the distance between us with deliberate slowness. When I reached her, I dipped down and brushed the lightest kiss against her forehead.

"Finché non incontreremo di nuovo, bella. Until we meet again, beautiful."

Then I turned and strode for the VIP exit, Ciro following close behind, leaving Cassandra sitting there—processing, catching up, trying to piece together the chaos I had just dropped on her. I grinned to myself. She was going to be livid when she caught up with what I just requested. But at least this way I could protect her while we slaughtered those bastards. Cassandra Bennett was a beautiful frustration that I'd come to realize I needed more than I ever thought humanly possible.

As we neared the exit of Inferno, I noticed movement in my peripheral—a bleach blonde with tanned skin and sharp overly painted light blue eyes. I'd seen her around before, a dancer at Inferno, but she had never once tried to get my attention.

Tonight, though? Tonight, she looked determined as she blocked my exit.

Ciro unabashedly checked her out as she flicked her hair over her shoulder, flashing him a sultry smile.

"What do you want?" I barked, already annoyed.

She straightened, looking up at me. "I need to ask you a favor."

Her voice was high-pitched, grating, barely cutting through the thumping music. My jaw tightened. How fucking dare this *puttana* ask me for a favor? Me. The fucking Don of the Italian mob.

"No." I pushed past her, but she stumbled, grabbing my jacket in a desperate attempt to stop me, I felt her sharp nails dig into the fabric.

She was lucky I didn't hit women. Because I was half-tempted to backhand her.

"How dare you touch—"

"It's about Angel."

Her words cut through my fury like a blade, and she quickly let go of my jacket, stepping back. That's when I noticed the worry in her eyes, and the slight tremble in her fingers.

I inhaled slowly, smoothing down my lapels. If this was about Cassandra, I'd hear her out. "Go on."

She stepped closer, lowering her voice. "Angel came in last week pretty beat up." Her eyes flicked over the room, scanning the crowd as if making sure Cassandra wasn't nearby. "She said it wasn't you…" She met my gaze again, her expression pleading. "I can tell she means something to you. Could you…maybe take care of whoever did that to her? She's special, you know?"

Oh, I knew she was special. She was priceless, something that could never be replaced, and she had a grip on my heart.

The woman's hands fidgeted in her hair, and before I could say a word, Ciro took advantage—pulling her into his chest, pressing her too-large fake tits against him as he held her tight.

"Don't you worry, *bella*," he murmured, stroking her hair. "We'll take care of it."

Fucking pervert.

"What's your name?" I asked, concealing the absolute fury clawing at my insides, because I already knew who broke my little *topo*, but to hear he had tried to break her again. He was a dead man walking.

"Candy," she mumbled against Ciro's chest, held so tight she could barely look up at me.

Ciro winked at me over her shoulder, mouthing, "Nice tits."

"Thanks, Candy, for letting me know." I turned, already picturing the thousand ways I'd make Declan McCalister beg for death. "Come on, Ciro."

Cassandra

"Angel, come here!" Sapphire shouted from across the main room.

At three in the morning, Inferno was finally empty. The lingering smoke from cigarettes and cigars still swirled and danced in the bright lights we always turned on to encourage stragglers to get the hell out.

My heels clicked on the black tiles as I made my way over, hands clutching two buckets filled with cash. The girls and I had a tradition

—if it was a good night, we counted our money and helped ourselves to top-tier liquor.

The club was nice, but it honestly looked higher end when the lights were out. With the fluorescent lights beaming on everything it really made every cheap fix and flaw stand out like a sore thumb. The dents in the wall from bar fights covered by black paint without filling them in, the scratches on the fake marble tiles beneath my feet that Vinnie liked to polish only once a year.

When I reached the glass bar that had a disgusting amount of smudge prints and cracks along the seams, Sapphire squealed, "Girl, I made a grand tonight!" She bounced in her seat like a little kid on Christmas morning, her pin-straight bob wig dancing around her heart-shaped face.

Well, I guess for Sapphire, it was Hanukkah.

"What'll it be tonight, Angel?" Grace asked, her deep brown eyes crinkling in the corners as she noticed the two buckets I placed on the counter next to Sapphire's.

Taking in the elegantly lit shelves that accented the bottles, I settled on one of our finest scotches. When I pointed to it, Grace smirked.

"My favorite."

Turning to Sapphire, I smiled. "Glad you made some dough tonight, Sapph. You worked really hard." I rubbed her overly glittered shoulder tenderly. "Your new routine kicks ass."

Her golden blonde hair swished as she fanned herself with the cash dramatically. "A few of my wealthy regulars were back from a business trip too. They told me they've been in London closing a deal and were successful." Her grin widened. "Showed by how much they tipped tonight that they were in a good mood." She ended with a wink.

Grace slid the crystal glass of honey-colored liquid toward me. "How was your night tonight, Angel? Saw Romano and a very handsome-as-fuck friend of his go up to the VIP." Her pierced brow arched in question—Grace was way too observant, though it also made her helpful when it came to handsy customers. We considered her our look out; she guarded us, but it was still annoying when she brought up things I didn't want her to talk about.

The cool glass pressed against my lips as I considered my answer, taking a slow sip and letting the scotch burn all the way down. Thoughtfully I set the glass on the bar and skimmed the rim with a manicured finger. "I had a—"

"He was handsome indeed." Candy's familiar voice cut in. "He hugged me and everything." She wiggled her brows, her baby blues lit with too much enthusiasm as she slid into the chair on my other side. "I'll take a glass of white wine—the driest you have, Grace."

I gave Candy a suspicious look, taking another sip before asking, "When did you speak to Leo and Ciro?"

Candy's over-injected lips curved into a mischievous smile. "Ciro?" She licked her lips. "Is that his name?"

Then she completely ignored my question, casually counting her cash, straightening a few bills along the edge and resting them in neat, organized piles.

"Answer me, Candy." My tone was controlled, but she fucking loved driving me up a wall. And she knew exactly which buttons to push.

Grace set the frosted glass of white wine in front of Candy, then leaned against the bar, her signature scent of sweet orange blossoms floating around us as her short siren-green hair fell over one eye, complementing her dark skin that sparkled with gold glitter.

She was the only one besides me without blonde hair. Grace was also from the west side of Chicago, running from her own Irish demons. She was cunning when it came to men, able to change her look and make it seem like she had vanished. With Vinnie's help, she had kept a low profile, and because all of us here at Inferno understood the risks, we kept our mouths shut.

The other girls—Fiona, Roxy, Vixen, and Emerald—joined us, taking their seats along the bar top. Grace swiftly took their orders, but I knew she was still keeping an ear on our conversation. Nothing was private here, but it was protected.

Candy continued stacking her bills neatly before finally answering. "After they finished with you." She glanced at me briefly, just long enough to catch my reaction.

My grip on the crystal tightened, the grooves biting into my hand, probably leaving indentations. That made her smile mischievously, and it only made me want to throttle her.

"Why?" I needed to know. Were they trying to get the other girls involved? Digging for more blackmail? I knew the girls would never sell me out—we were family here. None of us came from great places, but we'd found a sanctuary at Inferno.

"Candy, why do you always do this to her?" Roxy asked, clearly fed up with our usual back-and-forth.

But it wasn't me—it was Candy.

Candy just shrugged. "They didn't say much. Just thanked me for being so amazing to you." Her tone was so smug it made me see red. "Then that tall, sexy Ciro—fuck, I'd climb that man like a damn tree." She sipped her glass of wine like it would solidify a wish before finishing, "Hugged me in gratitude."

Bypassing the color red in my vision, a black cloud hovered over everything. Fucking black. I was about to freak the fuck out when Vixen chimed in.

"Candy, you're such a needy slut. You know those men aren't into you."

"Yeah!" Emerald let out a giggled agreement.

Candy's smirk slipped into a sneer, her eyes flicking over each of us.

"You didn't feel how hard he squeezed me. He was practically feeling up my breasts."

My empty glass hit the bar so hard as I slammed it down that the glasses underneath rattled. "You know what? I'm happy someone's finally paying those fake-ass tits some attention. God knows your cheating husband isn't."

The room went silent.

Fuck.

All the girls gasped, and I cringed on the inside.

Low blow, Cassandra.

"Shit, Candy. I didn't mean—"

She held up a hand. "Don't."

Her face was serious now.

Fiona slid off her stool, wrapping an arm around Candy in a side hug. Her pink-and-blonde hair contrasted sharply with Candy's bleach blonde. Candy patted Fiona's arm appreciatively. The two of them had always been close—I knew more than once they'd run away from their shitty husbands together.

Candy exhaled slowly. "Rick and I are...separated. Finally." Fiona squeezed her tighter. "The asshole finally fucked up on parole and got caught. He'll be in prison for ten years. Hopefully."

Shit.

I was a bitch.

I reached over and squeezed her arm lightly. I knew she didn't want an apology—it would sound hollow after what had just transpired, even if she deserved one. "I'm glad he won't be giving you any more grief, Candy." We all knew what *grief* meant. Every one of us had some man giving us grief at one point or another—it felt inevitable. Her shoulders relaxed, and I saw a small spark of light flash in her eyes, the kind that signified hope. It made my heart warm for her. None of us deserved these awful men we seemed to have such a bad appetite for.

"Me too!" Emerald exclaimed. "Let's celebrate!"

We all stared at her—seriously?

Emerald wasn't dumb, but she was sometimes deaf to social cues. Actually, out of all of us at Inferno, she was the only one with a college education—graduated with a degree in economics. But she'd gotten caught up in the world of crime, arrested for assisting in drug smuggling for her on-again, off-again boyfriend. She got off easy—two years in prison and two years of probation—but it ruined her chances of landing a decent job with a felony conviction. Add the mountain of student debt, and Inferno became her only real option. She started working here not long after me.

Then Candy threw her hands up. "You know what? This *is* something to celebrate!"

Emerald and Fiona joined in on the excitement. Vixen, Roxy, and I went back to counting our money, but we joined in for a few shots when Grace slid them across the bar. I was happy for Candy. Really.

Glad that one of the girls had escaped her abuser—envious, even. I mean, it's fucking hard. These assholes know exactly what to say to pull you back into their web, sweet-talking you right up until the moment they turn and beat you senseless. That's just what narcissistic womanizers do.

They wait.

They watch.

And they strike when you're at your weakest.

After drinking way too much, I had to call a taxi. The other girls kept celebrating, which had somehow turned into them dancing and giving Candy lap dances for her to judge. It was hilarious—especially since they were so drunk they wouldn't have passed a walk-and-turn test. So, to say they were doing a shit job balancing on a small couch was being generous.

The laughter and chaos no longer pulled at me the way it should have. The idea of joining in, of pretending this was just another night, felt exhausting. The weight of what I'd committed to with Leo sank deeper and deeper as the night dragged on, pressing into my chest until it was hard to breathe. It only made me more annoyed with myself. I caved too quickly.

What was it about that man? Besides his intimidating status.

Which, honestly, if I were God, I would've never made a criminal as hot as Leonardo Romano. That was just poor planning on their part.

Maybe that's why I caved. He'd sat there in that chair across from me—legs spread, an erection on full display like a goddamn all-you-can-eat buffet. I clenched my thighs together, as I waited for my cab it did nothing to control the heat building inside me.

"Miss Bennett."

A male voice cut through my thoughts. I snapped out of it instantly, my hand diving into my purse.

Since Declan had decided to use my face as his personal slapbox practice, I'd been more jumpy lately and seemed to pull out my pepper spray at any sound that startled me. Whipping it out, I aimed—and froze.

Dimitri.

Lowering the canister, I exhaled, both frustrated and relieved. "Hey, Dimitri."

The man in front of me had become almost like a regular at Inferno, and he was a big flirt to all the girls, bringing in chocolates for them to share and bouquets of flowers. He was smart too; he and I would have debates about politics and economic issues on my breaks. It was refreshing, and I enjoyed his company. I tossed the black cartridge back into my bag and clutched the strap tightly. My gaze flicked to his side, where I noticed the gun tucked into a holster. Yeah, my pepper spray wouldn't have done jack shit.

"Why are you here? Is Leo with you?" I swayed slightly on my feet. Thank fuck I wasn't wearing my heels anymore.

Dimitri tucked his hands into his pockets, leaning against the black SUV like he had all the time in the world. "No, the boss isn't here. But he sent me to come get you. You know, the agreement and all that." He pulled out a cigarette, lighting it way too slowly, like he already knew I was going to argue with him. Like he was waiting for it.

That pissed me off. Was I really that predictable now? I stormed toward him, stumbling a few times but still managing to get in his face. Dimitri wasn't short—average height for a guy, maybe five-nine —but he was built like a fucking tank. Tattoos from his knuckles to his face. Stoic as a gargoyle whenever he was with Leo.

But right now? He had that playful smirk he always wore around the club when he was there on business.

A dimple appeared. I squinted. Yeah. Definitely a dimple. Not a tattoo.

I scowled. "What's so amusing?"

Dimitri took another drag of his cigarette, exhaling a thick plume of smoke toward the sky before answering. "Just that Leo said you'd be pissed when you found me here. And he was right."

His too-white smile only made me want to punch him. I let out a sharp huff, gripping my purse strap harder. I wanted to stomp my foot, throw a full-blown, two-year-old temper tantrum—but that would just make him laugh harder. And I was sure Leo had already predicted this exact conversation. So I forced a smile—probably a sloppy one, but a smile nonetheless.

"How sweet. So Leo had an escort come and take me home?" My voice dripped with mock sweetness, but the way Dimitri's lips widened into an impish smile which told me he knew I was full of shit.

Tossing the half-finished cigarette onto the concrete, he stomped it out with the heel of his boot. Then, with a cocky glint in his dark brown eyes, he tugged on the back passenger door handle and gestured for me to get in.

"That's right, sweetheart. So be a good girl and get in the car so I can take you to your new home."

Good girl? How infuriating. Out of all our conversations we've had he had never antagonized me, but I wasn't going to let him see that it got to me. Flipping my hair over my shoulder with a tight smile, I climbed in, fumbling around in the dark for my seatbelt.

When I couldn't find it, I gave up, sighing and resting my head against the cool, overly tinted window.

Dimitri started the engine, blasting the A/C as he glanced over his shoulder at me. "Let me know if you're gonna blow chunks. Gio will make your life hell if you dirty up his baby."

I rolled my eyes before closing them.

Yawning, I settled in deeper. The leather seats felt extra snuggly and embracing, pulling me in. Maybe a little nap would help me sober up—but then Dimitri's words gripped me. *New home.* Oh shit. I wasn't going to my apartment. I was headed straight into the wolf's den, and knowing that did nothing to ease the stress piling up, turning my life into one massive shit sandwich.

Leo

Slam!

My head snapped up as the wooden office door flew open and ricocheted off the wall, leaving, if I guessed correctly, a gash in my wall. A disheveled, wild-eyed, nostril-flaring, chest-heaving Cassandra came barreling into my office with Gio and Dimitri staring after her as if stunned that she had gotten past them. Why the hell did they let her pass?

"You motherfucker!" she seethed, I signaled for Gio and Dimitri to leave it and shut the door. "You moved all my shit last night while I was at work? That wasn't part of the deal!"

Still dressed in the clothes she left Inferno in—skimpy high-waisted jean shorts and a black crop tank that read, "I'm nicer than my face looks"—she looked like pure sin. Her creamy-toned legs were on full display, her perfect tits hugged by that shirt that couldn't be more fitting if it tried.

I barely stopped myself from smirking at the contradiction standing before me. "Good morning, *principessa*," I purred, rising from my leather chair and meeting her halfway. She craned her head back to glare up at me, putting her delicate, flawless throat on display.

Dio mio.

My hand itched to wrap around it, to feel her fluttering pulse beneath my thumb as I kissed her senseless. I wanted to consume her, devour her.

But then—

"Hello? Earth to Leo?"

Cassandra crossed her arms, narrowing her eyes into pissed-off slits. She looked like an angry little kitten, and fuck, I wanted to pet her so badly.

"Our agreement had no timeline," I said smoothly, brushing a loose strand of her dark waves behind her ear. I didn't let go right away. Instead, I played with it, enjoying the silky texture between my fingers. Her fiery emerald gaze locked onto mine like Minerva ready for war, but I only continued, my voice rich with amusement.

"So I took the liberty of having my men do the hard part for you. All your furniture is safely in storage. Clothes should be neatly hung or folded in your room. And all your little trinkets are carefully packed away in boxes in your closet."

Her nostrils flared, her gaze flicking between my lips and my eyes. I couldn't resist.

Releasing the strand of hair, I slowly slid my hand around her neck—gentle, patient, controlled. I didn't want to spook my little *topo*. Not when I'd gotten this far. My thumb rubbed over her rapid pulse. Her pupils blew wide. Stormy green overtook her irises. Intoxicating.

An excruciatingly long beat passed before she licked her lips and spoke, her voice softer this time—a mix of honey and smoke. "You could have at least warned me last night."

If God didn't strike me down for what I was thinking, I wouldn't be able to control myself.

Leaning down, I brushed my nose against her onyx hair at her temple, inhaling the scent of vanilla and roses. My lips grazed the shell of her ear as I murmured, "And miss the dramatic entrance you just gave me?"

I lingered there, drinking in her heat, her scent, the wild rhythm of her pulse beneath my fingers.

She didn't move away.

She wanted this.

She wanted me. But I needed her to realize it too.

Sure, I'd stolen a few touches—tasted the smoothness of her skin here and there—but that had been to satiate the obsession I'd developed for Cassandra. Now, with her this close, my obsession clawed at my insides. Claim her.

"Leo," she breathed, her voice a mix of question and longing.

My grip tightened—just a fraction. "Yes, *principessa*?"

Her stormy green eyes flicked to my mouth again. "Don't get the idea that you own me, because you don't." She exhaled slowly, controlled—but still shifted closer. The motion pressed my hand firmly against her throat.

She liked this.

The danger.

If I had to bet my life, I'd wager that beneath those tiny fucking shorts, she was soaking wet for me.

"I wouldn't dream of saying that…." My voice dropped, dark and rough with need, *"principessa."* Heat bloomed up her throat, creeping into her cheeks. "Do you like feeling my hand around your delicate little neck?"

Her lips parted. She stared at me—entranced, breathless. "No…"

I nearly laughed at the blatant fucking lie. "Do I need to check for myself?"

My free hand slid down her side, tracing the curve of her upper ribs—thumb stroking just beneath her breasts, which I could see right away were bare underneath.

Fuck.

My cock hardened painfully.

She sucked in a sharp breath, her hands pressing against my chest. Her fingers danced deliberately over my flexed muscles beneath my maroon button-down.

God, I needed more of her touches.

"If you do, you'll be very disappointed." Her voice was a challenge. And I've never backed down from a dare.

Keeping my grip on her throat firm, I let my other hand trail lower, fingertips gliding over every ridge and dip of her perfect body.

We locked eyes.

Neither of us daring to speak.

Just touching.

Then, slowly—deliberately—she started unbuttoning my shirt as if we were playing some sexy game of chicken. Oh how I loved her little games.

By the time my hand reached the top hem of her shorts, her stomach muscles fluttered beneath my fingertips. In one swift move, I unfastened them. The zipper buzzed loudly in the quiet room.

I hesitated.

Waiting.

Daring her to stop me. But she didn't. Not one word. Just that same defiant, burning look in her eyes.

Tugging her shorts down, I let them pool at her feet, my jaw clenching at the sight before me.

A black lace thong.

Holy fuck.

I fought every primal urge to slide those panties to the side and take her then and there. She hadn't begged yet. She hadn't told me to stop.

"Last chance, Cassandra." I swallowed hard, my voice thick with need. "If you don't tell me to stop…" I couldn't finish the sentence. My mouth was dry, my pulse hammering. I searched her eyes. She only shook her head.

"Is that a stop…or a don't stop, *principessa*?" I flexed my fingers against her throat, feeling her overheated skin and the pulse racing beneath my touch. "Use your words."

Her throat bobbed as she swallowed. "Don't…stop." She undid the last button of my shirt, nails raking over the hard muscles of my smooth chest.

That was all I needed. I was going to ruin her.

And the best fucking part? She wanted me to.

Tearing away the fabric shielding her delicious pussy, my fingers immediately slid between her soaking wet slit, seeking her heat. When I found her core, I groaned. "Such a fucking liar, *principessa*." My voice was a low, feral growl, the most primal part of me taking over.

Her moans were mine, filling the quiet office as I sank two fingers inside her, my thumb finding the swollen, sensitive bundle of nerves and strumming it with slow, precise strokes.

"Christ, Leo," she whimpered, so softly, so breathlessly it made my cock ache.

I curled my fingers, hitting that perfect spot I knew would make her eyes roll back. And when they did, when she rocked her hips into my hand, her nails biting into my flesh, I knew she was already slipping.

"Devour me, Leo." Her voice—a desperate plea, a demand, a fucking prayer.

And I came undone.

I did just as she asked, my mouth crashing against hers, swallowing her whimpers as our tongues warred for dominance. Still buried deep inside her, I pulled my fingers free just long enough to back her against the nearest wall.

Our wanting sounds melted into each other, fueled by a hunger that burned hotter than anything I'd ever tasted. The moment her back hit the wall, my fingers found her again. Thrusting them inside her, rough and deep, my desire to see her fall apart around me taking over everything else. I needed to watch her shatter—to see her lose control for me.

Her hips writhed, her walls fluttering around my fingers, her hands clutching the back of my neck, bracing herself. Leaning back just enough to study her face, taking in the way her lips parted, the way her eyelids fluttered, the way my name left her mouth like a whispered sin.

"Fuck, *principessa*," I groaned. "Show me. Show me how you come undone for me."

She broke beneath me. Her head fell back, her breath hitched, and my name tore from her lips, breathless and raw. My fingers didn't stop. I pulled every last ounce of her orgasm from her, watching her fall apart in my hands, knowing she was mine now.

She could fight it, she could deny it all she wanted, but it wouldn't change the truth. Cassandra was perfection. And after having a taste— she would never be able to get away. I'd give this woman anything to keep her here with me, forever. I'd collapse everything I've ever built, everything my family has created, to have this one remain mine forever. And that was a vow I planned on keeping.

Her trembling breaths filled the space between us, her body slowly coming down from the high I'd given her.

"Leo," she whispered, her voice still unsteady, "you're going to be a curse on my soul." A lazy smile curved her lips. "I haven't decided if it's the good or bad kind, yet."

Still catching her breath, she slowed the roll of her hips against me. Smirking, I pulled my fingers from her, bringing them to my lips. The second my tongue met her arousal, my eyes rolled back, groaning at the sweet, addictive taste of her.

A gift from God himself.

Then, without warning, I shoved my fingers into her mouth. "Clean yourself off me," I murmured, voice dark and commanding. "Taste how fucking perfect we are together." She moaned, taking them eagerly, her tongue swirling around them before nipping the tips with a wicked tilt of her lips.

"Perfect, huh?" she teased, her voice still husky from our intimacy.

Keeping her caged between me and the wall, I pressed my strained cock against her, hard and unyielding. "Yes, perfect. And if you want more, you'll tell me about the Irish, my little *topo*."

I ground against her, feeling her body tense beneath me. She squirmed, and I grinned.

Cassandra

What is this, the ice bucket challenge? Because that was a fucking mood ruiner.

The Irish.

Of course that's what he wanted. This was just a tactic to lure out information. "Get off me," I demanded, done with this. The sensation of feeling used crawling over my skin, hot and shameful.

Leo didn't move. I wiggled insistently, trying to break free. "If you wanted the information, we could have withheld the sexual shit." I huffed, more frustrated with myself than with him. My own expectations got the better of me. What the fuck was I thinking? Did I seriously start believing this ruthless man wanted anything more than what he needed to infiltrate the Irish?

"*Principessa*," he said gruffly, pulling me closer and burying his face into my neck. He inhaled deeply, making a shiver run down my spine. What the fuck?

"Just tell me what I need to know," he murmured, voice thick with something I couldn't place. "While I have you in my arms. Please." He pulled back, and I found myself locked in his gaze—his stormy gray eyes dark as a sky before a tornado.

Then he lifted my right leg around his waist and ground against me—my exposed core, his evident arousal pressing into me. And yet... he had said please.

My brows furrowed. "Why do you need to hold me?" My voice was quieter this time, more uncertain. "You're making this more than it needs to be. And using my needs won't make me tell you more than what I was already going to give you."

It was bad enough that my body wanted him. I hadn't been able to shake the fantasies that had started about a week ago. With them finally manifesting I knew I had to get back to reality.

He sighed, reluctantly stilling his hips, though I felt the restraint it took him to do so. "I know, *amore mio*," he muttered, shaking his head. "You don't understand how badly I need you. Or how much power you hold over me."

My back stiffened. Power? Me? There was no way I had any power over Leo Romano—the Italian Don of Illinois. I was just some bottom-of-the-barrel stripper who had terrible karma and seemed to always find trouble.

I laughed, the sound disbelieving, bitter. "Stop bullshitting, Leo."

His lips seized mine and my eyes widened. The force of it stole my breath, every ounce of his passion, his hunger, his truth pouring into me like a confession without words.

When he pulled away, I was speechless.

"Cassandra, I don't bullshit." His voice was steady. "You, of all people, know I am not a man to lie. You are a woman I need, crave, want—so badly I'd burn everything I've built for you."

My mouth must have been hanging open, because he lifted a finger under my chin, tilting my face up. I shook my head.

No. I couldn't hear this. I couldn't be trapped in another relationship with a dangerous man.

"Leo, please..." Tears pricked the corners of my eyes. "I'll tell you what you want. Just let me go." I jerked my chin from his grasp, and this time, he released my chin.

Slowly, he set my leg down with care—still trapped between his body and the wall—I noticed the way his chest heaved, the way his stormy gaze shifted into something deeper. Longing. Desperation.

No. God, please. Anyone but him. I knew that look too well, and if

Leo was falling for me, I wouldn't have any chance of escaping Chicago. I'd be trapped again—controlled, owned. Just like every other bastard I'd mistaken for salvation.

I ducked under his arm before he could read too much into my expression, grabbing my shorts and pulling them on quickly, my panties ruined and left to rot in his office. Then I crossed the large office space toward the empty fireplace, the scent of cigars and cognac catching my senses. I studied my surroundings, noticing the red and gold Persian rug beneath my feet, which was a beautiful accent to the intricately carved mahogany desk in the center of the room.

My body collapsed into one of the leather chairs, the cold fireplace looking more like a metaphor for my heart than a piece that adds warmth and comfort. My hands rubbed together in my lap, my leg bouncing.

I couldn't look at him. My gaze flicked to the dark stone mantle that had a few photos, some with him in them, others without. It was an oddly homey detail for a man supposedly so ruthless. Not even Declan had pictures of him with his family or friends in his room at the mansion. Actually, when I thought about it, there were no family photos in any room of that giant building.

His stare was heavy as he approached, the weight of its meaning settling over me. He wanted me to fall for him, the same way I knew he was falling for me. It felt like a pressure tactic in itself. And I couldn't take that on. Not now. Not ever.

Leo didn't argue, didn't try to force me into anything. Not like Declan. Leo wasn't even angry.

Instead, he simply strode to the other leather chair across from me, sitting down with deliberate ease. His movements were calculated, controlled as he placed an ankle on his knee, steepling his hands over his stomach. A stomach still bare to my view. And I couldn't help but peek.

One last look. Perfect abs, a bare tanned chest—he looked like a Roman god.

Perfect.

Lifting my fist to my mouth I coughed awkwardly, tearing my gaze away, heat creeping up my cheeks. *Get it together, Cassandra.* "Let's get started," I said quickly, chewing on my lower lip, my eyes locked on my lap. Not only was I still fantasizing about Leo's stupid, godlike body, but I was about to help murder the people I considered family.

I was so fucked up I deserved to die right along with them.

The dark thoughts didn't stop. They coiled in my head like a tumor sending out tendrils, sinking deeper with each answer I gave. Every question Leo asked peeled away another piece of me, another layer of guilt pressing its way into my chest. By the time it was over, I was already suffocating in my own mind. I didn't even realize I had left until I found myself wandering the halls of Leo's estate.

Lost. Go figure. I was always lost.

I scanned my surroundings, searching for something familiar, but all I found was a long, dark blue hallway, its intricately decorated trim stretching toward a set of dark wood double doors at the end. The dim lighting from the sconces cast everything in a moody glow, making the corridor seem endless, almost unreal.

Hesitation kept me still for a moment. Then curiosity won. If I was stuck here, I might as well get familiar with the place. Or maybe even find out some secrets of my own—in case Leo and Ciro decided I was no longer useful. I gripped both handles and pulled.

Nothing.

Okay, let's try pushing. I cursed under my breath when they swung open. Idiot. Seriously, they need a sign for that.

Light flooded the room. Large stained-glass windows towered above me, their intricate designs of angels and saints casting shards of color onto the polished floors. They looked like they were from an old cathedral. It wouldn't have surprised me.

To my left, rows of bookshelves stretched horizontally across the space. Matte black. The contrast made the spines of the books pop, their rich colors vibrant against the dark shelves. Something about the sight stirred something in me. I used to love books. But I hadn't picked one up since getting my GED at twenty.

Back then, I wanted to go to school to be a social worker. Help other kids who grew up in a similar home to the one I did. But it wasn't in the cards—not when I was "rescued" by my first boyfriend. I thought I was in love with him. Turns out, he just needed me to help lift cars and bring them to chop shops.

I tried not to linger too long on my terrible luck. College just wasn't meant for me. That was why I helped the women I could, in any city I wound up in. It was the one thing that made me feel like my life wasn't a waste. That I was making a difference in this cruel world. That I had a purpose other than attracting criminals and psychopaths.

I drifted toward them, my fingers grazing the spines as I passed.

This place—this room—felt different from the rest of the estate. It wasn't heavy with power like the rest of Leo's house. It felt… untouched. Peaceful. I paused, pulling out a dark red book with gold-engraved lettering. I flipped it over, scanning the description.

Romance.

I huffed. Just what I needed—false ideas of love and devotion. I shoved it back in its place.

Where was the horror section? That seemed more fitting.

Leo

My jaw cracked, a sharp pain radiating to my temples. I stubbed out another cigarette, barely a second passing before I pulled a fresh one from the pack resting on my desk, placing the dry filter between my lips.

Ciro flicked the light on his Zippo, the corner of his lip curling in that usual smart-ass way of his. "Leo, if you keep smoking like this, you'll die at the ripe age of twenty-eight," he mused. "And if Mama's favorite *figlio* dies, she'll most likely follow close behind you. God forbid." He rolled his eyes dramatically.

The leather beneath me groaned as I leaned back; I hadn't moved from my spot since Cassandra drifted out of here in what looked like a daze. Blowing a slow billow of smoke into the air, I looked up at the painted ceiling of a replica of the Sistine-chapel artistry. Was my interrogation too harsh? I knew it wouldn't be easy for her, even a blind man could see her devotion to that family. I'm sure I would have felt the same if the roles were reversed.

Shifting my gaze back to Ciro, I refocused. "Where's Nico? He's late." My mind rotated constantly between Cassandra, the information she gave me, and the fucking war ahead. Ciro cracked his neck, rolling it from side to side, but before he could respond, Gio's head popped in through the door.

"Nico's here, Boss." His voice was clipped, stoic. I dipped my chin, giving him the signal to let him in.

The moment Nico stepped inside, I narrowed my eyes, pressing my unfinished cigarette into the ashtray resting on the side table between Ciro and me with slow deliberation.

"You made me fucking wait, Nico."

"I know, Boss." He exhaled, already heading for the empty chair Dimitri had dragged into the room earlier, completing our little semi-circle-of-knights-at-the-round-table bullshit.

"My old lady had a lot of bitchin' to do." He flopped down, his posture too relaxed for my liking.

"I don't give a fuck, Nico." I flexed my fingers against the arms of the chair, the urge to snap his goddamn neck creeping in. "If you keep me waiting again, your wife will know how it feels to be a widow."

"Christ, Leo," Ciro cut in, exasperated. "Tone it down. Sorry, Nico, Leo here is all flustered about his new pet."

My blood fucking boiled. I shot to my feet, cocking my gun and aiming it at Ciro's face in one swift motion. "Shut your fat fucking mouth, Ciro." The pounding in my ears wasn't just from my growing anger—it was from something deeper, something Ciro thought was funny to poke at, but I sure as fuck didn't. "Undermine me again and see what happens."

Ciro's expression shifted, the dark amusement in his eyes hardening into something challenging.

I didn't pull back. I'd never back down. I wasn't afraid of making an example out of my own cousin if I had to. I'd miss him, sure, but I couldn't look weak—and he knew not to step out of line in front of others.

The tension thickened, stretching into a dangerous standstill. Nico didn't say shit—he knew better than to jump in when I was making a point.

Finally, after a tense fucking minute, Ciro shifted his gaze to his drink in his hand. His other ran through his light brown hair, his signature smirk returning like I hadn't just been about to blow his fucking head off.

"Boss, so you got that info from your new broad?" Nico's thick Italian accent cut through the silence, his eyes hesitantly flicking between the two of us. He was watching our body language, making sure the fire was out before moving forward.

I kept my gaze locked on Ciro as I carefully sat back down, tucking my Glock back into its holster. Then, turning my head deliberately toward Nico, I gritted out, "You mean Cassandra? Show some fucking respect."

Nico nodded immediately. "Apologies, sir." His knee bounced, his fingers tapping the arm of the chair.

"Have a drink, Nico." Ciro leaned forward, grabbing the neck of the cognac bottle, pouring a glass, and sliding it across the table. Nico stopped fidgeting long enough to curl his fingers around the crystal, lifting it in salute before knocking it back. His face contorted from the burn, letting out a sharp breath before speaking.

"Boss, my father always told me emotions make a man reckless." His gaze flicked to me, wary but careful. He was testing the waters. I stayed silent, letting him continue. "Not that those Mick bastards don't deserve what's coming to them but…"

He trailed off. Didn't need to finish. I knew what he meant.

Hell, I was worried, too. Cassandra had burrowed so deep under my skin, and after tasting her earlier, my mind was fucking unpredictable. But it didn't change the fact that Finnegan had thought he could plan a raid next month at one of the Russian warehouses and blame it on us. He thought he was a step ahead of me, and soon he'd see just how fucking wrong he was.

"You have nothing to worry about, Nico," I said smoothly. "Let's get to business." I turned my head toward the doorway. "Gio, Dimitri —get in here."

Two ominous shadows peeled away from the hall, stepping inside like silent assassins. I reached for the bottle, pouring myself a two-finger glass, swirling the amber liquid before taking a slow sip.

"Let's start with how we're going to execute this plan."

Ciro was the first to jump in. "I think a silent infiltration of their mansion would be fun, hit them right in the heart." The glint in his darkened gaze was fucking maniacal.

But he was right.

Less mess. Less public attention. Fewer people to pay off.

"I agree," Nico said, leaning forward. "My only concern is how well we can trust Cassandra." His eyes cut to me, adding quickly, "Ain't personal, Boss."

I shrugged, taking another sip of the smooth, perfectly aged drink. "Cassandra is staying here for a while. If she gave me false information, I'll kill her myself."

Silence.

Then Ciro exhaled, resting his elbows on his knees. "Who do we go after first? Declan or Finnegan?"

His voice was serious now.

The amusement from earlier? Gone.

His dark promise remained.

"Finnegan." I didn't hesitate, then tipped back the rest of my drink, the glass close to cracking under my grip.

Then I added, "Declan's mine."

I wanted him to suffer. To pay for every bruise, bloody nose, and broken bone. I already had a plan of my own, ready and waiting for the moment I got my hands on Declan. He would wish he had never met Cassandra—and he would especially wish she had never caught my eye.

"Gio, Dimitri—get our crooked cops in place." I slammed the crystal down onto the table. "Nico—gather our people. Get them ready."

My gaze locked onto Ciro. "Get every weapon we have hidden in our safe houses and make sure they end up in the right hands. And talk to your contact with the Russians and give them a heads up on what we intend on doing."

Ciro nodded.

We knew what this was. All hands on deck. It was time to show the Irish exactly what it meant to fuck with the Italians.

I pushed to my feet, rolling my shoulders, the tension under my skin no longer frustration—but promise.

EPISODE 7

*E*pisode 7
Cassandra

My lips smacked together as I tried to swallow the dry lump in my throat—to no avail. Rolling over, I grabbed my phone, flipping it to check the time. I hissed as the too-bright light blinded me through the chaos that was my hair. Pushing it back, I squinted, noting that it was around 2:30 in the morning.

"Fuck me," I grumbled, tossing off the soft cotton sheets that adorned the almost-too-lavish bed.

My new room was nothing to balk at—definitely way nicer than the shithole I was barely keeping up rent with.

Swinging my legs over the side, they dangled, making me feel like a munchkin. I hopped down, the cool wood meeting my toasty feet and agitating me further.

Shuffling through the darkness with my arms stretched out in front of me, it felt like a game of Marco Polo with the furniture. I'd only been here three nights, and so far it was furniture: two, Cassandra: zero. My feet slid along the floor to prevent any more damage to my pinky toes—thanks, dresser.

As my eyes adjusted, my shoulders dropped, hopeful I'd make it this time without any casualties. When my hand touched the wooden door, I internally did a jig. Hell yeah. Fuck you, furniture.

Touching the smooth brass handle, I gripped it and tugged it open slowly. I was sure everyone slept in separate wings, but I didn't want to chance another intimate moment with Leo. Just as I crossed over the threshold confidently, my baby-pink silk shorts snagged on the handle, jerking me backward and causing me to bang the side of my head against the edge.

I muttered a slew of cuss words at it before adjusting my pajamas and continuing my mission to the kitchen for a glass of water, determined to pretend my failed attempt at being smooth never happened. But who was I kidding? I was not smooth, nor did I have the luck to make life easier. I mean, look at me—I was trapped in a mansion with a killer.

The hall was just as dark as my room, illuminated only by the electric sconces evenly placed along the wide space. Some of them lit up paintings that seemed fancy, while others highlighted family portraits of Leo and his relatives. From what I'd gathered, he had a classic Italian family—a beautiful younger sister, an adorable mother, and a stern-looking father who no doubt had been the previous Don. A part of me really wanted to know more about them, to learn their names, but then I reminded myself that this was just business.

Trusting Leo's words about burning down his empire seemed a little extreme for someone like him—unless he was secretly a romantic at heart, which I highly doubted. Once he accomplished his goal and got bored of looking at my face, he'd either kill me or dump me out on my ass in the middle of Chicago.

The shuffling of my bare feet echoed down the silent corridor, and as I rounded the corner to the stairs, I paused. I always admired the beautiful hand-painted family portrait that hung just over the vast dark oak doors. Just in front of it was a gorgeous chandelier with crystals that, when lit, cast sparkly rainbows on the ceiling. It was all too lavish, something I wasn't accustomed to.

Glancing over the railing of the white marble staircase, I made sure the coast was clear before beginning my descent. The double staircase seemed like overkill for a man who probably never had guests here, but I guess if you have the money, why not be boujee with it?

God, if I had this kind of money, I'd live large too—without a care in the world, on some deserted island. Alone.

Well, maybe with a vibrator or two. A girl's got needs.

Tiptoeing along the open space, my silk pajamas made a soft swishing sound against my skin. The kitchen was empty in all its immaculate glory. Again, it was overkill—modern cooktops and units, absolutely stunning black marble countertops, and equally dark modern cabinets. Everything I would want in my own deserted island mansion. Maybe instead of killing me, I could convince Leo to send me there to live out my days.

I snorted a laugh and quickly covered my mouth.

The kitchen was predictable, having investigated it yesterday afternoon before my shift at Inferno, so I knew where everything essential was. Reaching for a glass, I heard rustling. I quickly set the glass on the marble top and spun around, peering into the dark open space.

Fuck.

My hands started to sweat as I kept my gaze locked on the shadows, slowly opening the drawer where Leo kept all his fancy knives. I gripped the first handle I touched, clutching it in my hand without taking my eyes off the potential threat.

"I know you're there. Come out," I whisper-shouted.

My other hand guided me along the smooth counter as I circled the bar. "I have a weapon," I warned, hoping to sound intimidating. If it was Declan, he would have already laughed. If it was Leo, he wouldn't be playing games.

A man in a dark jacket with the hood up materialized from the shadows, his frame massive. My stomach twisted—I couldn't make out his features. "Who...who are you?" My voice was shaky as I continued moving away, my sweaty hand gripping the knife tighter.

A low chuckle rumbled from him. It sounded familiar—but not enough for me to place a name.

"Answer me!" I whisper-shouted again, more urgently.

"If I did that, it would ruin our game," the mystery man purred.

What the fuck?

He stepped closer, his footsteps slow and deliberate, like a panther stalking its prey.

"I'm not playing games, motherfucker." I waved the knife in my hand before realizing it was a butcher's cleaver.

Nice, Cassandra. What are we, fucking Leatherface?

I attempted to pretend I knew what I was doing, but then he pulled a shiny silver gun, its metal catching the faint glow from the under-cabinet lighting.

Cool. I brought a knife to a gunfight. I'm definitely going to die.

We circled the bar like some sick game of ring-around-the-rosy. "I'll fucking scream," I narrowed my eyes on his obscured face.

"And I have the ability of putting a bullet in your brain, but I'm not," he chuckled, shoulders shaking.

The sick fuck thought this was hilarious.

The more he spoke, the more I recognized an Italian accent. The deep timbre of his voice felt oddly familiar. Who the fuck was this? Dimitri? Gio? My mind scrambled as my heart pounded. My hands felt so slick that one wrong move and the meat cleaver would go flying.

Being on the side facing the living room now, I made a split-second decision. I ducked out of sight, ditching the cleaver in case I panicked and face-planted on it, crawling quickly toward the couch. It was dark—he wouldn't find me too fast, but I needed to move quickly.

Pressing my back against the couch as I crawled around, I held my breath, listening. The coffee table in front of me forced me to keep my knees tucked close to my chest.

Silence.

Peering around the corner of the couch, I noticed the mystery man was nowhere to be seen.

Shit.

Jerking back, I was caught off guard by a body slamming into my side, knocking me onto my back. His massive form pinned me down.

"Too easy," he murmured, his breath hot against my ear.

I went to scratch his face, but he caught my wrists, pinning them above me.

"Naughty, naughty, *piccola strega*."

I stiffened.

My eyes locked onto his—grey, wolf-like, just like Leo's.

"Ciro?" My brow furrowed in confusion.

His chest rumbled with amusement. "You really need to work on your escape and fighting techniques. Not that it would have mattered with me," he said smugly. His grip tightened as he pressed a knee between my legs. "I'm one of the best headhunters out there. That's why they call me *L'Uccisore*."

His smile was wide—too wide.

A cold shiver slithered down my spine. "Are you going to kill me?" I forced an annoyed tone into my voice to hide my unease.

"Not today." His voice was smooth, almost like he was picking up a girl at the bar.

Fucking psychopath. And yet, my traitorous body found it hot as hell. It was a survival reaction—I knew that much. That was why I always let these dangerous men get closer than I meant for them to. My God-given instincts kept me safe, and I knew exactly how to use them.

Shaking off my body's fucked-up lust, I shot him a glare, hoping it would convey just how much I hated this entire situation. "Then get the fuck off me," I snapped, flashing a tight smile to solidify my fuck you.

Laughing, he got to his feet in one swift motion, offering me his strong, tanned hand while pushing back his hood to reveal chestnut-brown hair. I smacked his hand away and got to my feet, adjusting my silk spaghetti-strap top and shorts.

I didn't wait for him to say anything. I came down here for water, and that's exactly what I was going to get. Filling a glass from the fridge's dispenser, I kept my eyes on Ciro, who leaned casually across from me, arms crossed over his broad chest.

He looked so much like Leo—minus a few differences in hair color and some softer edges that didn't quite match his psycho personality.

Feeling uncomfortable under his intense gaze, I finally broke the silence. "So, why are you down here being a creep?" I took a sip of water, my eyes trailing over his body. Even though he wasn't Leo, my body responded as if he were.

Jesus, I needed to put my vagina under lock and key. That bitch was confused.

Ciro didn't answer right away. He just stared, his eyes calculating, as if trying to read my next move.

It was unnerving.

Eventually, he responded. "I just got back from a rendezvous with a friend."

The way he said *friend* made me think twice about asking further questions, so I didn't. Moving to the sink, I set my glass down and turned—only to find Ciro invading my personal space.

His large, muscular arms caged me in on either side, forcing my lower back to press into the edge of the stainless steel basin.

Ciro inhaled deeply. "Roses and..." He leaned in close to my temple, scenting me again. "Vanilla."

His voice dropped into a low rumble, and I felt the vibrations through my thin top. My nipples hardened immediately.

Fuck.

Ciro definitely noticed because he smirked. "*Piccola strega*, you are a troublemaker."

I quickly crossed my arms over my chest to hide my betrayal and glared up at him. "No, it's just cold in here."

He laughed. "Sure, and the sky's fucking purple."

I shoved at his chest, but it did little to move him—he was solid muscle. If anything, it only caused him to step closer. My neck strained as I looked up at him.

"You're an idiot."

"Then tell me the truth, *principessa*."

The nickname Leo used rolled off his tongue just like Leo would say it. Only...it felt wrong. It looked wrong coming from him.

"Don't use that nickname," I growled.

Ciro's eyes crinkled at the corners. "Just what I thought. You've got it bad for my brother." His hand gripped my chin—not hard, just in a controlling way. A way that pissed me off even more. "How unfortunate for me," he mused, pouting mockingly, though his steel-grey eyes sparkled with mischief.

His head dipped lower, his lips brushing the shell of my ear. Goosebumps erupted along my skin.

"Unless you'd be willing to have both of us."

Ciro pulled back just enough for our faces to be inches apart, searching my eyes for a reaction.

Christ, this man was unhinged as hell.

Hardening my features, I said, "I'm going to bed. Goodnight."

Ciro slowly released me, stepping back to give me space. But I felt his eyes—those sharp, wolf-like eyes—follow me, watching.

I rushed off, his gaze burning into my back as I ascended the staircase two steps at a time. I didn't breathe until I was safely tucked inside my room, locking the door for good measure. My shoulders sagged at the sound of the lock clicking into place.

The pseudo-safety eased some of the tension in my body, but I couldn't shake the feeling that I was destined to be caught in this war —not just between the Italians and the Irish.

Leo

My tasty little *topo* had been avoiding me since our little rendezvous in my office. Glancing over at the wall where everything happened, I leaned back in my chair and loosened my tie.

Fuck, I needed to see her again.

Running a hand through my dark brown hair, I exhaled sharply. My watch caught the fading light of the sunset streaming in behind me. Cassandra's moans had taken over my mind—I hadn't had a restful night's sleep since. Every time I closed my eyes, all I saw was her leg wrapped around me, pressed against the wall, her lips parted, her body writhing. And the constant hard-on? Impossible to control.

I adjusted in my seat, already feeling the tightening of my pants.

"Gio," I called, my voice tight.

He was at my side in a second. "Yeah, Boss?" He adjusted his suit jacket, his freshly buzzed hair neat as ever. Gio was one of the best finds I'd ever laid eyes on when it came to soldiers—or bodyguards, depending on the day. His tailored suit fit his large frame perfectly, making him seem even more untouchable.

"You and Dimitri—go find Cassandra."

At the mention of his name, Dimitri poked his tattooed face into the doorway, his expression neutral. I nodded at him, and he reciprocated the gesture.

Dimitri and Gio were loyalty you couldn't buy. Not only that, but they were entertaining when I let them relax.

Gio strode out, and I watched as they both exited toward the south wing of the estate.

Not a minute passed before Ciro's smug grin graced my presence. "You look like you could use a drink," he said, his long strides eating up the distance from my doorway to the small liquor bar beside my desk.

I released a frustrated breath. "That's an understatement." I rubbed the bridge of my nose, my elbow resting on the desk.

Ciro placed a crystal tumbler in front of me, the ice cubes clinking as the amber liquid settled. Glancing up, I grabbed it quickly— desperate for a distraction from the stress that had been accumulating over the past week. Between the Irish and Cassandra, I was strung tight.

Ciro slid into the leather chair across from me, his posture relaxed but his eyes calculating.

I knew that look. It meant he was about to fuck with me. And I wasn't in the damn mood.

Growling, I said, "Don't fucking start with me, Ciro."

Reaching into my suit pocket, I pulled out my cigarettes. The crystal clinked against the desk as muscle memory took over— cigarette between my lips, lighter flick, inhale. The first drag settled my nerves slightly.

"I would never," he grinned wickedly, watching me lean back, my shoulders dropping from my ears for the first time today.

I shot him a glare. "I call bullshit."

Ciro pressed a hand to his chest in mock offense. "You wound me, *fratello.*" Chuckling, he shifted in his seat, crossing one ankle over his knee. The movement exposed his obnoxious, cartoon-themed socks.

I gestured to them. "You're second in command. Why the fuck are you wearing those childish things?"

Lifting my glass, I took a long pull, the ice rattling softly against the crystal. It was a pointless question, because I knew Ciro better than anyone. He was a killer through and through, but he also had a light heart. He knew how to keep moments light when it all felt heavy, not take things too seriously until he had to. I appreciated that about him. Hell, I loved that about him. It kept me in check on occasion when we were alone like this.

Ciro's gaze flicked to his socks before he hiked up his pant leg, exposing more of the abomination.

"You don't like them?" His mischievous smile widened. "Your sister got these for me."

"Fucking Alessia," I muttered, though the slight tug at the corner of my lips betrayed my amusement.

Ciro finished off his drink and reached for the decanter. It was a piece I'd bought in Rome five years ago while on business—Roman soldiers etched into the expensive crystal, classic patterns carved along the edges, and a soldier's helmet used as the stopper.

He tugged off the top and poured himself another drink, then offered me a refill. I obliged.

"*Piccola strega* was fun last night."

I stiffened. My steel-grey eyes locked onto his.

"What the fuck did you just say?"

She's mine. Only mine.

The primal part of me demanded I claim her, make it known to everyone that my little *topo* was protected by the don of Chicago. I wanted her to smell like me. Her rose-and-vanilla scent returned to the forefront of my mind as I took a slow drag from my cigarette.

My hard stare remained on Ciro as he chuckled.

"Cassandra," he clarified. "We played a little game of hide from the killer."

He fucking laughed like it was a joke. I stubbed out my cigarette and set my glass down hard—purposefully.

"Cassandra's mine!" My voice rose, matching the anger boiling in my veins. Ciro didn't flinch. His eyes held that unhinged glint, his signature grin still in place. That look unsettled most people, made them back off. But I was immune to his bullshit. He set his glass down slowly, leaning forward, elbows on his knees.

Fucking casual. Fucking calculating. Was he testing me?

"Is she yours, brother?" His tone was amused. "You haven't fucked her." He cocked his head slightly.

My teeth clenched so hard my jaw ached. My eye twitched.

Cassandra started off as just someone I wanted to fuck, but the more layers I peeled back, the more I found the soft pieces she tried so hard to hide. Somewhere along the way, I'd started falling for her. She wasn't someone you stumbled across twice in a lifetime. She was a gemstone too many people had used and never understood the value of.

"No." My voice was flat.

Ciro raised an eyebrow. "No?"

My knuckles turned white as my fists clenched against the desk. "You heard me. I said no. Test me again and see what happens."

He knew exactly what no meant. Don't fucking touch. But the glint in his eye told me he wasn't finished. He wanted to keep pushing.

Before I could call him out—

She entered.

My eyes shot to hers. I stood immediately, adjusting my suit and smoothing my hair.

Fuck.

Ciro only turned in his chair, giving her a too-familiar smile.

Her wide eyes reminded me of a deer that had just wandered into a predator's den by mistake. That look made my cock twitch. I needed to feel her in my arms.

Rushing to her, I reached for her waist—only to be met with a knee to the balls.

Cassandra

Sidestepping Leo's doubled-over form, I crossed my arms and popped my hip out. "I didn't give you permission to touch me," I stated, my voice void of any feeling.

Ciro laughed loudly, and I shot him a glare. "Same goes for you. Or you'll end up like Leo here."

He pretended to be scared, waving his hands in surrender, though his smug smile remained firmly in place. That man was both terrifying and extremely unnerving.

Caught up in glaring at Ciro, I didn't notice Leo standing—until his large, calloused hand gripped my bicep tightly, jerking me to face him fully. "How fucking dare you," Leo growled, his steel-grey eyes blazing with barely contained anger.

I wasn't going to give him the satisfaction of seeing me falter. I was a dead woman anyway.

"How dare I?" I jerked my arm, but his grip was too tight. If anything, it became almost bruising—more worrisome than the daggers he was shooting at me.

"You don't get to assume that I'm just some property you can touch," I snapped, nostrils flaring as I met his fury head-on.

Unlike him, my anger had an undercurrent of fear. Fear of what would happen if I pushed him too far. Would he hit me?

We faced off for what felt like minutes, though realistically it was only a few seconds. Then he released my arm. Sliding his hands into his slacks, his expression softened.

"Of course, *principessa*," he murmured.

My jaw must have been hanging open because Ciro chimed in, "If you keep that mouth open much longer, it might be considered an invitation."

He laughed again.

Leo clearly didn't appreciate the crude joke because his gaze snapped to him, fury returning.

Closing my mouth, I huffed. "What do you want, Leo? You had your goons retrieve me?"

When his attention returned to me, something was different. A look I wasn't used to seeing on his usually sharp features. One that made me soften inside, and I hated that.

Stepping closer but keeping some space between us, he leaned in. "I..." His eyes searched mine before he cleared his throat. For a fleeting moment, I saw emotion in his face. Longing.

The kind of longing I had to ignore was for me.

"Ciro will be escorting you to work tonight," he finally said, straightening. His face returned to its usual stoic mask.

I hated to admit it, but seeing the vulnerability disappear so quickly made my heart sink.

Get a grip, Cassandra.

Internally, I rolled my eyes at myself.

Leo's voice was tight when he added, "And he'll be on his best behavior." His gaze cut back to Ciro. "or I'll make sure you don't sit in on the next meeting."

The muscle in his jaw ticked. Something passed between them that I didn't understand.

My head swung back and forth watching them, nearly giving me whiplash. "Fine," I mumbled before settling my gaze on Ciro. "Let's go. I can't be late."

I glanced up at Leo, who was still close, our eyes locking again. "I'll... see you later." My voice came out gentle, with more meaning than intended, but for some reason it felt right. I wanted to comfort that part of him that seemed restless with longing.

He dipped his chin.

I didn't look back as I exited the room, leaving the two assholes to finish whatever conversation I'd walked in on—one I knew was about me.

Gio and Dimitri followed close behind.

"So, are you two coming along too?" I asked, keeping my focus forward as we descended the immaculate staircase toward the front door.

"Nah, you got Ciro, Angel," Dimitri said smoothly.

I didn't miss the way he used my stripper name. Looking over my shoulder, I found his sinful smirk waiting for me.

Gio grunted his opinion, which I assumed was agreement.

Reluctantly, I tore my gaze away from Dimitri's mischievous brown eyes to look at Gio—He had a military vibe about him. Shaved head, tall and lean, always serious.

Unlike Dimitri, he didn't have tattoos. Well any that I could see.

My need to push his buttons came full-on. "Man of few words, I see."

I'd been trying to get this big guy to laugh. Maybe I should lower my standards to a small twitch. He was tough to crack.

Dimitri chuckled, the low rumble sounding light. "Get a couple drinks into this lightweight, and he'll talk your damn ear off."

My gaze remained fixed on Gio's stoic expression. He opened the massive front door, and I paused in the sunset-lit doorway.

"Is this true? You're a gabber when you're drunk?" I smiled teasingly up at him.

He shrugged, his eyes meeting mine for the first time. I caught the twinkle of playfulness.

My smirk widened. I'd consider that a win.

"Good to know."

We continued to the SUV parked just beyond the stone steps. The fountain in the driveway was bathed in pinks and oranges, cascading down a naked Roman woman. Leo's estate was breathtaking, to say the least. Short, manicured hedges lined the cobblestone driveway, leading to a massive reinforced black gate. Bushes of varying-colored roses decorated the space, surrounding granite statues—each, unsurprisingly, Italian-themed.

Sighing, I mused aloud, "Hey, if you have any sway with the big asshole inside, convince him that instead of killing me, he should just buy me a home like this on a deserted island."

Yes, I was sticking with the deserted island theme. I really wanted to manifest that shit.

Dimitri laughed, and I heard Gio cough. But it was Ciro's voice—right in my fucking ear, no less—that nearly scared the piss out of me.

"I'll be sure to tell the big asshole that," he whispered.

My heart leapt into my throat, and my hand pressed against my chest. "Fucking Christ, Ciro. You need a fucking bell!"

All three of them laughed. I turned to Gio with wide, excited eyes.

I did it. I made him laugh.

A small smile tugged at my lips.

"Come on, *piccola strega*. Time to go." Ciro took the stone steps two at a time and opened the back passenger door for me, flashing a cocky grin.

Sliding in, I heard the heavy thud of the door closing behind me. Ciro rushed to the driver's side, and once he was settled, he roared the engine to life. Our eyes met in the rearview mirror—his steel-grey gaze crinkling at the corners.

"Ready?"

"Whatever," I grumbled.

He only smiled wider and drove off, circling the fountain and heading toward the gate. We left the safety of the Italian don's humble abode behind.

Ciro parked the black SUV at the back entrance of Inferno.

As soon as he stepped out to open my door, I noticed my coworkers were all outside gossiping—Sapphire, Grace, and Emerald—gawking. Their eyes flicked between me and him, checking if I was okay. I rolled my eyes dramatically in response.

"Do strippers get some sort of telepathy with the job?" Ciro joked, placing a hand on the small of my back to guide me toward the entrance.

The girls quickly scurried inside, avoiding any potential confrontation. Crossing my arms, I said, "Yeah, and they said you look like a fucking idiot."

Ciro shook his head, a shit-eating grin plastered on his psycho face. Leaning down, he murmured, his breath gliding along my cheek and neck. The scent of musk and pine surrounded me, but it only made me think about how he didn't smell like cigarettes and spice.

"Well, be sure to relay that I'm an idiot with money—and a fucking awesome cock."

I choked on my own spit, coughing violently as I shoved him away. "You're unhinged. You know that?" I wiped my mouth of the few spittle droplets resting on my lips.

He shrugged casually before gripping the steel door handle and tugging it open.

Inside, the DJ was already doing sound checks in the main room. Down the hall, fluorescent lights illuminated the dressing room doorway, where the familiar chatter and laughter of my Inferno family filtered out like a beacon.

Pink and purple lights flashed at the end of the dark, black-painted hall. The fresh scent of Pine-Sol told me the cleaning crew had already come and gone. As we reached the dressing room, the conversations inside died down. All eyes turned toward us. Many of the girls were topless, but none of them cared.

"Ladies, this is Ciro," I said nonchalantly.

Ciro, ever the charmer, flashed an award-winning smile, letting his shameless gaze land on each of them, lingering on those who were topless. "Hello, ladies. You all look… stunning this evening."

Christ.

Candy practically tripped over herself, her double-D fake tits bouncing as she reached him. "Ciro, so great to see you again, babe," she gushed, fluttering her lashes as she latched onto his arm like a damn sloth.

He chuckled, soaking up the attention.

Rolling my eyes, I turned and walked to my station, wanting nothing to do with their shenanigans.

Let them have him.

Candy and the others giggled and flirted while I focused on getting ready for my shift. When Vinnie walked in, announcing that clients were arriving, the girls groaned but quickly abandoned Ciro—though not before he gave them all a dramatic farewell.

Sitting on the bench where our lockers towered, I strapped on my platform heels. I straightened, adjusting my bra and giving myself a once-over in the full-length mirror on the wall.

Then I noticed him.

Ciro.

The three stacked grey lockers on either side of me boxed me in. Suddenly the narrow space felt more like a trap. He stood tall behind me, arms crossed.

Our gazes met.

And the look in his eyes was dangerous. Like something straight out of a sexy stalker movie. The hairs on my arms rose automatically.

He strode toward me, his casual white fitted tee straining against his muscled chest and shoulders, the dark denim jeans showcasing legs that had me weak in the knees. He didn't stop until he was right behind me.

It made me think back to the way Leo had prowled toward me in his office and caged me against the wall, or the feeling I got when I sensed his presence just behind me in the VIP lounge. When I looked at Ciro, all I saw was Leo, and it stirred a need in me that I kept burying.

He just stood there.

Staring.

Observing.

The tension coiled tight between us, thickening the air.

"Cassandra," he purred.

I barely had time to react before he spun me, shoving me against the lockers. A startled gasp left my lips. One of his hands gripped my hair at the base of my skull, pulling my head back. His other hand clutched my waist. His knee wedged between my thighs like it had the other night on the living room floor. My hands flew up instinctively, gripping his biceps for balance, and my eyes widened.

"What the hell, Ciro?" I breathed. A tone I did not want to be giving him. But fuck, my body was a treacherous slut.

A low rumble vibrated from his chest as he leaned in, nuzzling my neck. He inhaled deeply. "Vanilla and roses," he murmured. His hot breath against my skin sent shivers down my spine. "A scent I never thought would make my dick so fucking hard."

My stomach clenched. Christ on a cracker, this man was too much.

That was his M.O.

I squeezed my eyes shut and inhaled sharply. "Get off me," I ground out, trying to sound firm. "You know Leo wouldn't like this."

Ciro laughed. "Why would Leo not like this, *piccola strega*? "His grip on my hair tightened, keeping me in place. His lips brushed back and forth against my pulse point before he bit me.

Hard.

I yelped, slapping his chest. He growled. His hand on my hip squeezed tighter. And even though he was being rough—I wasn't scared.

No.

I was absolutely fucking loving it. Not because of what he was doing, but because when he pulled back and looked into my eyes, his steel stormy grey ones brought me back to when Leo looked at me like that, with his fingers buried deep inside me.

Ciro's tongue flicked out, soothing the bite with a slow, deliberate lick. Then he sucked at the tender skin. The contrast of pain and pleasure made my head swim. His hips ground against me, and my body responded in kind. He took that as an invitation, sliding his hand from my hip to my ass, squeezing it roughly.

"Fuck, this tight ass of yours," he groaned. He kissed along my jaw, nipping at my earlobe.

Panting, my fingers—traitorous things—slipped under his shirt, exploring hard muscle. I whimpered when he bit my ear. His chest rumbled in approval.

"You haven't answered my question, Cassandra." His voice a low, husky sound. His hand tightened in my hair, forcing me to look up at him. "Tell me. Why would Leo not like me touching you?"

His steel-grey eyes darkened. "Now."

His words made my head spin. How the fuck was I supposed to think straight with this happening?

My nostrils flared as I forced myself to breathe. I needed to regain some control. Our eyes were locked in a silent battle—who would break first?

His hand on my ass drifted lower before sliding up and over my mid thigh. Then slowly he grazed the inside of my thigh. Like a wicked game of chicken.

I refused to react.

I refused to acknowledge what he was forcing me to admit out loud. If he thought he could make me confess my feelings about Leo, he was wrong. I wasn't saying them out loud. Because once I did, they'd become real.

Ciro chuckled, watching me struggle. His rough fingers slid higher. Under my fishnet dress. When he hooked two fingers into the edge of my g-string—right above my clit—he rubbed his knuckles against my bare mound.

My eyes rolled back. A moan slipped out before I could stop it.

Fuck.

Ciro crushed his mouth to mine, and with no dignity or self-control, I kissed him back.

I was fucked up. Hooking up with Leo's fucking lookalike cousin.

We were all tongues and teeth, kissing with abandon. Ciro's fingers toyed with my soaked entrance, teasing, spreading, circling my clit—just enough to make me ache, but not enough to satisfy. I could feel his smirk against my lips.

"You are indeed a naughty girl, *strega*." His two fingers slid between my slick folds, teasing me mercilessly.

My leg—when the fuck had it wrapped around his hip?—tightened around him, pressing him closer.

"Are you letting me touch you because you want *me* to..." He nipped at my bottom lip before finishing, "...or are you letting me touch this sweet pussy because you're thinking of Leo?"

My eyes snapped open like a bucket of ice water had been dumped over me. "What?"

Ciro's fingers paused their teasing, his mischievous grin widening. "You heard me, *piccola strega*."

Shame and guilt crushed me like a tidal wave, drowning out the lust fogging my brain. I shoved him away.

"Fuck you!" I shouted, breathless and furious.

Ciro brought his fingers to his lips—and licked them.

"Delicious," he cooed. His cocky grin burned into my retinas as he patted my cheek with his still-wet hand. "Something to think about while you shake that perfect ass onstage."

Blinding rage replaced every ounce of lust in my body. "You motherfucker!"

"Angel!" Candy's voice cut through the air. "Your turn onstage!"

Ciro pressed a finger to his lips, winking. If I could have punched him, I would have. Storming away from the lockers, I nearly collided with Candy as I adjusted my clothes and brushed down my hair. She gave me a once-over, eyes narrowing.

"Were you masturbating?" Her nose wrinkled in disgust. "Because if so, you better not have been doing it near my shit."

"Shut the fuck up, Candy." I shouldered past her and into the dark hallway.

Candy followed, undeterred. "Have you seen Ciro? I really want to give him a lap dance."

Her annoying voice grated against my already fried nerves. My fists clenched. "Go check the fucking dressing room," I growled, not bothering to look at her.

She gasped, but I didn't stick around to hear whatever dramatic bullshit she had planned next.

What I did hear was the clack of her heels hurrying back to the dressing room.

Fuck Ciro. Fuck Leo. Fuck all these men.

Climbing onto the stage, I took my position, waiting for the DJ to introduce me. Inhaling deeply, I closed my eyes. Exhaling slowly.

I had no one to blame but myself. That reality was a bitter pill I refused to swallow.

These men. This lifestyle.

Opening my eyes, I scanned the main room. My regulars were at the front.

And then I saw him.

Ciro.

With Candy draped all over him, of course.

He waved at me.

Fucking bastard.

Candy clung tighter, her death glare locked on me—though in reality it just made her look constipated. Not caring, I flipped him off.

Cash flew onto the stage.

Fucking masochists.

Then the music boomed through the speakers. I let the bass sink into my skin, let the rhythm dictate my movements. Let the dance and music take over my thoughts.

Unfortunately…the thoughts won.

These cycles I couldn't break had taken a toll on my life. The danger I was in. The happiness I could have had if I'd never met them, if I'd never let my finger land on the open map I had splayed on a diner table a year ago. I was running again. The idea came to me after watching a movie on my phone in my car the night before. Closing my eyes, I allowed fate to choose my next destination.

Chicago.

At that moment, I thought Chicago was going to be the change I needed. But it's like they say—you can change people, places, and things, but if you aren't changing, the problem keeps following.

Leo's face flashed in my mind, and I stumbled onstage. Luckily, I recovered smoothly, spinning into the movement like it was intentional.

But fuck.

Leonardo Romano.

Why do I care so much about you?

Gripping the pole, I spun, flaring my legs out before locking my thighs around the cool metal. Leo had been nothing but kind to me. In his own mafia way. He'd never hurt me. Never forced himself on me.

He was the only one I trusted not to lose control of his temper. Leo had proven that time and again over these past two months.

No matter how far I pushed him…

He still called me his *principessa* and treated me as such.

A pang hit my chest. Not in a regretful way. Not in a what-the-fuck-have-I-done way. But in a longing way.

And somehow, that felt right.

Maybe I was changing. Maybe I was finally choosing someone who actually put me first.

Leo

Cassandra was always busy on weekends, and my days were usually occupied with business. But when Monday rolled around, I knew this was my opportunity.

I needed to see her.

Needed her like a damn drug.

Just one hit—just a small inhale of her scent—and maybe my mind would stop obsessing over her for five goddamn seconds.

I had her routine memorized. By now, she'd be in the estate gym, running on the treadmill—sweaty, focused, glistening.

Fuck.

My cock liked that thought.

Consumed by what I was going to say to her, I barely registered my arrival at the gym's private entrance. The glass walls and doors gave me a preview of what was inside, and I didn't hesitate.

Tugging the glass door open easily, my eyes skimmed over the top-of-the-line equipment—free weights, benches, stair climbers, and of course the boxing ring where Ciro and I trained. It was immaculate, just like the rest of my estate.

Cassandra always chose the farthest treadmill near the back wall by the stairmaster. Probably so she'd have enough time to react if someone tried to attack her. My cautious little *topo*. Too bad she blasted her metal music at full volume, completely oblivious to her surroundings. She was never going to hear me coming.

I moved along the glass wall toward the back corner, my Rolex giving me a general idea of how long she'd been running. Today was no different. She was training for her marathon. I knew this because my tech guy uptown hacked into her phone when she moved in and joined our Wi-Fi. It allowed me to look through her search history, and the most frequent page she pulled up was the Chicago Marathon that happened every spring.

She had never run it. I didn't know if she had ever run a marathon before, but it was something I wanted to learn about her. I ached to know everything from her lips—not this obsessive stalking.

Her arms pumped hard, her pace relentless. I could hear her heavy breaths, breaths so similar to the ones she made when she was moaning for me in my office almost a week ago.

Shoving my hands into my pockets, I slid between the stair master and the back wall until I stood directly behind her as she ran.

For a moment, I just admired her.

Her body was a vision, clad in black leggings and a dark teal sports bra. Sweat glistened on her fair skin, her toned muscles flexing with every stride.

Fuck, that ass.

When I finally got my moment, I would worship it. All. Night. Long.

Slowly, I stepped closer, positioning myself just to her side. Then, with a subtle wave—just enough of a warning to see how she'd react— I watched.

As expected, she startled.

Jumpy little *topo*.

Smirking, I waited as she scrambled to press the emergency stop button, her feet stumbling as the treadmill powered down. She gripped the sides for dear life, her chest heaving, her sports bra sticking to her damp skin.

"Fucking Christ, Leo," she panted, her voice breathless.

Just like she'd sounded when she was begging me to touch her. My lip twitched. "I didn't realize I needed to warn you before entering my own gym."

Her fingers pressed to the pulse at her neck as she checked her watch, irritation flashing across her features. "You fucked up my heart rate and time," she grumbled, narrowing her eyes at me.

But I could see the softness still. She wasn't really mad. If anything, she looked like she wanted to see me. Wanted to be around me.

Taking my chance, I stepped closer, keeping my hands in my pockets to resist the urge to touch her. I knew how much she hated that.

"*Principessa*," I murmured, my voice softer now. "I needed to see you."

I didn't bother hiding the vulnerability. She already knew how badly I wanted her—how deep her hold on me ran.

I would fucking move mountains for this woman.

Cassandra turned fully to face me, leaning against the treadmill's guardrail. Her emerald-green eyes gleamed, vibrant and alive, like polished gemstones catching the light.

Dio mio. I had it bad.

"Well," she said, a small smirk tugging at her lips. "Here I am." Then, as if catching herself, she shook her head and sighed. "I mean, I needed to talk to you too. So I'm glad you found me."

She must not have realized—I never needed to find her. I always knew exactly where she was.

Crossing my arms over my chest, I mirrored her stance, my expression playful. "Oh yeah? What could you possibly need to talk to me about?"

Her confidence wavered. She shifted slightly, inhaling deeply as if bracing herself. Then, locking her gaze onto mine, she said, "On Friday night, Ciro and I kissed and—"

My arms uncrossed instantly. My fists clenched at my sides. We kept our eyes locked, tension thickening between us, as I silently wrestled with the anger threatening to explode from my chest.

Cassandra noticed my reaction and hesitated before stepping forward. More trusting than I expected.

She reached out and touched my arm.

"I'm really sorry, Leo," she murmured, breaking our eye contact to look at the floor, shame painting her features. "I'm sure you hate me now."

My blood boiled beneath the surface at the betrayal. How could she allow something like this to happen? She was a good woman—I knew it. Cassandra had feelings for me. I knew it, even if she refused to admit it. And the sight of her now…with shame decorating her features only proved that she knew she'd made a mistake.

Which meant this wasn't her doing.

This was Ciro's fault.

Without another word, I grabbed her wrist and pulled her toward the gym exit.

"Leo! What the hell? Where are you dragging me?" She pulled at her arm, trying to resist, but I didn't stop.

My strides were long, determined, fueled by the rage threatening to burst from my skin. The sconces along the corridor flickered, matching the erratic pace of my heartbeat. When we burst into Ciro's room in the south wing, we found him lounging on his bed, scrolling through his phone like he didn't have a care in the goddamn world.

I released Cassandra, placing a steadying hand on her lower back. Her skin was still warm, still damp from her workout.

Or maybe that heat was fear.

I didn't know.

She glared up at me but said nothing.

"Apologize," I demanded, my jaw tightening.

Ciro sat up, lazily setting his phone on the nightstand. "Are we having a threesome?" he asked with a knowing curl of his lips.

I clenched my fists so tightly my knuckles ached. Cassandra moved forward slightly, her mouth parting as if to apologize.

My brow furrowed.

Why the fuck was she apologizing?

I reached out, touching her shoulder gently, stopping her before turning my glare back to Ciro.

His expression remained infuriatingly amused. A headache began to form at my temple. "I said, apologize."

Cassandra jumped slightly at the sharpness of my tone. Instinctively, I brushed my thumb over her shoulder in a soothing motion.

She whipped her head around to stare at me in shock.

"For what, Leo?" Ciro stood now, moving toward us, slow and deliberate. "For touching Cassandra?" His smirk deepened. "For the kiss?" He stopped right in front of us, his grey eyes flicking between me and her. "Or for making her admit to having feelings for you without saying them out loud?"

His voice dipped lower, darker, dripping with amusement.

Cassandra stiffened beside me. Her legs trembled slightly as she took a step back.

Before she could retreat any further, I swung.

My fist connected with his nose.

The sickening sound of my fist connecting to his nose echoed in the room as blood splattered over Cassandra and me. She shrieked, stumbling backward.

I didn't stop.

My second punch landed hard against his ribs, and Ciro just took it.

He fucking let me hit him.

Because he knew.

He knew he crossed the line.

"Leo, please, stop!" Cassandra's voice wavered, and something inside me cracked.

My fist paused midair, my chest heaving as I peered over my shoulder at her. Cassandra stood frozen, her shoulders hunched and arms wrapped around herself, her breath coming in uneven waves.

She was shaken.

I turned back to Ciro, who was sitting on the edge of his bed, head tilted back, fingers pinching the bridge of his nose. Blood smeared across his jaw, his shirt stained with it.

And the motherfucker was still smiling.

I took a step forward, fists still clenched at my sides and covered in blood, but Cassandra's soft voice cut through the thick tension like a knife.

"Leo."

Her voice was steady now, but there was something behind it—a plea.

I exhaled sharply, forcing myself to breathe. My fingers twitched at my sides before I flexed them open and closed.

Then I refocused on her.

Cassandra hadn't moved, but she was watching me carefully, searching my face like she was trying to understand what the fuck just happened.

I stepped toward her, closing the space between us.

She didn't flinch.

Was she trusting me?

Reaching out slowly, gently as if touching a frightened child, I cupped her cheek, my thumb brushing against her soft, flushed skin. Her eyes widened slightly at the touch, but she didn't pull away.

"Cassandra, you need to understand something," I said, my voice calm though the edge of my anger still lingered. "Ciro knew what he was doing. He was testing my fucking word."

My jaw ticked as I said it, the weight of those words thick in the air between us. I let my thumb continue to brush over her cheek.

"He manipulated you without my permission. And you deserve an apology."

Her emerald eyes flickered with something unreadable—something that looked an awful lot like admiration.

Or maybe something more.

"Oh…" she murmured, her gaze flicking briefly to Ciro before meeting mine again. "You're not mad at me?"

I shook my head instantly. "No, *principessa*. I mean I'm jealous, and a bit pissed off but I'm not mad at you nor do I hate you." My voice dropped lower, more certain. "You're mine. I know who you truly are under all your bravado."

Her lips parted slightly, eyes widening just a fraction.

Ciro let out a low whistle, wiping blood from his nose.

I ignored him, keeping my focus locked onto her. Cassandra was staring at me like she didn't know what to say, her lips slightly parted, her chest rising and falling.

The corner of my lip twitched. "Ciro is getting a warning because he's family," I said, my voice dipping into something darker. "But next time?" I leaned in to emphasize the deadly promise in my tone. "I won't hesitate to rip his dick off and shove it down his throat until he stops fucking breathing."

"Christ," she gasped.

"Seriously, that's fucked up, Leo," Ciro muttered, dabbing at his nose with the bottom of his shirt.

My stance remained firm, my hand still on her cheek, my thumb still stroking the softness there.

Then, without breaking eye contact with me, Cassandra did the most unexpected thing.

She stepped forward—and hugged me.

For a brief second, I didn't move.

A grunt escaped my lips, my body tensing at the unfamiliar sensation of having her this close by her choice—her warmth seeping into me, her head resting against my chest, her fingers curling lightly into my back.

Ciro stared at me from the bed, shaking his head like he couldn't fucking believe what he was seeing. He mouthed, "Hug her back, idiot."

Swallowing hard, I slowly—so slowly—wrapped my arms around her, pulling her against me. I squeezed her tight, holding her there, feeling the way her breath hitched as I did. Her ear pressed to my chest, right over my heart.

I knew she could hear it pounding.

"When you say you know who I am…what does that mean exactly?" she asked in a soft, skeptical voice.

Leaning down slightly, I inhaled—breathing in the rose-and-vanilla scent that had been haunting me for days. Then, unable to stop myself, I pressed a soft kiss to the top of her head.

"I know where your money goes, why you can't pay rent, and the things you've had to sacrifice in order to survive."

The hug didn't last long enough. Because nothing with Cassandra ever would.

The second she pulled back, I reluctantly let her go, my arms feeling fucking empty without her in them. Her green eyes penetrated mine, shifting between anger, annoyance, and relief. Like the fact that her mask had been removed gave her permission to let her true self show.

"You've been doing that much research on me?"

I nodded. "The moment I met you, I felt the need to know more about who you are."

Her arms shifted between wanting to cross and needing to hang at her sides. I could see her vulnerability, how uncomfortable she was exposing it to me and Ciro.

"I care about those women and their kids because I know what it's like being trapped." She bit her lip before releasing it, her left hand rising to rub her right arm soothingly. She peeked up at me. "I wish you didn't find this out," she whispered, the admission leaving her like a long sigh.

This wasn't what I wanted. She was supposed to feel peace knowing I understood. That her secret was safe with me. That I cherished this part of her—honored it, even.

But instead of trusting me with it, she was retreating—building walls where I wanted to tear them down.

Ciro cleared his throat dramatically. "Leo, why don't you invite her to family dinner."

Cassandra blinked. "Family dinner?"

I shot Ciro a glare. Fucking asshole. His smile was self-satisfied as he wiped more blood from his lip.

Cassandra turned back to me, curiosity lighting her features. "You mean the family in the portrait above your front door?"

She actually sounded excited.

I hesitated for half a second before nodding. "Yes." Then, cautiously, I added, "Do you... want to meet them?"

The idea of bringing her home to Mama, Alessia, and my father

Enzo—the former don of Chicago—made my stomach tighten in a way I wasn't sure I liked.

I had never brought anyone home before.

Cassandra tilted her head, considering the question. Then, to my absolute fucking shock, she smiled. "Yes," she said, nodding enthusiastically. "I do."

My chest tightened.

Ciro laughed, clapping his hands together. "Then it's settled. You'll come tonight."

Cassandra's lips parted slightly, but before she could say anything, Ciro continued. "You'll love Alessia. She's a firecracker, just like you. And Antonia? She buys the best wine."

My palms started sweating.

Like a fucking teenage boy.

Cassandra turned back to me, her smile still in place. "Leo?" she prompted.

Clearing my throat, I nodded stiffly. "Yes. Of course. We'd love for you to come."

Ciro grinned, clearly entertained by my discomfort. I shot him another glare letting him know he wasn't fully forgiven before turning back to Cassandra. "Come," I murmured, gently placing a hand on her lower back. "Let's get you back to your room so you can get ready."

As I led her out of the room, a small, ridiculous smile tugged at my lips.

My *principessa* was about to meet my fucking family.

And the craziest part?

She actually wanted to.

And so did I.

Cassandra

Ciro and Leo waited by the front door, their sharp eyes tracking my every movement, while Dimitri and Gio stood off to the side in their usual intimidating stance. I'd been around them long enough to see past it, though, and gave the two bodyguards a small smile and wave. Gio dipped his chin in acknowledgment, while Dimitri smirked, brown eyes gleaming with amusement.

It didn't go unnoticed by Leo. His posture stiffened slightly before he stepped forward, extending his arm like I was some goddamn princess in a fairytale. Rolling my eyes, I took it, his grip warm as he leaned in close, his breath tickling my ear.

"You look absolutely beautiful in that burgundy sundress, *principessa*," he murmured, his voice deep and smooth.

A blush crept up my cheeks, the unexpected compliment sending a flutter through my stomach. I almost stumbled in my wedge heels, but Leo's arms caught me instantly, wrapping around my waist, steady and secure. His hold lingered, his quiet chuckle vibrating against me.

I felt lighter, almost like I wasn't carrying everything alone anymore. Even though I didn't like the fact that Leo had been looking into my bank account and tracking what I'd been doing with the money, I appreciated the unexpected acknowledgment of my good deeds.

Sure, every woman I'd helped had been grateful and felt the need to give me something in return, but this was different. Leo saw who I really was, and although I wouldn't admit it out loud, I believed it.

Ciro gave me a predatory grin as he opened the front door. "You two are going to give me a fucking cavity."

"Shut up, Ciro," I muttered, trying to step out of Leo's embrace, but his arm only tightened around my waist.

He needed this.

Even after everything—after what I'd admitted to him about Ciro and me—Leo still held onto me like he was staking a silent claim. I'd let him have this tonight, but tomorrow I'd lock whatever feelings had risen back in their cage, because if I was going to break my cycles, I had to leave Chicago.

The warm Chicago air hit me as we stepped outside, the scent of an oncoming storm thick in the air—a much-needed break from the relentless heatwave. The city had been suffocating lately, the kind of heat that scrambled people's brains, making them do stupid shit.

Gio and Dimitri moved ahead, slipping into the front seats of the sleek black SUV. Leo held the back door open for me, his expression softer than usual, a warm smile replacing the usual hard edges of his face.

My heart did a stupid little flip.

Sliding in, I barely had time to situate myself before I saw Ciro open the opposite door.

He gave me a wry smile.

Oh, hell no.

I realized what was happening a second too late—trapped, sandwiched between two very large men. Before I could even adjust, Leo's strong arms grabbed me, pulling me onto his lap. I gasped, my gaze snapping to his, but he didn't budge. His steel-grey eyes darkened immediately, fingers locking around my hips.

"Be a good girl, *principessa*," he murmured, his voice thick with something that made my core tighten.

That was all he said before Gio started the vehicle, pulling us forward.

I couldn't relax—not with Leo's fucking dick right beneath me, the one I still secretly wanted to get to know better. Shifting slightly, I tried to get comfortable, but my body betrayed me, hyper-aware of every single inch of him.

Where the fuck was I supposed to look?

At Ciro? At the floor?

Ciro must have noticed my dilemma because he let out a low, amused laugh. "Relax, *strega*. Leo won't bite." He winked. Most of the swelling from earlier had calmed down, except maybe around his nose. It was taped in such a weird way, but the guy still looked good.

Which irritated me all to hell.

That earned him a glare.

"What?" he asked innocently, tilting his head. "Still pissed at me?"

Oh, he was loving this.

I kept my arms crossed.

"Fine, fine," he sighed, feigning defeat. "I'm sorry I was an asshole and got a little handsy the other day. Can we go back to being friends now?"

Why did Ciro have such a punchable face?

But deciding to be the bigger person, I flashed him a smartass smile. "You barely made an impression on me, Ciro. How could I be mad when your touch and kiss were so… forgettable?"

Leo's laughter rumbled through his chest, vibrating against my side, sending goosebumps across my skin. The rest of the car burst into laughter too. Even Ciro chuckled.

And just like that, I felt something shift—like I belonged. The tension, the guilt… some of it melted away in the warmth of their laughter.

"You're cruel, *piccola strega*," Ciro muttered, shaking his head before looking out the window.

Leo, however, pulled me even closer, his nose nuzzling against my neck. "You are something else, Cassandra," he murmured low enough that only I could hear.

A delicate admission.

Leonardo Romano had it bad for me, and two instincts hit me simultaneously—jump out of the car and run for dear life, or the louder one whispering for me to let him in just a little.

I sighed softly, my fingers threading into the back of his hair, petting him gently as the truck rolled through the streets to Leo's family house, a place I never imagined I would be heading to.

As soon as we stepped into his family's mansion, I was hit with the scent of garlic, rosemary, and simmering sauces. Laughter filtered from another room and through the air, warmth wrapping around me like a comforting embrace.

Halfway to the kitchen, my steps faltered.

"What if your family hates me?" My voice cracked slightly.

This sort of nervousness was unlike me. I didn't even feel this way when Declan brought me to his family house to live after he found me a year ago.

Leo turned, blocking my path, his large frame shielding me from view. Tilting my chin up with two fingers, he made me meet his gaze. "They're going to love you," he assured me, his voice steady. Then, lips curling into a smirk, he added, "And if they don't…"

My eyes widened. "You wouldn't," I gasped.

He laughed. "You think I'd off my own family just for not liking you?" His arm curled around my waist, pulling me closer. "Maybe."

My lips parted in shock.

Not at the words—but at the fact that he was joking.

"You make jokes?" I asked, dumbfounded.

Leo grinned. "Only when necessary."

His entire face softened when he laughed, making him even hotter, which seemed unfair. Was he always like this around his family? Because if so, I was in trouble. If I wasn't sure if I liked him before, seeing more of him like this might actually make me become obsessed with him, and all plans for leaving would be out the window.

I barely had time to come back from cloud nine before he whispered, "I'm going to kiss you now."

It wasn't a question.

It was a warning.

He waited—giving me enough time to say no.

I didn't.

His lips found mine, slow and sweet at first before shifting, his tongue sliding over my bottom lip, seeking permission. When I opened for him, we were gone, completely consumed by each other. My fingers tangled in his hair, my body pressing against him, and fuck —I could have jumped him right there in the hallway.

A female voice cut through the moment.

"Get a room."

I froze, breath catching in my throat.

Leo, however, smirked against my lips. "That," he murmured, "would be my sister, Alessia."

Shoving at his chest, I stepped back, cheeks burning as I tried to fix my dress and smooth down my hair.

Leo only laughed. "You look great. Stop worrying so much."

"Easy for you to say."

Peeking around his broad frame, I caught sight of a stunning woman with a wine glass in hand, hazel eyes crinkled in amusement.

She smiled knowingly.

I immediately ducked back behind Leo.

"Fuck, I'm such an idiot," I hissed, slapping his chest. "Why did you have to embarrass me like that?"

Leo grinned, then turned to his sister. "Alessia."

"Leonardo," she drawled, her accent thick, before flicking her gaze to me. "So you're the girl who's got my brother's balls wrapped up tight."

Oh. My. God.

Leo and I both coughed at Alessia's blunt statement, completely caught off guard. From another room off to the side, Ciro roared with laughter, another deep chuckle joining his.

My face burned, and I mentally cursed myself for thinking I could make it through this dinner without being absolutely humiliated at least once.

Alessia smiled wide, unfazed, her hazel eyes flicking between me and Leo like she knew exactly what she was doing.

Before I could respond, a warm, lilting voice filled the space, speaking in rapid Italian.

I turned just in time to see a striking woman appear in the hallway —beautiful in the same way Leo and Alessia were, with steel-grey eyes and an air of quiet authority.

Leo's mother.

I immediately liked her, because something about her warm smile made me think of my mother. I missed the way she would smile at me when it was just her and me. We were always happier when my father wasn't around.

She spoke again, her tone gentle but firm. Though my Italian was limited, I caught the meaning—she was telling Alessia to behave and leave me alone. Alessia rolled her eyes but didn't argue, just winked at me before disappearing through a doorway, where I could already hear her and Ciro launching into some ridiculous banter.

Leo's grip on my waist tightened as he guided me forward. "Cassandra," he said smoothly, "this is my mother, Antonia." Then, in a tone so full of admiration it made my heart ache, he added, "She's the world's best cook and an even better mother."

Antonia blushed at the praise, playfully swatting at Leo before turning her full attention to me.

I swallowed, nerves fluttering in my chest. What the hell was I supposed to do?

After only a second of hesitation, I stuck out my hand, offering a polite smile. Instead of shaking it, Antonia tugged me into a tight hug. I floundered for a moment, completely caught off guard, before I finally relaxed and hugged her back.

It took everything in me not to start tearing up as Antonia held me. I hadn't had a passionate hug like this in…God, I didn't even know how long. I remembered hugging Declan's mom, Abigail, but it had been cold and swift. Like hugging a robot on autopilot—the movement was there, but the meaning was missing.

She murmured something softly in Italian, her voice warm and affectionate, then, sensing my limited grasp of the language, translated —welcoming me into her home.

I giggled, the tension in my shoulders easing. I responded with the little Italian I had learned from my mom, "*Grazie per avermi ospitato, Antonia.*" Carefully, I hoped I wasn't butchering the pronunciation. Then for good measure, in English, I translated, "Thank you for having me."

Antonia gasped, eyes widening in genuine surprise. Then, in true Italian fashion, she pressed the tips of her fingers together and bobbed her hands up and down in an exaggerated display of emotion.

"Why didn't you tell me this beautiful woman could speak *Italiano?*" she demanded, turning to Leo.

Leo chuckled, shaking his head. "I only just learned this myself. I knew she had some knowledge, but still…" He trailed off, his gaze flicking to mine, something steamy and undeniable swirling there.

Our eyes locked.

Mine? Playful.

His? Hungry.

I swallowed, suddenly feeling very warm.

Quickly, I averted my gaze and blurted, "Antonia, I hear you have the best collection of wine."

Antonia laughed, looping her arm through mine. "Come, *bella*. I'll show you," she said, guiding me toward the kitchen.

Leo followed behind. I felt his gaze on me the entire time, burning into my back like a brand.

And God help me—it wasn't scary.

It was hot.

BY THE TIME dinner was ready, I was well acquainted with Antonia and Alessia.

And very tipsy.

Carrying a dish into the dining room, my wedge heels thunked softly against the marble floors as I took in the gorgeous space. The walls were a warm beige, hand-painted with intricate murals of grapevines and sprawling Italian landscapes. A stunning crystal chandelier hung above the tan table, its tiers refracting the dim lighting in delicate rainbows across the cherub-painted ceiling.

I inhaled deeply—immediately regretting it when my gaze landed on the three men already seated at the table.

Two I already knew.

The third?

I recognized him from the portrait above Leo's front door.

Leo's father.

I froze.

The heat drained from my face, my breath catching as my stomach dropped.

The former don of Chicago.

And he was terrifying.

His sharp hazel eyes were unreadable as he rose from his chair, his long strides eating up the distance between us in mere seconds. His presence was suffocating—controlled, lethal—his tailored black suit only adding to the severity of his features. The deep chestnut of his wavy hair emphasized the sharp angles of his face, and for a split second, I thought I was about to die.

If it weren't for the hot dish in my hands forcing me to keep my composure, I would have definitely looked like a deer in headlights. Instead, I carefully set it down on the table before straightening, preparing myself to officially meet the most feared man in Chicago.

"It's a pleasure to meet you, Cassandra Bennett. I'm Enzo Romano," he said smoothly, his voice deep and velvety, laced with just the right amount of rasp.

I blinked.

He used my full name.

Fucking hell.

Wiping my palm discreetly against my dress, I extended my hand, hoping to God he wouldn't notice the slight tremor.

"It's an honor, Mr. Romano," I said automatically.

The second the words left my mouth, laughter erupted around the table.

Leo and Ciro both lost it, their deep chuckles mixing together in a ridiculous display of amusement.

Even Enzo—who had been all stoic and intimidating just a second ago—pressed his lips together, trying to suppress a smirk.

I stood there, my extended hand empty, my lips pressed together as I glared at the two assholes laughing at my expense.

"Shut up," I snapped. "It's not every day you meet one of the scariest dudes in Chicago."

That only made them laugh harder.

Enzo, however, raised a single brow, his voice turning dangerously amused. "Scariest dude, huh? Are you saying my son isn't doing his job right?"

The room stilled, my empty hand falling to my side. His smile vanished, replaced with a blank, cold expression that sent chills down my spine.

For a second, I thought he was serious.

Then, just as quickly, he laughed.

"All of you are not right," I muttered, dropping into the seat Leo had pulled out beside him.

"I agree," Alessia said breezily, setting two bottles of wine on the table.

"Sorry, *cara*," Enzo said with a smirk, joining us at the head of the table. "I don't get to use my intimidation tactics like I used to."

Ciro nudged my leg under the table, whispering, "Enzo's a big softie."

Enzo snorted. "Is that so, Ciro?"

The warning in his tone was subtle but effective. Ciro held up his hands in mock surrender, grinning.

I exhaled slowly, finally relaxing.

Maybe this wouldn't be so bad.

As soon as Antonia entered with a large, immaculate plate of stuffed chicken, potatoes, and carrots, the energy in the room shifted. The teasing faded, replaced by something warmer, something more intimate. This wasn't just a meal—it was a tradition, a ritual, something built over years of family gatherings.

Antonia set the dish down at the center of the table, her movements practiced and precise, a quiet pride in the way she placed each element with care. Enzo, still sitting at the head of the table, gave her a soft, knowing smile.

"Looks wonderful, *amore*," he murmured.

Antonia shot him a look—one that clearly said, *Of course it does. I made it.*

I couldn't help it. I laughed. Antonia's gaze swung to me, and her lips curved into a smile.

"This is normal for you guys, huh?" I asked, glancing around at the effortless way they interacted.

Ciro smirked. "Dinner at the Romanos? Yeah. Always a show."

Enzo took a slow sip of his wine before setting it down, his expression turning more serious. "Before we eat—" His gaze shifted to Leo, something silent passing between them. "Leonardo, will you do the honors?"

Leo straightened slightly, nodding as he looked around the table. The conversation died down, a quiet respect settling over the room.

Even Ciro shut up.

Leo exhaled softly, then clasped his hands together. "Heavenly Father," he began, his voice steady and deep, "thank you for this meal, for my beautiful family, and for an even more wonderful woman by my side."

What?

My eyes flew open, my head snapping toward him.

Leo's gaze was already locked onto mine, dark and unreadable, something heavy and certain in the way he looked at me. My breath hitched, my pulse hammering so hard I could hear it in my ears. Heat crept up my neck, spreading fast.

I quickly looked away, staring down at my empty white plate with green leaf patterns around the edge as the table echoed a quiet "amen."

Ciro was smirking. Alessia's lips twitched like she was dying to say something.

And Enzo?

He just watched me, his expression impossible to read.

Leo Romano was slowly stealing my heart.

And so was his family.

EPISODE 8

Cassandra

Conversation flowed effortlessly as plates were passed, dishes were shared, and glasses of wine were refilled over and over again. The laughter never stopped, the teasing was endless, and the warmth in the air was something I hadn't felt in a long time.

Everything just felt easy, natural. Alessia and Ciro spent half the meal bickering, throwing insults at each other in a way that only made them laugh harder. Antonia watched them with soft amusement, occasionally scolding Ciro when his language got too vulgar—which only made him smirk and apologize insincerely.

Enzo was mostly quiet, sipping his wine, observing. His presence felt more than heard.

And Leo? Leo barely let me out of his sight.

Or his touch.

His hand remained on my thigh beneath the table, his thumb idly tracing slow, deliberate circles against my skin. His grip was firm, his touch possessive, tightening every time I shifted. Subtle, but clear. *You're mine.*

I didn't mind it, if I was honest. I'm sure the alcohol lowered my inhibitions enough to tolerate the caveman-like claim, but I also felt something different—a sense of safety when I was with him and his family. It was terrifyingly unfamiliar, and it made me curious how the don of Chicago could make such an emotion exist at all.

Surely Karma was right around the corner, readying her traps and sharpening her blades. I just had to wait for the other shoe to drop. But until then, I'd try to enjoy this temporary feeling of protection and let this man take care of me—just for tonight.

"Alright," Alessia announced, leaning back in her chair, her fifth glass of wine in hand. "Since we finally have a new face at the table—" her hazel eyes flicked to me—"Cassandra, tell us how the hell you've managed to put up with my brother for so long."

I choked on my sip of wine.

Leo sighed. "Alessia—"

"No, no, this is a great question," Ciro interjected, grinning. "Because we all know he's an asshole."

Leo shot him a look that should have been enough to shut him up. It wasn't.

Antonia huffed dramatically. "Ciro, language."

"Sorry, Mama, but let's not pretend Leo isn't the grumpiest motherfucker in Chicago."

A burst of soft laughter escaped me, and I covered my mouth. Leo tensed beside me, which only made me laugh harder. I mean—he *was* the grumpiest motherfucker in Chicago.

Alessia leaned forward, smirking. "So? Answer the question, *bella*. How do you tolerate him?"

Chancing a glance at Leo, I found his steel-grey eyes already locked onto mine. I could have made a joke. Could have brushed it off with sarcasm like I always did. But for some reason, at that moment, I didn't want to. I wanted to be honest.

Tilting my head slightly, I said, "I guess…" I chewed on my lip before continuing. "He makes me feel like I can be myself. And no matter how much I poke at him, I know he'll protect me."

The table went silent.

I didn't blame them. Hell, even I found myself staring inward, stunned at my own audacity for admitting that out loud. I wasn't supposed to do that.

Leo stilled like one of the marble statues on his front lawn. A tightness formed in my stomach, the weight of my own words settling heavily in my chest. But it was true—at least for now. Until he eventually got bored of me and cast me aside. I was just some low-life stripper, after all.

The weight of those words hung in the air until Antonia sighed dramatically, sipping her wine before shaking her head with a knowing smile. *"Dio mio,"* she murmured, "she's already in love with him."

The sound of my fork clattering against my plate mixed with my coughing fit, the suffocating words landing far too dramatically. "What! I didn't—"

Alessia cut in. "Oh my God, Mama, you can't just *say* that!"

Antonia shrugged, completely unfazed. "What? I'm right."

My eyes bounced from person to person as my face heated. When my gaze landed on Leo, he was smiling dangerously at me, his fingers tightening on my thigh just above my knee, as if telling me he was both supportive of my embarrassment *and* approving of the observation. One I hadn't even confessed to. I mean—no, not confessed…fuck.

Ciro coughed, poorly hiding his laugh.

My face felt like it was on fire, the room suddenly squeezing in on all sides. I grabbed my wine and took the biggest sip possible, avoiding everyone's gaze.

Ciro laughed outright. "Aw, *piccola strega*, you're blushing."

Setting my empty glass down I gave him the sharpest death stare I could possibly muster at him.

He winked.

I groaned, pressing my fingers to my temples. This family was going to ruin me.

THE NIGHT LASTED LONGER than I expected, but by the time Leo finally led me outside, my stomach was full, my cheeks ached from laughing, and my head was pleasantly buzzed from the wine.

The air was still warm, the pavement damp from the earlier storm.

Leo walked beside me, his hand firm at the small of my back as we made our way toward the SUV.

"Did you have fun?" he asked, his voice softer now.

I hesitated, then nodded. "Yeah. I did. Well—except when your mother decided to embarrass me."

Leo stopped walking.

I turned, confused—and suddenly I was pinned against the cooled metal of the SUV. My breath hitched, my hands gripped his shirt as he leaned, one arm wrapping around my waist while the other cradled the space between my neck and head, steel-grey eyes dark and intense, focused on mine.

"You belong with me, Cassandra," he murmured, the smell of red wine heavy on his breath and mine.

I swallowed hard as I tried to gain control of my rapid heart beat.

His lips brushed mine in an intimate, claiming way.

"Say it," he urged.

The seconds felt like minutes and when I opened my mouth to say something, anything, the back passenger window whirled down and from inside the car, Ciro called out, "Can you two not fuck against the car? Some of us actually want to go home tonight."

I groaned, heat rushing back to my cheeks. Worse, it throbbed low between my legs—but that wasn't something I was going to think too far into. Not again.

Leo sighed. Then, gripping my chin, he kissed me deeply—slow and possessive, making sure I felt every bit of his frustration.

My traitorous body melted into it, especially when his tongue glided over my lip—a subtle ask for access, for more of me. I obliged, unable to even tell my body—the little slut—to say no. He tasted just how I remembered, but instead of scotch or cognac, it was rich Italian wine. My eyes fluttered closed, and my grip on his jacket shamelessly tightened, pulling him closer.

What was I even doing anymore?

Nothing made sense. I trusted him. I felt safe with him—for now. But I also knew this wasn't going to last forever. I sure as shit didn't love Leo Romano. I couldn't.

When he pulled back, the corner of his mouth lifted on one side, exposing a dimple near the soft pink scar on his cheek. "You'll say it soon."

It was a promise—one I knew, somewhere deep down, he would keep.

And fuck, if it didn't mess with my head.

Because I knew he was right.

I was weak like that.

Leo

My mother had always told us stories before bed each night—many of them about love. It had been her favorite genre, actually. But one story stayed with me more than the rest. It was about a blind prince who fell in love with a baker in his kingdom—a forbidden love. And although the story ended sadly, the moral was rooted in an old Italian saying: *"L'amore non guarda con gli occhi, ma con l'anima."* Love didn't look with the eyes, but with the soul.

My favorite part was what the prince said to the woman before they exiled her. "We will find each other in the next life, my love. Because with you, our souls are forever interwoven. No matter the distance or time that separates us, I will always be yours—and you mine."

I used to listen to those stories with wide eyes and open ears because I believed in true love—in the wanting of the heart. That was before I had to grow tough. Cold. Just like my father had as don. It wasn't to say he had always been like that. No. He had softened for my mother, loved her with every fiber of his being, and would have done whatever it took to make sure she knew it.

Even then, deep down beneath the surface of the wolf, I still believed in love. And Cassandra was mine to love and cherish. It was fate, written into our souls. My heart had always belonged to her. I could feel it. And I knew she was slowly warming to me, her eyes opening, finally seeing that I was as much hers as she was mine.

Hearing her confess that she felt safe with me at dinner the other night had set my heart burning for her. The way she let me in, allowed me to feel her skin beneath my hand as we gathered around the table with the others. And especially the way she melted into my arms when I kissed her, with every ounce of need I possessed for her—an unspoken branding of what I knew to be love. A feeling I had never thought my heart would experience. But it all made sense then.

My obsession had never been a flaw. It had been a mask—one my aching soul wore while waiting to be woven with hers.

The vibration of my cell phone made me refocus. My gaze found the screen as it lit up with Ciro's name. I knew it could have been important, but with him, he could just as easily have been calling to bust my balls. I decided to answer.

"What?" My tone came out unamused as I leaned back in the leather chair behind my office desk. Files and papers were piled in neat stacks across the surface. My eyes flicked to the grandfather clock in the far-right corner—five in the afternoon—its ticking created a steady pace for my heart rate.

His chuckle on the other end told me he was calling purely for his own entertainment. "I thought you could use a distraction."

A click of the wooden office door revealed his smug smile. Pulling the phone away from my face, I ended the call and set it down.

Rising, I adjusted my sleeves, leaving my suit jacket draped over the back of the chair. "A distraction?" My brow arched incredulously.

"Don't give me that look, Leo. It hurts my feelings." He gave a mock pat to his heart, but his smirk never faded.

I crossed my arms over my chest. "Just tell me what you want. I'm busy." I gestured to the work spread across my desk.

His eyes swept the room, then he shook his head in disbelief—which should have offended me, but he was also right. I hadn't been busy. I'd been daydreaming about Cassandra.

"She is downstairs, you know." He stopped in front of my desk and plopped into the chair opposite it before kicking his polished black dress shoes onto the surface. He knew that irritated me, but I ignored it—for now. "Cooking." He added it with a grin that bordered on wicked, clearly poking to see how I'd react that day.

But the idea of Cassandra cooking in my estate, of my kitchen filled with the scent of anything she made, had my heart racing. Ciro must have caught my hesitation because he chuckled. "Want to know what she's wearing, or do you want to find out yourself?"

I didn't let him finish. I rounded the desk, my strides full of purpose and eagerness to catch a glimpse of my little *topo* doing something as mundane as cooking. Maybe she was even cooking for me. The thought had me nearly sprinting, Dimitri and Gio hot on my heels without a word.

When I finally reached the kitchen, my breath faltered and my stomach fluttered, forcing me to lean against the doorframe to steady myself.

What a sight to behold.

Cassandra stood in a white apron, her silk-dark hair tied back into a loose ponytail as she pulled something from the oven—roast, maybe. It smelled divine, like rosemary, thyme, and citrus.

Her movements were graceful, just as they had been when she danced at Inferno. When her eyes found mine, my world stilled. Those emerald eyes pierced into me as I followed the way she set the pan down, slipped off the oven mitts, then leaned back against the counter and crossed her arms. That stare turned into a challenge instantly.

"Take a picture, Leo. It'll last longer."

Her voice cut through the spell, and I smirked, pushing off the frame and straightening.

Steadier now, I took a slow inhale, catching the aroma again as I replied, "I see you've made yourself at home, *principessa*."

Cassandra rolled her eyes, and if I'd been closer, I would have kissed the attitude right out of her. Instead, I shoved my hands into my pockets and stepped closer—just enough that she still felt in control.

"I was sick of eating takeout." Her voice was unamused, but the way her eyes searched mine told me she was waiting for me to push back.

Part of me wanted to.

The other part—the one that had fallen for her—couldn't.

Carefully, I took another step, reaching out to uncross her arms. I pulled her into my embrace, one hand settling at her lower back, the other cradling her cheek. "Thank you." The words came out gentle as I searched her eyes and watched them soften.

Then, just as quickly, she pushed out of my grasp. I let her go—but my heart sank.

She needed more time.

"It wasn't for you. But…" She looked past me. I glanced over my shoulder to find Dimitri, Gio, and Ciro watching in their own ways. My jaw tightened as she added, "If you're all hungry, I made plenty."

"Don't mind if I do," Ciro's smart-ass mouth cut in like a blade.

He sauntered past me, ruffling her hair as he went. She batted him away and told him to set the table. Gio and Dimitri moved to my side.

"Boss, want us to leave?" Gio knew exactly what was happening, and I appreciated the offer. But she liked them, and I wouldn't deny her that.

Shaking my head, I said, "No. Please, join us." I gestured toward the table, then turned back to help Cassandra serve.

It was a small win. A glimpse of what life could have looked like if we spent every day together.

For the rest of our lives.

Cassandra

It had been over a week since I got there, and I was starting to feel a little cooped up. Leo had been paying me not to go into Inferno, for reasons he seemed unable—or unwilling—to explain, which was a pain in my ass. But the money was good, and I couldn't complain about making my salary while sitting around all day.

However, I had this gut feeling that something was off. I hadn't been receiving my usual messages from Declan, which maybe I should be grateful for—but it also made my heart break a little. Had he moved on?

I must have been out of my mind if I missed getting threatening messages from a man I once loved.

My hands brushed along the dark blue walls of the hallway that led to Leo's office. I paused, rubbing my fingers together—no dust particle in sight. Everything was too perfect here, too manicured and controlled. It made me want to crawl out of my skin while simultaneously curling up into a Snuggie and sipping hot tea.

Infuriating.

This mental tug-of-war between wanting security and hating it.

The heavy wooden door to his office opened suddenly, and my eyes landed on Leo. One hand was shoved into his pocket while the other ran through his dark brown hair, gripping the strands when he reached the back of his skull. He looked frustrated. Tired. The lines of his face were more defined, his complexion a little paler.

Gio stepped out beside him, catching me standing a good distance away. He gave me a subtle acknowledgment before getting Leo's attention and pointing in my direction. I felt rooted in place—nervous, even. I knew exactly how Leo was going to look at me. The way his body would relax. How those normally intense gray eyes would soften. It only made the reality of my feelings resurface, and if I was acknowledging how I felt towards Leo then that meant I was more likely to stay and that couldn't happen.

His steps were sure as he closed the distance, stopping just out of reach like he always did when initiating conversation. My chin lifted so I could peer up at him. "I need to ask you a question."

He kept his attention on me, unwavering, studying me. "Anything, *principessa*." The hand in his pocket came out, as the phone in his other slid easily into his breast pocket.

Taking a steadying breath and ignoring the way my chest felt like a drumline, I asked, "Are you hacking my phone?" My arms crossed, my chin lifting higher even though I wanted to turn and run in the opposite direction.

The tick of his jaw told me everything—but I wanted to hear him say it. To be honest with me. He shoved both hands into his pockets this time, something I'd noticed he always did when calculating his words. "Yes."

One simple word had me boiling. "Why." My teeth clenched painfully.

"Because." He stepped closer, his eyes flicking between mine and my mouth. "You don't need to be involved in what's happening."

It was so discreet. So infuriatingly protective. "What the fuck does that even mean, Leo!" I couldn't stop myself from raising my voice. He was just so...aggravatingly controlling.

Leo didn't move. Didn't flinch. Didn't change that expression of longing on his face. It made me want to punch him. "Declan's been threatening you. And you don't deserve to be spoken to in such a manner." That was when he closed the distance, my heart picking up a different beat entirely.

Strong arms enveloped me in a warm hug, and my own arms automatically reciprocated. "You have no right—"

"Shhh, *principessa.*"

A shudder left me as warm liquid slid down my cheeks. It startled me. He must have felt it because his hold tightened. "I don't have any right to deny you privacy, but this—what he's saying—this isn't about you. It's about the war, which has everything to do with me."

I pulled back to look up at him, and his hands immediately came to my face, brushing away the evidence of my vulnerability—not to dismiss it, but to show support. Understanding. Patience. "How long have you been doing this?"

"Since you logged onto our Wi-Fi. I'm sorry, *bella.* It wasn't meant to be malicious—only to keep you safe. Emotionally and physically." His hands slid down to rest on either side of my neck, his thumbs gently circling the pulse fluttering there.

Our eyes connected again. "Gio, leave us." His Italian accent was deep and rich, wrapping around me like a spell. I didn't see Gio leave, but I knew he had by the way Leo kissed my forehead—so tenderly. "*Ti desidero più di quanto dovrei.*"

The whispered confession—I desire you more than I should—

made my hair prickle as heat rushed south. Every nerve ending felt electric. Every breath felt heavy.

I didn't know how to respond.

And I wasn't sure I needed to.

Leo

My little *topo* was as furious as a summer thunderstorm. There was no yelling—only the sharp clap of her door as it slammed shut behind her, and the rumble of her pounding feet as she rushed to find me.

The anticipation of that first lightning strike sat right at the precipice as I remained seated at the head of the dining table, just in front of a mural of the Roman goddess Venus in all her glory. My afternoon espresso was gripped between two fingers as I poured in sugar. Gio read the newspaper while Dimitri polished his gun at the opposite end of the table from where I held space. We were all waiting —but only my eyes were glued to the entry door, expecting it to burst open at any moment.

Then, with a flash and a crack, Cassandra stormed in—all five foot six inches of her. She wore the most adorable soft gray T-shirt and high-waisted black jeans. It made her look so normal. So sweet. A stark contrast to the determined expression set on her face.

I swirled my spoon through the espresso as I mixed the sugar, the clink of porcelain sounding like the catalyst to an argument I fully intended to win.

"I'm going to work," she demanded, her white tennis shoe stomping as if to solidify her decision.

My brow arched, but I remained calm on the outside. I had to. She was trying to leave—didn't she understand the danger she was in? For a week and a half now, I'd been paying her well to stay here, at least until the war with the Irish was settled. Declan's intercepted messages, ones my tech guy had pulled, made it clear he knew exactly where she was—and he was fucking furious.

Selfishly, that thrilled me.

But it also kept me on edge.

I'd doubled security around the estate, installed more cameras in and around her room to ensure no one slipped in or out without my knowledge, and I hadn't been sleeping more than five or six hours a night. I was at my breaking point. But my little *principessa* didn't deserve to see that side of me. She was precious. Sacred, even.

Calmly, I lifted my espresso and took a sip before setting it down. "No."

As if she'd expected it, she came in guns blazing. "You can't keep me from work, Leo. That wasn't part of our deal."

"Our deal was that you stay with me until further—"

"Notice. Or until it was safe. Nothing about me being trapped in some golden cage like a damn bird." Her words were thick with resentment, fear, and old pain—battles I knew she'd been fighting long before me. It was what kept her from opening her heart completely.

Cassandra was smart, but her instincts were on high alert. When she felt threatened, she attacked. When she was scared, she cowered and sought comfort. And when she felt powerless, she reached for control.

I released a long breath, leaning back in my chair and steepling my hands in my lap. "It's too dangerous, *amore*." Outside, the clouds thickened, dimming the sunlight filtering through the front windows of the estate. "Declan knows you're here. I can't risk it. I can't risk you."

My fingers turned white as I pressed their tips together, jaw flexing under the weight of that truth. I hadn't wanted to tell her—but she'd left me no choice.

She began pacing in front of the dark wooden double doors opposite the windows, the dimming light sharpening her tension. I studied her, noting the way her fingers flexed and clenched at her sides. She looked like a caged cat.

Her steps stilled. Then she surged forward, planting her hands on the table. The scent of vanilla and floral musk hit me like the first cold burst of a storm rolling in. Her shoulders were drawn tight.

"I'm not asking, Leo. I'm telling you."

Her emerald eyes flicked between mine with a desperation I knew well—and hated seeing in her. She didn't like feeling stripped of autonomy. And she wasn't ready to be one hundred percent mine yet. Her internal war with her heart was far from won.

My hands fisted in my lap. "*Principessa*, you know I've been patient. I've been understanding. But you will not speak to me—"

"Boss."

My gaze snapped to Dimitri as he stood from the far end of the table.

"What the fuck do you want?" My tone was pure warning.

He slid his polished gun into his back pocket and crossed his arms. "I'll go with her tomorrow night. I know that club inside and out. I'll bring a few other bodies, too."

Dimitri glanced at Cassandra, who looked surprised by the offer, before turning back to me. My attention shifted to my little *topo*. She'd stepped back from her attacking stance, arms crossed defensively—ready for another round if I pushed.

I stood, running a hand through my hair before shoving it into my pocket. Logistically, it made sense. If I let her go, she'd feel heard. If Dimitri—one of my best—went with her, I knew she'd be safe.

Just like she always was.

My eyes locked on Dimitri. "You don't let her out of your sight for any fucking reason. Understand?"

The warning was clear. I'd kill him if he failed her.

I hated this. It went against every instinct screaming to keep her here, under my protection, under my watch. But the way her body visibly relaxed—how fury melted into hope—made me override that deep-seated need to control.

"Thank you, Leo."

Her voice snapped me back to the moment.

I closed the distance, one hand cradling the back of her head as my fingers tangled in her silky black hair, the other wrapping firmly around her waist, pulling her into me. I needed to hold her. Needed to feel that she was still with me.

Her hands fisted in my suit jacket like they always did. I loved how she clung to me as if I were her lifeline. My head dipped to her ear as I breathed her in, committing her scent to memory.

She was mine. I knew it in my soul.

"*Senza di te non sono niente,*" I whispered, for her alone.

Her breath hitched—I knew she understood. *Without you, I am nothing.*

My nose brushed her cheekbone until our eyes met, breaths mingling, heavy. "You shouldn't say things like that." Her voice contradicted itself, because I could see in her green irises how much she adored being wanted like this.

I grazed the tip of her nose with mine. "One kiss, *amore*. I beg of you."

I didn't care how desperate I sounded. Not to Gio. Not to Dimitri. With her, I needed her to see that she and I were inevitable.

Those green eyes darkened. Heat flared between us like gasoline meeting flame. Then—slow, timid, devastating—my little *topo* blessed me. Her soft pink lips met mine, her hands clutching my lapels as she pulled me impossibly closer. She melted against me like the first warm day after winter.

She was beautiful.

And I was never letting her go.

Cassandra

The next night, Dimitri and I drove silently to Inferno. I was grateful he had stepped in and made Leo see reason, and being able to feel like I still had some ability to choose my own path took a heavy weight off my conscience.

Honestly, accepting Leo's little violations of my personal life went against everything I'd been striving for since Declan. I needed to take back my power. My dignity. And Leo was no exception—even if he was constantly declaring his love and his need for me.

My cheeks flushed as I thought about the kiss we'd shared after we compromised. Fuck. He was burrowing deeper than I wanted him to go. But the moment he begged me…I was putty in his hands.

Dimitri was a great escort, efficient and unobtrusive, and I didn't miss the five other goons stationed around the back entrance, waiting for us. They weren't there for show—I knew they'd be patrolling all night until I returned home… I mean, to Leo's estate.

After dropping me off at my station in the dressing room, Dimitri slipped easily into place, flirting shamelessly with a few of the girls like he belonged there. Then he caught my gaze in the mirror and gave me a subtle nod. *I'm here.* Close enough to matter.

It was comforting—almost like Leo was here with me.

When I'd left for Inferno earlier, Leo had been waiting at the door with Ciro and another man—Nico, I think he'd said—heading out to handle some business. It explained why Leo had seemed so upset about me being away from the estate. He wouldn't be able to keep his eyes on me at all times.

Spritzing my wrists and neck with my favorite Chanel perfume, I felt a familiar comfort settle in—like embracing an old friend after too much time apart.

"You're practically glowing."

Candy's reflection appeared behind me, her sharp eyes meeting mine in the mirror. She wore a pink glitter bra, a white cowgirl hat, and matching pink assless chaps. Her bedazzled cowgirl boots reflected the fluorescent lights, nearly blinding me.

"That noticeable, huh?" I murmured, setting the bottle down. As much as I wanted to deny it, the truth was impossible to ignore. Since meeting Leo, I'd felt…revived.

A rare smile spread across her lips, softening her usual hard edges. "Yeah. Very." She stepped closer, reaching for the brush on my vanity. "Here. Let me."

She ran it through my hair slowly, gently—the way I imagined an older sister might.

Her smile didn't fade. "You love him?"

Our eyes locked again.

Did I love him?

I wasn't sure I even knew what that meant. And since Antonia had brought it up at dinner a week and a half ago, I hadn't been able to stop ping-ponging the thought around in my mind.

"I don't know," I whispered thoughtfully. "How would you describe being in love?"

Candy's hand stilled, her eyes flickering with something distant.

Haunted. God, if only I knew what she'd been through. Most days she was a pain in the ass, but moments like this—when she was like this—I could appreciate her for what she really was.

A friend.

"I'd say it's a feeling you get in your gut," she said at last, resuming her strokes. "Not like when you're horny," she snorted, more to herself, flashing a mischievous curve of her lips.

I rolled my eyes.

"Like butterflies," she continued, her voice shifting. "They're all you think about. All you want to talk about." Her exhale was long, heavy. "I remember loving one man so much I knew I would've given my life to save him."

Her voice turned solemn, her eyes glistening. I reached up, touching the hand she'd unconsciously rested on my shoulder. She gave me a sad smile, then shook her head like she was forcing something down—burying it where no one could reach.

The show smile returned, but it didn't reach her eyes.

"Anyway," she said, brushing my hair again, nails carding through the strands. "Is that something you think you feel?"

POP! POP! POP!

The sound echoed through the main room.

BANG! BANG!

A retaliating shot fired back.

Screams erupted. Girls ran in every direction, panic breaking out as they ducked and rushed toward the emergency exit at the back of the building.

Candy's grip tightened on my shoulder. "What the fuck do you think is going on?" she asked, her voice rising—but not screaming.

Grabbing her perfectly manicured hand, I dragged her toward the bathroom inside the dressing room. I knew better than to expose us in a narrow hallway during a shootout.

"I don't fucking know," I whispered harshly, shoving her inside and locking the door behind us. "But stay quiet."

The cleaning supplies were separated by a cheap black curtain in the small tiled space, so I pulled us into the corner, forcing us into a crouch behind the mop and bucket. We clung to each other, trembling as chaos erupted just beyond the door.

"I'm scared." Her voice came out small. Vulnerable. Something I hadn't heard from her before—not even when her ex had been beating on her.

My sweaty hand tightened around hers as I met her worried expression. "Me too." I forced a tight smile, offering what little reassurance I could when I wasn't feeling it myself. "But we should be safe here."

Her chin dipped as she gave me a tight smile too, mimicking mine —one I was sure was also just for show. "I'm sorry for always being a pain in the ass. I know I come off as annoying and high maintenance." She spoke like someone who knew something was coming to an end, and I didn't like it.

With as much confidence as I could muster, I replied, "Don't talk like that." I pulled her closer, one arm wrapping over her shoulders protectively. "You're less of a pain in the ass than you think, and besides—" I rested my cheek against the top of her head. Her cowgirl hat had been lost somewhere in our escape. "I know it's all an act. You've been like a sister to me. You pulled me in when I was at my lowest." Tears pricked my eyes, and I inhaled deeply, forcing them back. "You all mean so much to me. Like family."

Her hand flexed against mine as she pulled back to look at me, her eyes red and glassy. "You mean that? You've always been kind of a bitch to me."

I couldn't help the smirk that tugged at my lips. "Yeah, I know. I'll try to fix that."

Then—

"Don't you fucking dare."

Dimitri's rough voice echoed through the room, followed by a deep grunt.

Shit. Was he in trouble?

Leo and Ciro had business tonight. Gio had a family emergency. That meant Dimitri and his five men were the only ones here to protect me, since the Inferno bodyguards didn't arrive yet.

He was in danger.

POP!

BANG!

"Fuck!" an unfamiliar voice yelled. "Fuck you, you fucking wop!"

Another shot fired—loud. Final.

Silence.

Candy sobbed quietly, silent tears streaking through her makeup as her manicured hand clamped over her mouth. I couldn't cry. My adrenaline was too high. But my body shook like a damn earthquake.

Then a voice froze every drop of blood in my body.

"Come out, come out, wherever you are, Cass."

I felt a small embarrassing warmth spread in my pants before I could stop it.

Candy looked at me, eyes wide. "Is that—?" she mouthed.

I nodded.

"Baby," Declan continued, voice unhinged, "if you come out, I won't kill the rest of the stupid bitches in the hallway."

Terror surged. I was a selfish idiot. I shouldn't have come. Leo was right—Declan was furious. I should've swallowed my pride and stayed.

Candy grabbed my arm, shaking her head violently, tears spilling freely. *No. Don't go.*

But I had to.

My eyes pleaded with hers.

Her fingers tightened around my wrist painfully. I gently pried them away, motioning for her to stay quiet.

Rising, my legs felt numb, fear sinking into my bones, my bloodstream—into everything. I could still feel the dampness between my thighs, but there was no room for shame.

My Inferno family was in danger.

And I was the only one who could stop it.

I took a single step toward the door—

BOOM!

The door shook under the force of a kick, the handle rattling violently.

"Get the fuck out here, Cass! Now!"

His rage was rising. If I didn't comply, he'd start shooting again.

With shaking fingers, I twisted the lock. The second it clicked, the door flew open, the force knocking me backward. I slammed into the curtain, cleaning supplies crashing—

Exposing Candy.

She screamed.

My eyes widened in horror.

Declan sneered.

Our gazes locked as he aimed the gun at her.

Without breaking eye contact, he pulled the trigger.

The shot exploded through the space. My ears rang so hard I thought my skull might split open. Time slowed as my eyes followed the bullet's path.

Candy's body jerked.

Blood splattered across the wall, the mop bucket—some of it on me.

She crumpled. Lifeless.

Her beautiful face frozen in fear against the wall she'd knelt beside. Permanently.

Before I could process it, rough hands seized me. I hissed as he yanked me upright, fingers fisting my hair. My vision blurred, sound cutting in and out as he dragged me into the blinding lights of the upturned dressing room.

The first thing I saw—

Dimitri.

Slumped against the lockers.

Blood oozed from his side, from his mouth, as he wheezed.

His regretful eyes met mine. "Sorry," he coughed, blood spilling from his lips as my heart sank.

Declan laughed mockingly. "You fucked him too, you fucking slut?" He yanked my hair again, forcing my gaze back to him.

"I didn't Dec! Please stop, I need to help him." My voice was full of urgency, he jerked my head back to Dimitri making sure I watched him die slowly. He had become a part of the Inferno family, a part of my small world. All our short talks during my breaks here, or when he escorted me around. The laugh he made when I would say a good one liner to Leo. It all seemed to fade away along with the light in his eyes.

Declan jolted me forward, causing my neck to whip around too fast and create a pinching feeling that radiated up to my brain. "You're not helping anyone, if anything, this is your fucking fault Cass." He tsked with his disappointment in me. Like he truly believed that I was the reason he stormed this place, that I personally forced his hand and the hand of his other goons to shoot my friends, my family.

Shock consumed me as my hands clutched his wrist, trying to ease the pain at my scalp. But I deserved more than this physical pain, because this was entirely my fault, all because I fell in love with the wrong person, and didn't listen to the one man who had my best interest in mind.

Tears poured freely.

Fear wracked my body.

My friends were dying.

The people I cared about were dying.

And it was all my fault.

"Come on," Declan sneered. "I'm taking you home."

Disgust twisted his features as he dragged me forward, making sure I saw every body—every person injured, dying, or dead.

The smell of gasoline filled the air.

Soft, broken whimpers echoed from the girls trapped inside.

As we stepped into the sunset, the city bathed in the most beautiful golden light I'd ever seen—cruel humor only Karma could manage—I knew one thing for certain.

My martyrdom didn't save a single fucking soul inside Inferno. It doomed them.

EPISODE 9

*C*assandra

Shifting, the clanking of my chains felt heavy on my limbs, making them numb and unbearably cold. Every part of me ached, and my breaths rattled in my chest. Maybe this was Hell. I was a sinner, after all. And after watching Dimitri and Candy die because of me, and seeing the entire facility go up in flames—murdering the people trapped inside—I deserved every ounce of this pain.

Their faces before they died haunted me. The way Dimitri had looked at me—his normally hardened, handsome features softened by something almost unrecognizable. Regret. The helpless, fearful expressions on the girls who were tied up and bloody in the hallway, caught mid-sprint for the exit.

And Candy… fuck.

The pained flash of her eyes as she screamed, just before her brains splattered across the wall behind her. I shivered at the memory, my eyes squeezing shut as if I could physically will the visual out of my mind. God, she had only just regained some semblance of freedom after her ex was imprisoned. In death, she was freer than most.

Fuck, that was dark.

I hissed as I curled into a fetal position on the concrete floor, my ribs screaming in protest. They were definitely broken. A slow, shaky breath escaped me as another wave of guilt and agony crashed over me. But my eyes were dry. I had cried all I could.

After arriving here hours ago, I had shed every tear possible. I was dehydrated and throbbing in every limb. Declan hadn't gone easy on me. The moment he threw me down here, he whaled on me with fists and feet, screaming about how pathetic and worthless I was, how I had betrayed him by staying at Leo's, and running my mouth. I tried to explain that I wasn't getting his messages, that they had hacked my phone, and threatened me if I didn't tell them everything but that only fueled his anger like lighter fluid.

He was trying to break me.

"Those girls burned alive because of you. If you didn't spread your legs for every rich prick that walked past you, this wouldn't have had to happen!"
Thud!
His boot connected with my ribs again, sending blood flying from my mouth as I tried to crawl away. My arms gave out beneath me, and I collapsed, instinctively curling up to shield my head and face.
A sharp yank on my scalp.
Crack!
Pain exploded in my skull as he slammed my head against the cement floor. White and black spots swarmed behind my swollen lids. I prayed I would be able to recover from this.
"D-Declan," I rasped through the blood in my mouth. "Please… stop." I was so tired. So fucking tired.
For the first time, he listened—but not before he spit on me. He left me there, sprawled on the cold ground, either to die slowly or to wait until he decided to finish me off. The clang of the cell door echoed through the suffocating silence.

I was certain this miniature prison was beneath Finnegan's estate, which was hard to process since I had lived here for a year and never knew. Every night, I could smell when they had dinner. The memories of my time here tormented me—the home-cooked meals, the laughter, the idea of family.

The McCalisters.

And tonight was no different.

Slow, deliberate footsteps prowled down the stone steps. I curled in tighter, protectively, the chains scraping on the ground. I couldn't open my eyes—not out of fear, but because the swelling had forced them shut.

"Hello, Cass." A slow purr, dangerously close. My stomach twisted. If there had been anything in it, I would have hurled. But I haven't eaten anything since dinner at Leo's. "You look stunning."

With a shaky, filthy hand, I lifted a middle finger in his direction.

He chuckled. "Still as feisty as ever."

The cell door groaned open, and the scent of Declan's cologne filled my senses—like a living nightmare instead of how it used to make me feel. At home. He crouched in front of me. Rough hands clamped around my arm, yanking me up, and rattling the chains taut. A scream tore from my throat as my body protested, pain lancing through every nerve. His other hand gripped my jaw tightly.

"You might not be able to open your eyes," he murmured, his breath fanning over my face and smelling of whiskey, "so I want you to listen carefully."

My breaths came in rapid, shallow gasps. A slick sheen of sweat clung to my skin, mixing with filth, blood, and the rancid stench of me urinating. Any humiliation around it had left the moment I could only focus on the nonstop stabbing pains in my sides and face.

"Tonight will be your last fucking night on this earth." He leaned in closer, his lips brushing against the shell of my ear. "I'm going to treat you so good, baby."

Tonight? That meant it had to be morning by now. Leo must know what had happened to me. Fuck, I knew I didn't deserve to be saved, but a small part of me still hoped he would come to my rescue.

His tongue flicked against my skin, and a violent shudder ripped through me. My empty stomach heaved.

Declan laughed. "Then I'm going to fucking kill you. And the best part?" He paused, savoring it. "Leo will get this precious head of yours as a little present."

I whimpered, trying to push away, but I was weak.

Declan yanked me closer, dragging me into a mockingly gentle embrace. My body stiffened in excruciating protest, but he shushed me, stroking my matted hair.

"I'll be sure to paint your face nice and pretty with my fucking cum before I send you off. No need to worry."

His maniacal laughter sent bile crawling up my throat again—but this time I actually vomited what little liquid I had left all over him.

"Fucking bitch!" He shoved me backward, my skull cracking against the bars with a sickening *thwak*. A final slap sent me sprawling onto the cold, unwelcoming floor.

The cell door slammed shut.

Declan's footsteps stormed away, his curses echoing down the hall before his furious voice called out to someone, "Clean that bitch up— she smells of piss and shit!"

The sound of the chains scraping as I balled up again on the floor, paired with the continuous drip of water somewhere nearby, echoed through the now-empty space.

The one word I managed to whisper came out like a desperate prayer.

"Leo…"

Leo

My head snapped back as I hit the ropes, the impact knocking the wind from my lungs. Across from me, Ciro bounced on his feet, a cocky grin stretched across his blood-streaked face. The open cuts on his brow, bloody nose, and swollen lower lip made him look like Rocky Balboa after a match.

I swiped the back of my hand across my mouth, dark red smearing over my olive skin. I had built this ring specifically for when I needed to relieve stress, and Ciro was always my sparring partner when he was free from doing my dirty work. When he wasn't available, Dimitri was more than happy to throw a few punches. But he was dead now—

just like half the girls from Inferno. My jaw clenched, and I let the pain seep into me, distract me from the other emotions I didn't want to face just yet.

"Again," I snapped, pushing off the ropes and raising my fists.

Ciro laughed like a maniac, mirroring my stance. He wasn't enjoying the reason we were in the boxing ring—no—but he did enjoy pain. A masochist through and through. Ever since we started boxing at ten years old, he had fallen in love with the art of fighting. He craved a challenge, and I was the only one at his level.

We circled each other, my rage fueling every movement. Lunging forward, I threw a jab. Ciro weaved right, sliding in to thrust an uppercut. Anticipating his move, I pivoted and struck the side of his head with my elbow.

Ciro grunted. "Fuck. Is that it? You could've easily followed that with an uppercut to my chin, brother." He shook his head in disappointment. "Or is your mind still on Cassandra and how she's probably fucking dead?"

"Fuck you!"

The words tore from my throat, raw and guttural. I attacked faster, hitting him with combo after combo. I knew he was just trying to help me release the anger and frustration I had pent up. But his methods were brutal and heartless. He knew I loved Cassandra—I had told him how I felt when we drove to the warehouse the night she went into work with Dimitri.

Ciro only laughed, dodging, blocking, taking a few hits in vulnerable spots. Then, with a front kick, I sent him flying into the corner.

"That's enough," I muttered between heavy breaths.

Ripping off my knuckle guards, I tossed them to the ground. "Ciro, I can't stop thinking about her. I know she isn't dead, but if we wait any longer, she will be."

I leaned against the ropes, arms crossed over the top, my head falling onto my forearms. Deep inhales. Shaky exhales. *amore mio* had been gone for twelve hours, and I knew I was running out of time. If we didn't act soon, I'd never fucking see her again. And that was an unforgivable thought—because I couldn't wait another lifetime for her. My soul needed her now.

A loud clap landed on my bare back, the sound sharp against my damp skin.

"Our men are ready to go tonight," Ciro confirmed, his voice void of its usual amusement. Almost empathetic. It made me lift my head, peering at him through sweat-slick strands of hair. I normally wouldn't let myself look defeated, weak, and wounded. But I trusted Ciro, and I couldn't stop the fracture in my chest from widening.

The guilt I felt—my stupidity. I should have never caved to Cassandra's demands or Dimitri's suggestion. If I had held firm and not let my emotions for her get in the way, one of them would still be alive, and the other would be in my arms.

"Good." I swallowed, my throat thick with emotion.

Ciro dipped his chin, gripping my shoulder and pulling me upright. "Come on. Let's get some food in you. You'll need your strength for when we go kill those motherfuckers."

Nodding mindlessly, I followed him out of the ring.

FINDING out that Inferno had been infiltrated while I was busy with other business burrowed under my skin, filling me with a rage so potent it scorched my soul.

His last message wasn't a threat to her, but to me.

You fucked with the wrong property, Romano.

He had always been a loose cannon, and storming the place with a full army of Irish, despite knowing it could escalate the war, only confirmed it. Dimitri was dead, along with the other men who had gone with him.

The girls we found in the wreckage? We didn't even know if they were dead before or after the fire. I'd never know. Their bodies were nothing but ash and a few bones. My dirty cops confirmed that Vinnie had been on his way through their street cameras when the event happened. He was devastated—the poor bastard loved those girls like his own daughters.

I had to reach out to the Russians myself. Inform Aleksander that we were moving tonight and prepare for any aftermath. We had an agreement that he would take in Rowan, Maeve, and Abigail whether they wanted to go or not. I honestly didn't give a shit about them, but my little *topo* had a kind heart, and I'd made a promise to her.

We were also preparing to split Irish turf after the war was over, so Aleksander had no qualms about me ending Finnegan and Declan's reign early.

My jaw clenched. My hands curled into fists. Ciro gestured for me to sit at the sleek black bar stool, but the pristine, modern kitchen only agitated me further. I slammed my fists against the granite, rattling the décor and knocking a few items to the floor.

"Having a temper tantrum isn't going to change the fact that she's in that fucking basement at the McCalister mansion," Ciro said calmly, yanking open the fridge and rummaging through it.

Gio entered, standing stoically at the kitchen's entrance. He didn't speak—just waited to be addressed. He was taking Dimitri's loss harder than any of us. They were cousins after all.

I jerked my chin and rose. "Come here."

His black boots thudded with each purposeful step. My arms pulled him into a tight embrace before I released him and held his shoulders firmly.

Gio sniffed, trying to get himself together. "I just heard from Nico. The soldiers are ready, we're just waiting for our inside man to give us the information we need."

Grinding my teeth, I dipped my chin, dropping my hands to my sides and shoving them into my pockets.

Ciro grunted in approval. He already knew. He turned on the stove, cracking eggs into a bowl and tossing in chopped vegetables. "You hungry, Gio?" he asked over his shoulder.

"Sit," I ordered, motioning to the stool beside me. I left no room for argument.

Gio moved with ease, his broad shoulders brushing mine as he settled into the seat.

Running a hand through my damp hair, I sighed. "Any beers in the fridge, Ciro?"

Ciro set the bowl down, grabbed three beers, and twisted off the caps with ease. He slid them in front of us.

I lifted mine.

"To Dimitri. And the poor *bellas* we lost at Inferno." My voice tightened as I fought back the burn in my eyes.

"D was a good man," Gio murmured. "A cousin. A friend. A father."

Dimitri was a good dad to two kids, even if he and his woman weren't together anymore. He spent every waking moment outside of his duties to me with them and paid for anything his girl asked for, even when some of the demands were ridiculous.

Ciro dipped his chin. "He was a fucking terrible poker player, but the funniest bastard I'd ever met. Besides me, of course."

A small, sad chuckle left Gio and me.

We clinked our bottles together and took long pulls, the silence between us heavy with unspoken memories of Dimitri.

Ciro continued cooking, the scent of eggs filling the air. But all I could taste was the tension—the weight of the coming war.

Gio's voice was full of sympathy as he spoke directly to me. "She's a fighter. Full of piss and vinegar." He gave me a sad smile, one I returned. "We'll get her back… alive."

Fuck, I hoped so—because if we didn't, the fucking Irish were going to pay for it in more than blood. I would find a way to resurrect them over and over again just to kill them slowly, until they begged the angel of death to destroy their souls.

Cassandra

The faint, familiar scent of fresh linen and scotch stirred me from a pain-induced slumber, my body unable to handle anything more than what it had already endured. The cold, damp floor beneath me sent a dull ache through my limbs, its unforgiving surface pressing against my battered bones. A faint flicker of candlelight danced against the stone walls, casting shadows that made the cell feel even more haunted.

A draft slipped through the door at the top of the basement steps, sending a shiver through my already frozen body. Rats skittered in the corners, their tiny claws scraping against the cement, reminding me I wasn't alone in this hellhole. My head pounded with each weak beat of my heart, my breathing shallow as I struggled to stay present.

"Lass, wake up."

The sweet, elderly voice coaxed me from the abyss—gentle, yet firm.

My swollen eyes cracked open through the crust that had formed there, my vision blurring against the dim lighting. I forced my cracked lips to part, my throat raw from dehydration.

"Finnegan?" The sound of my voice was hoarse, barely above a whisper.

A brief sense of relief and hope washed over me. He was here. This man—who had once been like a father to me—had finally come. He hated when Declan beat me. I knew it. He'd always protected me before. My freshly cleaned fingers—from the creep who had roughly scrubbed me and redressed me in sweats and a baggy shirt—reached for him, trembling.

But then I remembered this was different, they found out I ratted them out. He wasn't my savior anymore, he was my enemy.

He stepped back.

My hand dropped to the cold floor as I tried to push myself upright, my body screaming in protest. I managed to get halfway up, my bleary gaze lifting to meet his. His features—once weathered with warmth—looked sharper now. Harsher. The ice-blue of his eyes, so much like Declan's, had lost all familiarity.

I didn't know this man.

"You're in a heap of shit, lass." His voice was cold, his narrowed gaze slicing through me like a blade.

"Finne—"

He cut me off. "Save your last breaths, you traitorous wench." He spat, the thick glob landing on my face, the crude gesture making me flinch.

Humiliation burned through me, the heat of it stark against my frozen skin.

"I came to say goodbye," he continued, his wrinkled hands clenching at his sides. "You were like a daughter to me... once."

The betrayal in his rigid posture made my stomach sink.

"Please, Finnegan, I didn't have a choice." My voice cracked, desperate, pleading. "But I—I asked them to spare your wife and daughters."

I had tried.

I had done everything I could.

His eyes darkened. "You're a rat." His voice was thick with disgust, and before I could react, his boot connected with my collarbone.

A sickening crack echoed through the cell.

Pain detonated through my chest, radiating down my arm and into my neck. A strangled scream tore from my throat as I collapsed, clutching the useless limb, my body convulsing from the impact.

"I'm so sorry, Finn," I choked out, though my eyes remained dry—no liquid left to shed. My head throbbed in sync with my fractured bones, my body drowning in agony.

I never thought my life would end like this.

A lifetime ago—when I was fresh out of an abusive relationship with an ex-con who had nearly killed me—I thought my suffering was over. Until Declan found me in an alley behind a dumpster, where my piece-of-shit ex had left me to die from a stab wound. He carried me to the McCalister estate, where Finnegan and Abigail called in their family doctor.

They let me rest.

They let me heal.

Declan stayed by my side the entire time.

Back then, I hadn't known he was a monster. But that's what narcissistic psychos do. They love-bomb you, ensnaring you in a web of lies. And by the time you're too deep to escape, they strip away the mask—revealing the monster beneath.

The year I spent with the McCalisters had been a dream. Or so I tricked myself into believing. I thought I would marry Declan one day. I thought I was happy.

It had never been all rainbows and happy endings. Being down here for probably more than twelve hours had been a nightmare—one that felt never-ending. And when I wasn't being tortured by Declan or his men, I had time to think back on the year I believed this place was a haven. I finally saw the cracks. The Frankensteined memories I stitched together to convince myself Declan wasn't as bad as my other boyfriends—most importantly, that he wasn't like my dad.

I was fucking wrong.

Finnegan exhaled sharply, shaking his head. "Save your apologies for God, you wretched whore. I curse you and your soul. I hope you rot in hell."

The venom in his words stung worse than any of my injuries. Then, without another glance, he turned and left, his footsteps fading into the distance, leaving me alone in the cold, rotting cell.

I lay there once again, consumed by the shame, the guilt, the self-loathing that had been festering.

How could I deny it?

I *was* a traitor.

I *was* a whore.

Not only had I let Leo touch me, but Ciro as well. I had outed the McCalisters to save my own skin. I was selfish. I was pathetic. And my actions had cost the lives of my Inferno family—and Dimitri.

My stomach twisted under the weight of my thoughts. Leaning over, I dry-heaved onto the cell floor, my body too weak to even purge the sickness inside me.

EPISODE 10

E pisode 10
Cassandra

The smell of dampness and coppered air made me think of the last moments I spent with Mama when I was a teen.

Her cold fingers clutching my arm like a warm blanket as I held her limp head, blood dripping profusely near her temple and onto the old off white carpet, staining it this deep crimson color. My dad had been arrested multiple times for battery and spousal abuse, but they never held him long. He always came out more aggressive, and each time he came home, Mama was always just a hair's breadth away from death.

A glance around told me she had fought this time—furniture tipped, the corner of the coffee table smeared with red splatter. She never retaliated, which told me she knew this time was going to be different. And knowing Mama, she had been thinking of me—how she couldn't leave me alone with the unhinged man she married out of convenience. Next to the door was the go-bag we had packed when I was just a kid, its contents raided and spread haphazardly across the entry, the door wide open, letting in the sound of cicadas and heavy humidity.

As I stared into her fading eyes, I knew she wasn't going to make it before the ambulance got here. He had known it too—ran the moment she fell, he left her lying there for her to die alone or for me to find her and clean up his mess. I didn't even process the tears sliding down my face until her shaky hand reached up, covered in blood, and swiped them away.

"Sempre e per sempre, amore mio." Her voice was raspy and wet. A soft cough came from her, and I choked back a sob as blood trickled from the corner of her lips.

I gripped her hand with my free one, pressing a kiss to the back of it. "Mama, I am so sorry. I wish—"

"Non permetterti di portare questo peso." She coughed again, her deep green irises dulling, lids blinking slower.

A weak, pathetic smile twitched at the corners of my lips. I didn't care what my mother said. I would always carry this weight—that maybe I could have done more, that maybe if I had been home, I could have saved her life…again.

The sound of sirens in the distance echoed—everything did in the countryside of North Carolina. And no doubt our small town would know what happened and keep their heads down like they always did. No one was willing to protect us, not with my father's old family influence. Mama and I were alone here, completely and utterly helpless to a monster who used his fists against the weak and his words against the strong.

The moment—a breath that came too late, lingered too long, a pause after the rattle that stretched…longer…longer…until her body remained still. The wail that burst from me didn't sound like me; whoever was making that broken sound made my heart weigh so heavy with such a deep sorrow that I wasn't sure I would be able to swim back to the surface. That's when I felt myself out of my body, looking down at the scene of me clutching her body to my chest, rocking her as if I could somehow wake her up—bring the only woman who had ever protected and loved me back to me, because I didn't want to think about how hopelessly alone I was without her.

Loud footsteps thundered down the stairs, sounding like the distant warning before a storm actually strikes. My mind was foggy, my body numb from the amount of pain I had endured, and my heart…that was in shambles.

"Get up! Get the fuck up now, Cass!"

Declan's voice ripped through the suffocating silence, sharp and venomous. The cell door was already open. They didn't even bother locking it. After Declan had his goon clean me up hey didn't even chain me up. Not when I was too battered to run, too weak to fight, and close to succumbing to the inevitable end waiting for me.

A fist tangled into my matted black hair and yanked me to my feet. A scream tore from my throat, similar to the one I gave that night, but this was for me—for this half-life I had been condemned to. Agony exploded through my ribs, my collarbone grinding in protest as he dragged me upright.

"Fuck, Declan! I'll come!" I rasped, my voice hoarse, barely carrying. My trembling fingers clawed at his grip, but he only tightened his hold, making sure I felt every ounce of his control.

He released me with a violent shove, only to seize my shoulders, dragging me in close. His breath, hot and acrid with whiskey, fanned over my cheek. "I sent a beautiful photo to your little Italian lover," he spat, his lips grazing my ear.

I stiffened, nausea curling in my gut.

His fingers slid through my tangled hair, brushing it back like a lover's touch. Mocking. Cruel. "Made sure he knew exactly who you belonged to."

Declan straightened, his grip shifting to the back of my neck. He squeezed—tight, punishing. White-hot pain shot up my spine as the broken bones in my clavicle ground together.

I sucked in a sharp breath, my teeth clenching against the scream threatening to rip free. He chuckled darkly at my pain. His hand on the back of my neck didn't loosen as he forced me up the stairs without a care. I was starting to feel that familiar sensation of leaving my body, that floating dissociation that almost felt like freedom.

We stepped into the main house, and the sudden shift in atmosphere made my stomach twist in on itself like a jolt. The stark contrast between the dungeon's cold, damp rot and the polished opulence of the mansion I once called home made me feel filthier—undeserving.

The high ceilings, the pristine marble floors, the lingering scent of expensive cigars and aged whiskey—it was all so surreal, like I had stepped into a dream I no longer belonged in.

Be small, Cassandra. Just stay small.

Declan knew I felt it.

He straightened his shoulders, rolling them back with satisfaction. He was parading me now, like a fucking trophy. My head hung, and I allowed my hair to fall in front of my face, shielding the shame that burned my cheeks and neck like fire licking at my skin.

As we passed through the grand hall, I caught glimpses of movement. More foot soldiers than I'd ever seen there. They scrambled, boots squeaking on the marble floors, the clicking of their chambers ricocheting off the high ceilings as they checked their weapons. Orders barked into phones from all directions, disorienting.

The beehive had been kicked.

Something was coming.

Declan's grip on my neck tightened painfully, jerking me forward. He picked up the pace, his steps more erratic. His paranoia was seeping through the cracks now—jaw locked, nostrils flared, shoulders rigid.

If I'd had more energy, if it had been anyone else with their claws in the back of my neck, I might have asked what was going on. But honestly, what was the point anyway? Karma and fate had my life planned out already...and I had always been meant to have the ending of a tragic story.

We climbed the grand staircase, his movements growing rougher, more frantic. Every hurried step sent fresh waves of agony through my battered body. I'd never seen him that frazzled. I'd seen him angry, sad, worried even—but this kind of unraveling wasn't like him.

Something was coming.

Declan shouldered his bedroom door open, the wood crashing into the light-blue painted wall and deepening the hole already there, then threw me inside. I stumbled forward, my body screaming in protest. My arms wrapped around my ribs as I sucked in a shallow, ragged breath.

"Move to the bed."

I hesitated, my eyes darting between him and the neatly made bed. Each shallow breath made every nerve ending feel like an individual knife.

The king-sized bed loomed like a guillotine. I could still smell his cologne lingering in the air, clogging my sinuses.

My gaze snapped back to Declan.

His eyes gleamed with something unhinged—fury and hunger. The kind of twisted look only a maniac wears when he knows he has nothing left to lose.

"Now!" he roared.

Flinching, I forced my legs to move, my body trembling as I approached the bed. I stood facing it, refusing to turn back.

I didn't want to see it coming.

Didn't want to look into his eyes when he killed me.

The heat of his body pressed against my back, my stomach sinking. His hands hovered over my shoulders, tracing down my arms until they reached my waist. His grip tightened. Hard.

At another time, I would have melted under his touch.

But when he touched me this time—

Revulsion crawled through my skin like insects, bile rising in my throat. My body rejected this, every nerve screaming in protest.

"Here's what's going to happen, Cass." His voice was low, thick with something far worse than anger. "You're going to let me fuck you one last time, and you're going to take it like a good girl." His thumbs pressed into my hips as he yanked me closer. His nose brushed my hair, his breath ghosting over my ear.

I gagged, my stomach flipping violently, but I had nothing left to purge.

"Show some fucking appreciation," he growled.

Then—

Gunfire. Just outside. Close.

The sharp, rapid crack-crack-crack of automatic weapons rang through the night.

Shouting. Screaming. Barked orders.

The mansion was under attack.

Declan's hold tightened instantly. His fingers twisted into my hair, slamming my face into the mattress.

Pain detonated through my skull. My collarbone was a cracked, brittle twig, pain climbing into my throat and cutting off my breath. My body arched in protest, my lungs burning like I'd swallowed fire.

The sheets felt endless as I clawed at them, struggling, my limbs flailing. Panic flared. Survival kicked in, adrenaline masking the worst of the pain.

Declan shoved me down harder, kicking my legs apart.

More gunshots—closer now.

Fabric tore as he sliced through my sweatpants. A cool breeze brushed my thighs. I thrashed, but my vision swam, black spots flashing behind my eyes. My chest tightened as oxygen slipped away.

"Stop fighting, Cass!"

Declan's voice sounded distant now, warped by the ringing in my ears.

My limbs grew heavy. My arms wouldn't move. My legs went numb. And then the memories came.

First, Candy's sweet, high-pitched voice. *"Angel, you know us girls at Inferno are always on your side. No matter what."* Her too-white smile flashed as she leaned in. *"We'd help you bury a body—as long as it didn't ruin my nails."*

Then Dimitri's brown eyes, that arrogant smirk he wore every time he was about to win at checkers when we played in the library on Wednesdays. A tradition we started after he caught me digging for information on Leo and Ciro—which I never did find.

My body relaxed.

I saw myself beneath Declan, like an angel or a haunting ghost watching from above. Then Leo's rumbling Italian accent filled me with fragile peace. *"Principessa, I'll always protect you, no matter what it costs me. You're mine. Sempre e per sempre."*

"Finally," I heard Declan murmur into my ear. "Gonna fuck you to death," he whispered, laughing. "And send the video to Leo."

It felt like having a front-row seat to my final moments and saying goodbye to my future escape to Florida. Sort of fucked up. I wondered if this was how everyone experienced their death, because if it was, I planned on filing a complaint with the higher-ups.

A roar.

The door slammed open.

A gunshot.

The world tipped into silence.

Then—nothing.

Leo

Our men had already stormed the McCalister mansion. They looked like an agitated ant nest—drones crawling out from every part of the estate while the masked soldiers of my mob gunned them down like special ops.

Ciro trained our *soldatos* alongside Nico, just as my father had trained us, and his father before him. We come from a long, blood-soaked lineage of fighters dating back to Roman soldiers. It's not just in our blood—it *is* our blood. I wear that legacy like armor. It gives us our edge, our code, our ruthlessness. It's why we dominate and why our enemies fall. We don't just go to war—we conquer. And it's why my men moved like a damn symphony of destruction through this place, swift and clean, cutting down anyone in our path.

As soon as Nico, Ciro, Gio, and I jumped from the SUV, the stifling Chicago humidity of the evening mingled with the chaos erupting around us. Cocking our guns in sync, we held them chest level, angled down and primed to shoot. We were ready for anything.

The three of them covered my back as I plowed through the crowd with one goal—to retrieve *amore mio*. She had suffered enough at the hands of these bastards, and I'd never forgive myself for the unnecessary pain I'd brought into her life. Cassandra had started as an obsession, but she'd become something more—someone. Someone fate had shoved into my path, a blessing to counteract the underground criminal life I lived.

She was an angel—one the demons fed on but never protected.

Me? I was her Archangel, willing to fight through hell to bring her to safety.

POP! POP!

Nameless faces crumpled before me like deflating inflatable tube men. My shots were precise, ruthless, fueled by fury. Nobody was stopping me from getting to her. My gun was hot in my hand, and I gripped it tighter the moment my tactical boots hit dirt and blood-stained marble.

I had only a few seconds to scan the area. That's when I spotted a seriously wounded Irish member slumped against the wall near the staircase. I moved with purpose, grabbed his blood-soaked shirt with my free hand, and yanked him closer to my face.

"Where is Cassandra?" I snarled, my eyes flicking between his darkening ones as death slowly pulled him under.

He coughed—blood splattered across my bulletproof vest. "Fuck you," he rasped, his accent thick.

I shook him hard. "You're already a dead man, motherfucker. Just tell me where she is."

His eyes rolled back, losing the fight. I gave him one more shake before tossing his limp body against the wall. "Fuck!" I growled, my jaw clenched tight.

"She's upstairs!" Ciro called from another room.

My eyes locked on the staircase and I charged without hesitation, kicking in door after door. I wouldn't rest until she was in my arms, under my protection. Once she was safe, I'd never let her out of my sight.

Ever. Again.

The last door on the right.

My boot connected with the door and it flew open. That's when I saw her—half-naked, bent over the bed, face smashed into the mattress. Declan's cock was out, primed to thrust into her.

I roared.

Without hesitation, I pulled the trigger. Time slowed as the bullet tore into his neck, blood spurting in every direction. He clutched at the wound and collapsed to the floor, near Cassandra's limp body passed out on the bed.

I stomped forward, gun aimed at his fucking head.

"As much as I wish I could torture you nice and slow, I'll take solace in knowing your cock will never come near *amore mio* again." My voice was tight, cold, full of deadly promise.

Declan tried to speak, only to gurgle and choke on the blood pooling in his throat. But I saw the defiance still burning in his ice-blue eyes.

Still trying to win.

Sick of the sight of him, I pulled the trigger. The bullet tore through the center of his eyes and out the back of his skull.

A slow grin spread across my face.

That was for her.

Then I turned.

Cassandra was still bent over the bed, unmoving.

My gut twisted into a knot. I moved fast, yanking a sheet from the dead asshole's bed. Wrapping her up, I took her in—really took her in —and my stomach bottomed out. Her face was swollen, bruised, nearly unrecognizable. Her body was limp and broken, from the photo he sent me I knew I had to be gentle. I brought my fingers to her pulse point on her neck and nearly collapsed with relief. She was unconscious, but alive.

I scooped her up bridal-style, holding her like glass, and carried her from the room. Ciro waited in the hallway. His dark, murderous gaze softened the moment he saw her.

"Let's go," I forced out. My voice scraped past my throat like it didn't belong to me. My eyes flicked between her broken face and the hall ahead. The gunfire below still echoed—but it was thinning out, the last gasps of a war we'd already won.

When we hit the pavement outside, my grip on her tightened. The closer we got to the bulletproof black SUV, the more anxious I became. I needed her safe. Needed her far from this nightmare.

Gunshots cracked behind us.

Pain exploded through my left side.

Fire bloomed where Cassandra's body had shifted my vest just enough to leave me exposed. The impact stole my breath, but I didn't fall. I wouldn't. I held her tighter, refused to go down with her in my arms.

"Die, ye guido bastard!" Finnegan's rough voice shouted behind me.

Ciro spun.

One shot.

That was all he needed.

I didn't look back. I didn't have to. Finnegan was dead. Ciro was at my side a second later, helping me carry Cassandra the rest of the way to the truck.

"Leo, want me to hold her?" he asked as we climbed in.

I hissed, pain ripping through me with every breath. I knew a vital organ had taken the hit. I could feel the warmth of blood soaking through my clothes, pulsing out of me like time running out.

"No!" I snapped.

Nico and Gio piled into the front seats.

"Drive the fucking car. *Now!*" I barked, urgency snarling in my throat like an animal ready to tear its way free.

Cassandra

My vision was blurry as I blinked my eyes open slowly. My limbs felt heavy, and my hearing flickered in and out like a dying signal. A raspy groan slipped from my lips as I tried to move my arm, and the sharp prick of needles and the tangle of tubes stopped me.

"Try not to move, Ms. Bennett," a soft female voice came from my right.

It took effort as I turned my head slowly, my vision clearing just enough to make out a pale, freckled woman with strawberry-blonde hair tied back into a tight bun. She looked middle-aged, calm, and efficient. The sun was low, casting a backdrop of light that made her look like an angel.

I must've looked confused because she added gently, "My name is Stacey. You're at the Romano estate, being treated for some serious injuries." Her warm smile crinkled the corners of her eyes, showing her age.

"How—" I coughed, my voice dry and rough. "How long have I been here?"

Stacey, who I assumed was a hired nurse, handed me a plastic cup of chilled water. I took it gratefully, swishing it around my mouth to fight off the desert that had taken residence in my throat.

"Four days now," she said as she took the cup back and set it on the nightstand. She moved to check my IVs, and only then did I fully notice them. "We're treating you for three broken ribs, a fractured collarbone, and two hairline fractures in your skull." Her warm hands adjusted the straps on my immobilized arm. "You'll need to take it easy. You're on pain management, but your injuries were quite serious."

"Stacey. Where's Leo?" I asked, scanning the bedroom I recognized as the one I'd been using before I was taken.

A familiar voice filled the doorway. "What, you don't want to see me?"

My head whipped toward the door, and I immediately hissed at the sharp pain that shot through my side.

"Easy," Stacey scolded gently as she checked the bandages on my face like a fussing mother hen.

"Ciro! Where's Leo?" I asked urgently. Stacey helped me shift upright despite the pain. I couldn't lie there like a corpse when asking about him—I needed to see him.

He felt like home, he was home, my home.

Ciro chuckled, but the sound was strained. He muttered something in Italian that I didn't catch, my brain still foggy with meds and pain. "He's… resting," he finally answered, his voice low and somber. His gaze shifted to the floor, avoiding mine.

My brows furrowed. "What does that mean?" Worry crawled up my spine and into my chest like barbed wire.

Ciro exhaled slowly and signaled for the nurse to give us a moment. He sat on the edge of the bed near my legs, placing a hand gently on my knee. The gesture was meant to be comforting, but it only made my stomach clench. My eyes searched his, like I could steal the answers straight from his brain.

"*Bella*, you need to understand what happened that night we found you." His gray eyes flicked between mine, serious and dark, and the unease in my gut began to curdle into something colder. "Our crew infiltrated the McCalisters. A few of our men died, some injured. Only a handful of the Irish got away." His thumb rubbed over the blanket in slow, grounding circles on my knee—it felt more for him than for me. "We kept our promise. Abigail and her daughters are alive. Declan and Finnegan are dead. *Una benedizione*," he muttered under his breath.

A blessing, indeed. After what those bastards did to me, I hoped they were rotting in hell already. I never thought I would feel that way about Finnegan or Declan, but they had been worse than I ever imagined possible.

"What about Leo?" I pushed, my hands gripping the sheets at my sides. The beeping on the heart monitor increased a fraction.

Ciro nodded slowly. "On our way out, Finnegan…" He swallowed hard, and I already knew what he was going to say. "He shot Leo in the left side—hit his kidney and pancreas."

My breath caught. My eyes widened as I tried to sit up straighter. A spike of pain lanced through my ribs mixing with the burning protective anger pulsing in my heart. I cried out softly, clutching my ribs with my free arm. If I could bring them back to life and murder them myself I would, good fucking riddance to those assholes.

"Cassandra, please. Be careful." Ciro held out a hand to steady me. "Leo's stable. He's strong. But… he's been unconscious for four days. Just like you."

"I need to see him. Now!" I threw the blankets off my legs in a panic, the heart monitor screaming its urgency.

Ciro grabbed me gently but firmly. "Hey! No, you don't. You're in no condition to be walking around."

"Then carry me, Ciro," I demanded. My voice was steel, even as my eyes stung with fresh tears. If Leo was seriously hurt after saving me, I had to see him. I needed to see him. I owed him everything for saving my pathetic life, one that had escaped death more times than it deserved.

I'd grown to care for Leo more than I ever expected. He wasn't just some mafia asshole. He protected me. Saw me. Respected what I wanted. I trusted him with my life, and I knew he'd never hurt me. He'd proven that over and over again, especially when I pushed him past his limits.

Tears welled in my eyes. "Please, Ciro," I choked out, my lip trembling fiercely.

He looked at me, and to my surprise, empathy flashed across his face—something I never thought Ciro was capable of. The man was a certified psycho on most days. But not at that moment. He seemed like a normal human being—a worried cousin, a compassionate friend. It made my heart warm, and more tears spilled free.

"Stacey, come in here, please," Ciro called out, his eyes never leaving mine.

The nurse rushed in, her brows furrowed as she scanned me, trying to assess the situation—no doubt worried about the heart monitor's alarms and my tear-stricken face.

"Yes, sir?"

"Can you help me move Cassandra to Leo's room? She'll continue treatment at his side." His tone left no room for argument.

Stacey hesitated, worry flickering across her expression as she took in my fragile state, but she didn't protest. "I'll get a wheelchair and increase her pain medication. It should be enough without causing further injury." She disappeared to prepare for the move.

When Ciro, two nurses, and the on-site doctor settled me onto Leo's massive bed, I broke.

Ugly tears.

Leo had a breathing mask over his face, shirtless, with clean bandages wrapped around his torso. He looked peaceful—but help-less. I hated it. Hated seeing him like this. This was my fucking fault. I had to go into work, had to defy Leo at every turn just to prove a point. And there he was—my Italian hero.

The room was dimly lit, the soft amber glow of a bedside lamp casting long shadows across the floor. A portable heart monitor beeped steadily near the window, its wires trailing toward the head of the bed like lifelines. The faint antiseptic scent mixed with the deeper, familiar trace of Leo—cologne, leather, warmth.

Everything felt still.

Waiting.

"Any update today, Dr. Harris?" Ciro asked, arms crossed as he scanned his cousin from head to toe.

Dr. Harris, an average-looking man with swept-back hair, adjusted his round black glasses and moved to the monitor, his eyes flicking between the numbers. "Vitals are stable. The infection we were worried about is already responding to the steroid treatment." He pulled a clipboard from the nightstand, scanning it before jotting a few notes. "I'm hopeful he'll wake in the next week or so."

"A week?" I hiccupped through my tears, scooting closer despite the IVs tethering both of us. I placed a trembling hand on his warm chest, needing to feel the steady thump of his heart.

Dr. Harris looked at me kindly, though his voice remained profes-sional. "Yes, Ms. Bennett. Mr. Romano suffered significant blood loss, and after emergency surgery, he developed an infection we had to bring under control. His body needs time. He needs rest."

I nodded slowly, unable to take my eyes off Leo's pale but still-handsome face. The scar I'd noticed the first time we met was barely visible against his washed out sickly skin tone. Seeing him like this ignited something inside me—a protective flame that burned deep in my chest.

Leaning forward despite my own pain, I pressed a soft kiss to his forehead. "Thank you. For treating him, Doctor," I whispered as I brushed a few strands of hair away from Leo's brow. My eyes were rimmed red, but filled with nothing but admiration.

Dr. Harris nodded. "Of course. It's our job." And with that, he exited the room, leaving Ciro and me alone with Leo.

I stayed close, interlacing my fingers with Leo's free hand, careful not to tug on any of the IVs.

Ciro's voice was quiet when he finally spoke. "Do you love him, *bella*?"

My gaze softened as I met his steel-gray eyes. "You'll know when I tell him first." I smiled, giving him a knowing look before returning my attention to Leo's face.

I did love him. I knew I loved him the day he kissed me and I wandered these halls, lost and reeling. But if I was going to admit it out loud, it wouldn't be to Ciro.

It would be to Leo.

Leo

The scent of alcohol, vanilla, and roses hit my senses as my vision began to clear. Female voices stirred around me like a flock of birds. One voice in particular perked my ears. I rolled my head to the left and caught a glimpse of a waterfall of black hair and emerald-green eyes.

"*Principessa?*" My voice came out hoarse, unrecognizable. I reached for her, but hands stopped me from the other side.

"Mr. Romano, please don't move. You'll rip out your IVs," a soothing, unfamiliar female voice said from somewhere to my right.

I didn't care. My focus was only on her as I pulled them from my arm haphazardly, feeling the slight sting. The nurse tensed and only helped to clean up the small amount of blood.

The emerald eyes leaned in, her breath warm against my cheek. "You better be a good boy, Leo," she whispered, teasing.

My heart immediately took off, and the monitor next to the bed confirmed it with a rapid series of beeps. She was okay. Alive. And still feisty as ever. When I held her limp body in my arms on the way to the estate, I prayed for God to protect her—especially her mind. I knew she would carry trauma from this, but I didn't want it to completely shatter her.

"*Principessa*, if you don't want me getting a hard-on, you better stop." My voice was low, raspy, dry.

Her sultry chuckle didn't help. A masculine cough from the foot of my bed caught my attention, and instinctively I turned toward it with a possessive edge.

My gaze landed on a man in a white lab coat—a doctor. The tension in my jaw eased.

"Mr. Romano," he started, quickly averting his eyes. "I'm pleased to see you're awake and… well." He cleared his throat and looked down at a clipboard.

"How many days has it been?" I asked. A nurse moved quickly to hand me a cup of water. I sat up enough to down it in one go. She refilled it, but I waved her off, already shifting slowly. Cassandra assisted me despite the pain I saw flicker across her face.

The room was dim but warm as my vision continued to clear, golden light filtering through partially drawn curtains. Everything felt still, quiet, grounding. It was different. Not that I wasn't normally comfortable in my own home, but I knew without a doubt it was because Cassandra was beside me. From the moment she arrive, she made this place feel like relief. She completed a puzzle I hadn't realized I'd been longing for.

When I looked at her again, I finally saw her. Faint bruising surrounded both eyes, her lip was busted, and one cheek still looked tender. Deep purple marks trailed beneath the strap of a black spaghetti tank top, disappearing beneath the sling on her arm. Her collarbone was visibly swollen. And yet, the top still clung to her curves, doing little to hide the way her body made mine react.

My dick twitched. I casually moved a hand to cover myself.

"A week and a half, sir," the doctor said as he stepped closer to check the vitals on the monitor. "You should calm yourself. You don't want to stress your body unnecessarily."

I chuckled, my darkened gaze flicking to Cassandra's mischievous eyes. "That's a little difficult, Doctor."

She leaned forward, wincing slightly. Her breath ghosted my ear. "Should I leave?" Her teeth nipped the edge of my ear.

Dio mio, this woman. What has gotten into her?

"Settle down, girl." Ciro's voice cut through the haze like a thunderclap.

My eyes shot to him and the corner of my mouth lifted.

"Shut up, Ciro. I'm just making sure he doesn't fall back to sleep," Cassandra replied playfully.

Ciro and I both laughed, the sound echoing through the room like the last rumble of a storm.

"I'll leave you three alone," the doctor said dryly, "but do try to remain calm." He gave me a pointed look. "No strenuous activity." His eyes flicked toward Cassandra in warning.

She raised her hands in surrender. "Scout's honor."

Once the doctor left, Ciro stepped closer to the bedside. "I'm assuming she gave you a boner," he said, brow arching accusingly as he gestured with his chin toward the hand still covering my crotch.

"Not quite," I laughed. "But it was a hell of a way to wake up."

Cassandra's expression softened. Her eyes misted, her voice cracking. "I'm so grateful you're awake."

I hadn't realized she'd inched closer, but she had—impossibly so. I lifted my hand to her face, brushing my thumb gently over her bruised skin. The warmth of her body soothed the last fractured parts of me.

With a content sigh, I replied, "*Principessa*, we have unfinished business." I smirked. "I'm not leaving until I collect."

She gave me a pointed look. "I'm over here worried about you, and here you are being a pervert." Her lips twitched, the bravado crumbling into a smile.

"Says the woman whispering in my ear to be a good boy," I shot back playfully, my gaze dropping to her lips before meeting her eyes again.

"She hasn't left your side since she woke up—about eight days ago," Ciro added, taking a seat at the end of the bed. "Glad you're back." His hand rubbed the back of his neck. "Doing your job has been a pain in my fucking ass."

My hand fell from Cassandra's cheek and I laughed, catching the truth beneath his words. He was worried. He just wouldn't say it. Ciro had been by my side since we were five. Chosen family. Ride or die until the end.

"Glad you understand my suffering when it comes to managing you and all these other assholes," I fired back, my eyes glittering with appreciation and brotherly affection.

He slapped my leg just above the knee, firm and familiar. "You'll get my bill."

Then his tone shifted. He glanced between me and Cassandra, nodding. "I should get back to work." Stepping closer, he placed both hands on either side of my head and pressed his forehead to mine—a silent, loving gesture only family would understand.

"I'll come check on you later, *mio fratello*."

Dipping my chin, I watched him stride off, his hands deep in the pockets of his navy-blue jeans. I waited for the door to close before turning back to *amore mio*.

"Cassandra." My voice softened. "I…" I paused, words catching in my throat. I had never stumbled like this before, never hesitated—especially not when I'd been meaning to say it for months.

Despite the pain living in her bones, she leaned toward me before I could finish. The moment our lips met, the pain faded. The room, the machines, the sounds around us—they all disappeared.

She kissed me like it would be her last—like she finally understood how hungry she'd been for me. Pulling the last of the medical restraints off—the heart rate monitor—I wrapped one arm carefully around her waist while the other sank into her hair at the side of her head, my thumb resting against the pulse in her neck.

Her heartbeat fluttered beneath my touch, fast and frantic like the wings of a hummingbird, making my own heart pound in response.

When her good arm reached up and rested against my chest, I knew she could feel it—the deep, resonating love I carried for her. It was undeniable. Unmistakable. And I had every intention of making that clear.

Pulling back to say the three words, "Cassandra, I—"

"I love you, Leonardo Romano," she said, cutting me off.

My eyes widened, then softened. A low, easy laugh slipped from my chest. "You always need to prove you have control, *principessa*."

She interlaced her fingers with mine. "No, I just…" She looked deep into my eyes, hers misty and shimmering like morning dew on a white lily at dawn. Fear lingered there, mixed with a profound weight of unspoken emotion.

"My little *topo*," I whispered against her mouth, pressing my forehead to hers. "You don't have to say anything."

Her hand slid up to cup my jaw, her eyes steady and determined. "I need to." Her voice shook. "You have no idea how scared, confused, and absolutely crazy in love I am for you right now." She clenched her eyes shut, tears finally breaking free.

My heart felt rapid and still all at once as I waited, breathing her in. I would always wait for her—every second, every lifetime. She was worth it.

When her gaze locked onto mine again, she whispered, "I thought I would never find true safety. True love. Not because it wouldn't happen for me, but because I thought fate decided I didn't deserve it— and I believed her." Her lips trembled as she fought back tears, and the sight crushed me.

My sweet little *topo* thought she didn't deserve happiness or safety. Rage flared in my chest, my grip tightening in her hair as I pulled her close, but I let her speak.

She bit her lip to steady herself, stealing reassurance from my touch. "I had every intention of leaving Chicago, and I almost had the funds in my savings account…" She averted her gaze, shame flickering across her face—shame born from survival, from love, from men who had hurt her. From me.

It broke my heart seeing the shame on her gorgeous face, but hearing her finally admit what her little nest egg was for didn't surprise me. And I knew staying here with me—choosing me— couldn't have been easy for her.

"Look at me, Cassandra." My tone was firm but full of love. "You will not be ashamed. You will not self-deprecate. You will not hide or run from yourself any longer, because you are not alone."

My hold on her waist tightened because she needed to feel me—feel the truth in my words.

"You are fierce because you fight. You are strong because you persist in the face of adversity. And this life of crime and danger may be a death sentence, but to me it has been a blessing."

I locked my eyes onto hers, forcing her to see my conviction. "You are my blessing, because without ever meeting you I would never have been able to soften. And I will only yield for you. I will destroy myself before I ever allow my world to crush your spirit, *amore mio*.

You are my Proserpina to my Pluto—my equal, my queen of life and renewal."

Heat radiated between us as we remained pressed together, breath heavy, foreheads touching, lips brushing. The heart monitor beeped wildly in the background, distant and unimportant.

"Do you hear me, Cassandra?"

It took her a moment. "Yes," she whispered. "I hear you."

My forehead pressed more firmly against hers. "And if you run from me, it will destroy me," I breathed. "But I will not become the monster you're afraid of. "

She whimpered—not in fear, but in that same broken, needy way I remembered from having my fingers buried deep inside her, making her arousal drip down my hand.

"Fuck, *amore mio*," I growled. "If I wasn't under strict orders, I'd fuck you until you couldn't remember your own name—until all you could scream was mine."

Her lips closed the short distance between us, kissing me with reckless passion. She winced with each tilt of her head, each roll of her body as she greedily pressed closer. I should've stopped her. Protected her.

But I was fucking selfish.

EPILOGUE

*L*eo

The smooth skin of pale knuckles beneath my grazing thumb kept me grounded as I listened to the laughter and banter around the dinner table at my family's home. My sister Alessia and Ciro were the life of the conversation, as per usual. I didn't mind, though—my full attention was on *amore mio* beside me.

The heat of her body, the smell of her rose-and-vanilla perfume—it drove me mad. It had been three long, agonizing months of celibacy. With both of us recovering from our injuries, and since we had finally gotten the all-clear just before this dinner, we were inseparable.

Cassandra Bennett had made me feel like a goddamn teenager these past few months—with the makeout sessions, groping, and dry humping—carefully, of course. My gaze met her emerald green eyes, the crystal chandelier above the table reflecting in them like gemstones. She was stunning, and completely mine in every sense. Her onyx-black hair was perfectly styled, falling over her right shoulder. The way she winged her eyeliner emphasized her round eyes, and those fucking lips—plump, red, and screaming for me to bite them.

Her grip tightened on my hand, probably noticing the way I was eye-fucking her face. Even I could feel my eyes darkening with lust. It was obvious I was craving her; my dick was hard as hell beneath the table. Hopefully, my mother didn't ask me to stand anytime soon. Cassandra wet her lips before they parted slightly, her pupils dilating a fraction—she wanted me too.

The clink of forks on porcelain, the soft laughter of my family—it all blurred behind the pounding rush of blood in my ears.

My name being called pulled me from our connection.

"Leo, tell me what the doctor said about your and Cassandra's injuries. Has he given you the all-clear?" My mother's Italian accent was thick with concern and hope as my gaze met hers. She gave me a warm, sweet smile—so familiar and soothing—but it didn't do shit for the storm building inside me.

"Yes, we have both been cleared," I said. My voice came out lower and raspier than I intended. Ciro caught it and decided to leap at the opportunity to poke fun.

"I'm surprised you two decided to grace us with your presence," he said, arching a brow as he leaned back, draping an arm over Alessia's chair while swirling his wine glass. A smug grin played on his face.

My mother looked between Cassandra and me like she was trying to catch something the doctor couldn't. "What do you mean, Ciro? They seem perfectly healthy." Her hands gestured animatedly toward us.

Alessia and Ciro both laughed, my father joining them.

"Oh, Mama, you are so pure," Ciro forced out between breaths.

"Leave your mother alone," my father scolded after a moment, noticing her cheeks growing red and her brows furrowing—the telltale sign she was about to lose it.

The smell of roasted garlic and red wine floated up from the table, but all I could focus on was Cassandra's hand drifting to my lap. Her fingers slowly grazed the fabric of the blue jeans I wore. The muscles beneath tensed, and I had to use every ounce of my training as the don of Chicago to remain stoic. It took every bit of control not to drag her away and make good on every fantasy that had haunted me since the day I met her.

"Leo, you never did give me a tour of your parents' home the last time I was here," Cassandra said, sipping her wine casually, a dark look in her eye. She knew exactly what she was doing—knew the game and played it like she wrote the rules.

My mother quickly interjected, "Oh, please, let me do the honor."

My father, catching the shift in atmosphere, patted her hand gently. "*Amore*, let our son do it," he said with a warm smile as she frowned. He leaned over, pressing a kiss to her temple before whispering in her ear. She smiled brightly, making her look younger. The sight made my heart swell, grounding me for a second—until Cassandra's pinky brushed closer to my cock, and I forgot how to breathe.

"I'm happy to assist," Ciro added playfully, winking at me.

My eyes snapped to his, and I growled, "I'm sure we can manage," shifting in my seat to adjust myself before rising. I extended a hand to Cassandra, offering to help her up. When her warm, delicate fingers touched mine, a shudder ran through me. I inhaled deeply, attempting to control myself, but her fingers curled ever so slightly around mine, like a promise.

I followed my little *topo*, my eyes glued to her ass in those denim shorts. My chest muscles flexed beneath my fitted white tee as I rolled my shoulders. The soft click of her sandals on the hardwood echoed down the hall. We both knew we weren't going on a tour of the house, and I was more than eager to fulfill her demands.

Cassandra

I couldn't wait any longer—these three months had been agony. Even with our heavy petting and makeout sessions, I needed more, and I knew Leo did too. The heated looks he gave me during dinner had me losing my appetite for food and craving something far more indulgent.

As soon as we were out of earshot, Leo surprised me by scooping me up and flinging me over his shoulder like a sack of potatoes. He smacked my ass so hard I had to cover my mouth quickly as I yelped.

I giggled like a schoolgirl. "Leo, this seems very caveman—even for you." My hands pressed against his back as I lifted my head to stop the blood from rushing down. His hand tightened on my thighs.

"At this point, *principessa*, I am reduced to my basic instincts with you." His voice was low, filled with velvety promises. My core pulsed between my legs—God, please save me.

We never went on the tour. Instead, Leo drove us back to his estate —thank God, because the things I needed this man to do to me would have been mortifying if his mother heard them.

HIS STEPS WERE confident as he strode through the house, continuing his caveman-like mission with me slung over his shoulder and up the stairs to his bedroom in the north wing. If I was honest, I liked it. Something about the primal act made me want to meet him in his intensity.

He gripped the handle, opened the door with force, and kicked it shut behind us.

Everything happened so fast—he tossed me onto the bed, then his massive frame hovered over me. His masculine scent of cigarettes and cognac filled my nose, and I inhaled deeply, sparks shooting through every nerve ending. I groaned, my hands grabbing the sides of his face, pulling him into a rough, messy kiss.

Leo's hips ground against mine, his hands tracing my curves with possessive hunger. He pulled away, lips brushing my ear before nipping it, then murmured something sinful in Italian—something I loosely translated as *You're mine, principessa.*

Then he licked the column of my neck before sinking his teeth into the flesh between my neck and shoulder. My eyes rolled back, my back arching. "God save me," I prayed.

"You don't need God to save you, my little *topo*. I'm going to have you praying for this to never end," he purred, trailing open-mouthed kisses over my collarbone and chest, just above the line of my tank top.

Sitting back on his heels, he peeled my thin straps down my arms. Thank God I didn't wear a bra—specifically for this moment. The look in his eyes, the deep, hungry rumble from his chest when he looked down at my breasts—that was the hottest fucking thing I'd ever seen or heard.

I watched as he slowly pulled his shirt over his head, exposing his perfectly sculpted chest and abs. A faded scar decorated the left side of his olive skin—evidence of what happened three months ago.

I wet my lips, thinking of how long we'd waited for this moment. If I was honest with myself, I'd wanted this since the first time I danced for him in the VIP lounge at Inferno. The soft pink scar on his right cheek was still there as he crashed his mouth against mine again.

"Cassandra, you have no idea how often I thought of this moment with you. How many nights I touched my cock thinking about this body and your fiery attitude," he growled, biting my lip and tugging it between his teeth.

Holy shit. The image of Leo stroking his thick cock to thoughts of me had me soaked. The don of Chicago—on his knees in his mind for me. The power that gave me was intoxicating.

"Oh really? Tell me, Leonardo Romano," I purred. "What sort of things were you doing to me in those sexy thoughts?"

Our eyes locked, wild and dark, breaths ragged with barely controlled restraint. His voice was hoarse when he finally replied.

"Let me show you—just a few highlights. We have the rest of our lives to play out the others."

And then he pounced like a predator. His kisses seared my skin, his hands pushing my breasts together, then his tongue swirling over each nipple before sucking them into his mouth—one at a time, desperate, needy. He teased with flicks and nips, lavishing them with worship and raw hunger.

"Fuck, Leo," I gasped, my hips grinding against him as his clothed erection rolled between my spread legs. The barrier of fabric was unbearable.

As if he heard the frustration in my breath, he trailed kisses down my torso, licking and nipping along my flushed skin. He glanced up at me, fingers hooking into the waistband of my shorts.

"You fucking wet for me, *principessa?*" he growled, popping the button open and peeling them down my legs before tossing them aside.

"Yes—so fucking ready for you, Leo," I whimpered, propping myself on my elbows to watch him, one hand slipping into his tousled dark hair.

His nose brushed against the soaked fabric of my panties, inhaling deeply before nipping my swollen clit through the lace. My hips jerked. He chuckled darkly, then hooked his thumbs beneath the strings and ripped them apart like they were nothing.

I hissed as the cool air hit my overheated skin. Leo gripped my thighs, spreading them wide before placing the flat of his tongue at my entrance and dragging it up to my clit, where he danced around it.

He groaned. "So fucking delicious," his voice muffled against me.

My head tipped back as he swirled his tongue, slow and torturous. I moaned, gripping his hair, holding him there.

"Leo, God—don't stop," I breathed.

He was right. I'd be praying for him to never stop. The hunger in the way he devoured me was more than lust—it was obsession. His finger teased my entrance as his mouth latched onto my clit. Then he thrust into me, and I cried out, already trembling.

I rolled my hips against the rhythm of his mouth and fingers.

"That's it, *amore mio*. Use me. Show me how much you fucking need me."

My walls fluttered at his words. I was so close—right on the edge. He pumped faster, the headboard knocking against the wall with the force of it.

With an earth-shattering cry, I came undone. "Leo—Christ—I'm cumming!"

He sucked my clit, drawing out every last tremble of my orgasm. When he finally pulled back, his lips were glistening.

"Such a good fucking girl," he purred.

I collapsed against the pillows, chest heaving, stars bursting behind my eyelids. Leo stood and stripped off his pants in one smooth motion.

"I'm going to fuck you hard, raw, and fast, *principessa*."

He grabbed the backs of my calves, dragging me to the edge of the bed. With one swift movement, he flipped me over, gripping my hips and arching my back. He leaned down and murmured into my ear.

"You're on the pill, correct?"

It wasn't a question—it was confirmation. I wouldn't have been surprised if he knew my full medical history, including my birth control.

"Yeah, I am," I whispered, panting.

Leo nipped my ear. "Good. Because I'm going to pump every last drop of my cum into this pussy. I want to see you thoroughly claimed —and leaking."

Then he spanked me sharply before plunging hilt-deep into my dripping heat.

My cry of pleasure rang out, loud and desperate, as he did exactly what he promised—fucking me raw, hard, and fast. It was primal, animalistic, and hot as hell.

Leo

The Chicago weather had finally released us from its suffocating grip as the cooler, more tolerable air of autumn rolled in on a gentle breeze. It fluttered a few strands of Cassandra's luxurious black hair, and I watched as she tucked them behind her delicate, pierced ear. The motion—so simple, so her—made my chest ache.

The skyline from the Michelin-star restaurant stretched across the glass like a living painting. I'd chosen this place intentionally, buying out the entire space for one reason. One moment. Candlelight flickered, twinkling in her bright eyes as she looked at me from across the small, private table.

"You're breathtaking tonight, *principessa*," I murmured, reaching for her slender, warm hand and pressing a feather-light kiss to her knuckles. She always looked beautiful—but tonight? Tonight, she looked like fate itself had dressed her for me.

I'd had Alessia take my goddess on a full day of pampering— massages, nails, shopping at the best stores downtown. I wanted her to feel radiant. Worshiped. And in that deep green velvet dress, she looked like a siren carved from dreams. Tantalizing. Untouchable—until I touched her.

Cassandra smirked knowingly. "You're in a good mood tonight."

Shrugging, I replied, "That's because tonight is special."

Her eyes sharpened, searching mine, trying to read between the lines. I chuckled softly, then pushed my chair back and rose to my feet. Her breath caught as I lowered to one knee beside her.

The gasp—and that wide-eyed, stunned expression—was everything.

Slowly, I reached into the inside pocket of my suit jacket and pulled out a small black velvet box, popping it open between us.

"*Amore… principessa…* Cassandra," I began, my voice low and steady despite my heart pounding like a war drum. "You—and only you—hold the power to undo me. To destroy everything I've built. And yet, without you in it, my life would mean nothing. An emperor without his empress has no empire at all."

Her lips parted, tears shining in her eyes. I smiled softly and continued, emotion threading through every word.

"I want to face everything life throws our way with you. Every joy. Every storm. Every breath. I promise to protect you always and to love you more than I could ever truly express."

Gently, I lifted the ring from the box and reached for her outstretched hand. My fingers were steady as the day I met her as I slid it onto her ring finger, the fit perfect—like it was made for her, because it was. I had searched for months for this gem, my broker finally finding it in Roma. The delicate silver band bore vine-and-flower carvings, and the four-carat princess-cut diamond was as clear as a Tuscan night sky. The ring was made more beautiful simply by her wearing it.

"Please… bless me with the honor of being your husband. Be my wife, *mia regina*—and the mother of our future children."

A tear slipped down her cheek as she nodded eagerly, her voice rough but soft, filled with awe. "Yes, Leonardo Romano. I'll marry you."

I placed a hand on her cheek, brushing the tear away with my thumb, and leaned in to kiss her deeply—gentle, reverent. But that never lasted long with us.

The kiss turned heated almost instantly.

"My insatiable fiancée," I murmured against her lips, grinning.

"Do you blame me?" she replied, her chuckle low and breathy, eyes burning with desire.

Shaking my head with a wolfish grin, I turned and told the waiter to clear the staff for the next hour. When I returned, I scooped her up and set her atop the nearest empty table. Her fingers clawed her dress up to her waist, as desperate for me as I was for her.

Stepping between her legs, I gripped the back of her hair with one hand, my other locking onto her hip. I tilted her face to mine, heart thundering like it was trying to escape my chest.

"I want you to scream my name so loud," I growled, voice dark and hungry, "that all of Chicago knows who the fuck has claimed your heart."

Then my mouth collided with hers in a kiss that claimed every inch of her soul. Her moan bled into my mouth, her body melting against mine. And I knew—this woman, this fire, this future—was mine.

Cassandra

I had no idea what Leo had planned tonight, but when he dropped to one knee beside me, everything inside me stilled. The world fell quiet. Candlelight flickered against the skyline behind him, painting his sharp features in gold, and in that moment, I knew—I would say yes a thousand times over.

Tears blurred my vision the second he said my name.

Amore... principessa... Cassandra.

The words that followed unraveled me. Leo never did anything halfway—not in business, not in bed, and certainly not when it came to love. His love came like a thunderstorm: loud, wild, inescapable. But this? This was something else. His voice was so full of truth and devotion that I physically ached to hear it.

When he slid the ring onto my finger, I didn't just see a future—I felt it. A whole life. Marriage. Babies. Laughter. Us.

"Yes, Leonardo Romano. I'll marry you," I breathed, the words a little broken, a little breathless—but absolute.

The way he cupped my cheek so tenderly before kissing me reminded me of every reason I fell for this dangerous, obsessive, maddening man. My heart was still trying to catch up when the kiss shifted, turning heated and greedy. He always tasted like heat and ownership, and I never wanted it to stop.

"My insatiable fiancée," he whispered against my lips.

"Do you blame me?" I shot back, grinning even as my breath hitched.

Next thing I knew, the restaurant was ours. Staff dismissed. Lights dimmed. He lifted me effortlessly and set me on a nearby table, the cool surface shocking against the backs of my thighs as I gathered my dress to my waist.

He stepped between my legs like he belonged there—and he did.

The possessive grip on my hip, the way his fingers twisted into my hair, the low growl vibrating against my throat—every piece of Leo was claiming me, carving this night into my bones and my heart.

"I want you to scream my name so loud," he said, voice like silk over fire, "that all of Chicago knows who the fuck has claimed your heart."

His mouth slammed into mine before I could breathe, before I could respond—but I didn't need to.

Because he did claim my heart, it was his.

Dangerously devoted. Entirely.

ACKNOWLEDGMENTS

I would like to acknowledge everyone who stayed with me on this journey. This book holds a dog-eared place in a time when my world felt small, trapped, and uncertain. Writing it gave me the strength and the therapeutic space to let it all out.

I'd also like to thank you—the reader—for purchasing this book or reading it as an ARC. As an indie author, it truly means the world to me.

To my wonderful friends, Molly and Skylar, thank you for contributing your knowledge, laughter, and excitement while I explored the depths of what the underground of Chicago holds in this universe.

My editor, Eve, has also been an incredible person to learn from and work with. Thank you for your patience, guidance, and support through this second publishing journey.

And last, but never least, my dearest husband. You are, and always will be, my number one fan and greatest support. Thank you for standing by my side unconditionally. I love you.

ABOUT THE AUTHOR

I WRITE FROM LIVED EXPERIENCE—FROM MOMENTS THAT BROKE ME, HEALED ME, AND RESHAPED ME. MY STORIES ARE ROOTED IN REAL EMOTION, REAL STRUGGLE, AND REAL CONNECTION. WRITING FESTIVAL OF DREAMS AND THE MAN IS A CACCIATORE WASN'T JUST STORYTELLING—IT WAS THERAPY, SURVIVAL, AND SELF-DISCOVERY.

WITH A BACKGROUND IN ADDICTION COUNSELING AND A HEART THAT FEELS EVERYTHING DEEPLY, I CREATE CHARACTERS WHO ARE MESSY, INTENSE, AND HUMAN. DARK ROMANCE, FANTASY, OBSESSION, HEALING, LOVE—EVERY PAGE CARRIES TRUTH.

IG: Jrmoss_author